NEVER SAY *goodbye*

FELICE STEVENS

DEDICATION

To my family.

And to the planet. We only have one. Let's stop screwing it up. Save the animals.

ACKNOWLEDGMENTS

Thank you always to my fabulous editor, Keren. Thank you to Hope and Jess from Flat Earth Editing for never settling until everything is as perfect as it can get. And to Dianne from Lyrical Lines, you're the best of the best. And last but never least, thank you to Reese for making every cover a gift I can't wait to open. And the special fairy dust.

And always and forever to my readers—thank you, thank you. You are the reason I get to do what I never dreamed possible.

CHAPTER ONE

DELAYED
CANCELED
DELAYED
DELAYED

"Crap." Ren Stewart dropped his knapsack from his shoulder to rest on his rolling case as he studied the departure board. His flight—originally due to take off at 5:14 p.m.—had been delayed until 6:38. It now showed the time pushed back even further, to 7:23. Never a good sign.

Weather-wise, February was always one of the worst months to travel, but it couldn't be helped. Ren went where the jobs took him. Now that his assignment was over, he'd gotten the hell out without considering what the weather at home might be like. Traveling was no big deal to him. If he got stuck in an airport, he'd make the best of it. Not the first time it had happened and it wouldn't be the last.

He spent more time inside airline terminals than in any apartment; they were his home away from home. With a pang, Ren realized he couldn't use that old saying. Like the foster child he once was, he no longer had an apartment or a place to call his own.

His stomach growled, and he decided to get something to eat. And drink. That was a definite necessity if he was going to be stuck in New York for any length of time.

The hostess sat him at a two-seater on the outer edge of the rapidly filling restaurant, and he ordered a beer. He scrolled through the weather app on his phone. "Dammit."

"Not looking too good out there," a deep voice spoke over his shoulder, and he glanced up.

And liked what he saw. A tall man—early to midforties if the silver brightening the dark hair at his temples was any indication—wearing a black sweater under a puffer jacket and soft jeans showcasing long, powerful legs. His face was best described as unconventionally handsome—rugged, with hard dips at his cheeks and a strong nose and chin. Not a man to give away his smiles easily.

"No," Ren agreed. "And the way things are shaping up out there, I'm thinking my flight's not going to take off tonight at all. It's already been delayed twice." Ren rubbed his face and frowned. "I figured I might as well get something to eat and wait to see what happens."

"You're most likely right." The man peered at his phone screen. "Third time's the charm, and then they usually cancel." His eyes narrowed, their color as wild and stormy gray as the sky outside. "It is pretty ugly out there. They won't want to take the chance."

"I get it. I wouldn't want to compromise safety over my need to get the hell away from the snow and ice."

The man had a nice, comforting laugh. "I gather you're going somewhere warm?"

"Yeah. Southern California."

The man's brows rose. "I am as well."

Their eyes met, studying each other, and Ren caught that subtle awareness between two strangers that maybe they had more in common than they thought.

"What flight're you on?" Ren asked. A five-and-a-half-hour trip would be more palatable if he had this man to chat with. *Stranger things have happened.*

"Flight one sixty-five to Santa Ana."

A slow grin kicked up his lips. "Fancy that." He tipped his head. "Why don't you come in and join me? Unless you're with someone?" He wondered if he was coming on too strong. It had been months since he'd had a proper dinner companion. Traveling around the Serengeti, looking for the elusive Eastern Black Rhino, wasn't the most conducive to a social life, and sex was a fleeting memory.

"I'm not, but I don't want to interrupt your meal."

"I do like my burger rare, but I don't expect it to talk back to me. Safe to say, I think you'd be a much better conversationalist."

Red-faced, the man nodded. "Okay. Sure, thanks." He pulled a black carry-on behind him, and within a minute Ren saw him maneuvering between the scattered tables. When he reached Ren, he remained standing and extended a hand.

"I'm Schaeffer."

"Ren. Put your carry-on next to my stuff by the wall here."

Schaeffer did as suggested, taking the seat opposite him. Awkward silence rose between them. Luckily, it didn't take too long for the server to come over. Ren ordered a burger and fries. Schaeffer ordered a beer and the same meal. He took off his jacket and hung it on his chair. Damn, the man had beautifully sculpted muscles, outlined perfectly by the tight black sweater clinging to his biceps and broad shoulders. Desire he'd sidelined for the past year and a half stormed its way to the surface.

"So, uh, are you visiting family in California, Schaeffer?" Small talk had never been Ren's strong suit, and after so much solitude, he was rusty at social interaction, but he gave it a try.

"Yeah. We're originally from New York, but we moved when I was eleven, after my mother passed away. My brother and father still live in California, but I moved home to New York. How about you?"

"Lived here all my life."

"What about your family?"

His heart squeezed tight. "No family."

Not anymore.

"Oh. Sorry to hear that. So…visiting friends in California?"

Schaeffer's drink came, giving Ren a chance to craft a response.

"No. I just wanted to get the hell out of the cold and be somewhere where I could see the ocean and hear the waves. Watch the sunrise over the horizon."

"So what you're saying is you're a beach bum." Schaeffer's lips twitched. "Do you surf?"

"Surf, sail, swim…I love it all."

"I hang out on the sand. More of a people-watcher."

"No better place than a California beach. All the bikinis and board shorts you can handle…depending on what you're into." He grinned and watched a red blush rise on Schaeffer's cheeks, though his eyes still retained a combination of interest and wariness. This night was getting better and better.

Their food came, and they each ordered another beer. They ate in silence, but on several occasions he found Schaeffer's gaze on him and felt that tug from before. An understanding. He wondered if it was too fast to suggest a get-together in California. If they even got there, that was. With dismay, Ren realized he hadn't checked the airline app for updates. He did so now, and his phone told him the bad news.

"Shit."

Chewing the last bite of his burger, Schaeffer looked up from his plate. "What?"

"The flight's been canceled." Ren spied the server and motioned her over. "There's nothing else for the rest of the evening, either. We're stuck here." He gave her his credit card.

Troubled eyes met his. "Hopefully they'll give us a hotel room—they don't have to these days. Here, take this." Schaeffer tossed him several bills, and he stuffed them into the pocket of his jeans.

"Yeah? God. Let's try anyway. I can't even imagine the lines." Half standing, Ren scribbled his name on the receipt and grabbed his backpack and case. "The customer-service area is a few gates away. Maybe we'll be lucky."

"Right behind you." At a swift pace, Schaeffer followed him out of the restaurant.

Ren's heart sank at the enormous crowds milling about, but Schaeffer pulled him. "Come this way."

They wove through the passengers standing around and made it to one of the booths set up for help. The line snaked down the terminal, and he groaned.

"We're gonna be stuck here all night."

"You never know. Sometimes passengers get lucky. I figure we'll be here about two hours."

Ren gave him a side-eye. "You sound like you have experience at this."

Schaeffer gave him a half smile. "I fly often."

Often enough that he proved correct. Ren felt sorry for the harried agent when he stood before her, so he tried to be as nice as possible.

"I'm sure there are no flights out tonight, but any chance for tomorrow?"

She clucked her tongue. "Nothing until Tuesday. I can put you on standby for flights on Monday, just in case you get lucky."

"Sure. Do you have a hotel voucher I can use?"

"Who said today wasn't your lucky day? Here you go. The shuttle bus will pick you up outside baggage claim."

"Thanks."

Ren moved aside as Schaeffer stepped up and leaned in to speak with the agent. They had a low and rapid conversation, but she continued to shake her head. He frowned and came away with the same voucher as Ren held.

"No luck?"

"Nothing until Tuesday, but—"

"Standby for Monday," Ren finished. "Same story I got." He held up the voucher. "Looks like it's a hotel for us."

"Let's get going. It's bound to be a zoo out there for the shuttles."

They pushed through the crowds, and as predicted, it was a madhouse outside. Finally, they got on the bus, and with the snow still coming down heavily, it inched toward one of the hotels nearby.

"God, what a night," he groaned. "Now we'll wait in line here to get a room."

Another hour went by before he made it to the front-desk clerk. Poor guy. His face shone with perspiration, and his tie lay limp and twisted. The phones never stopped ringing, and he was muttering to himself.

"Uh. I have—"

"Yeah. A voucher. Sure. Name?" He punched in the name. "You're lucky. It's our last one."

"Last one what?"

He handed Ren one of those little envelopes with a cardkey inside. "Room. We're sold out."

Ren glanced over his shoulder at Schaeffer, who was waiting patiently. "But...other people have vouchers, and they're still waiting for a room."

The clerk shrugged. "Not here. They're outta luck. And I heard the Crowne Plaza is also out. They'll have to go farther away from the airport. It's not only you guys. People were booked here, and when they saw the weather, they decided to extend their stays. We even got strangers sharing a room." The man's eyes lit up. "I see some pretty ladies you might wanna ask, ya know? It's a queen-sized bed." He snickered while Ren rolled his eyes.

"Yeah. Give me a second card key, please."

"Oh, damn. You got someone already in mind, huh?"

"Just please get me another one. I'll pick it up in a minute."

While he scanned another key, Ren walked over to Schaeffer. "Listen. They're fully booked—I got the last room—and he said the other hotels on the airport grounds are the same."

"Shit." His shoulders sagged. "Well, I guess it's back to the airport for me." He reached for his suitcase.

"Not if you don't want to. I told the clerk to give me an extra key." He held Schaeffer's stare. "We could share the room. If you're okay with that."

"Y-you don't have to do that. I'm a stranger." But the spark in Schaeffer's eyes indicated he'd like that to change.

"Not after we share the room." Schaeffer blinked, and Ren continued. "There's only one bed, but I don't mind…"

Schaeffer's face turned fiery red, and Ren winced. *Shit.* Had he guessed wrong?

"Hey, I'm sorry. I didn't mean to come on so strong. But we can still share. I don't want you to have to sleep at the airport."

But Schaeffer surprised him. "I'd like that. I'd like to stay with you. And share the bed." The last part was said in a hushed tone, their eyes locked. Ren's heart pounded at the shocking thrill Schaeffer's words released. He returned to the clerk and picked up the second card, ignoring the clerk's leer.

Ren handed Schaeffer the little envelope. "The sign says the elevator is this way. We're on eight."

They passed by people sharing snowstorm travel stories and waited for the elevator, then rode up to the eighth floor in silence and found their room at the end of the hallway. Ren unlocked the door and stepped inside the dim space.

It was a standard, midlevel hotel room—two hundred square feet, a queen-sized bed with a nightstand on either side, a dark comforter to minimize the sight of stains, a fiberboard dresser with a flat-screen above it, and the slightly musty smell of the hundreds of people who'd passed through there and failed to avail themselves of the body wash provided in the shower. The heavy curtains were half-drawn, letting in the pale light from the streetlamps. Snow fell steadily out of the night sky.

Schaeffer closed the door behind him and locked it.

"How—" Ren turned, his voice catching at the intensity of Schaeffer's stare and the hand circling his nape. A random, terrifying thought came to mind: *What if I just let a killer in the room with me?*

Schaeffer's fingers slid up to his jaw, and Ren, trembling and aching, nodded once. Nose to nose, their breaths mingled until Schaeffer guided their mouths together and their lips touched. Gently at first, then with increasing hunger. Teeth clashed and tongues pushed and played as desire exploded between them.

Ren tugged at Schaeffer's sweater, watching as it slid over his head. He had a nice amount of chest hair and abs that were defined but not cut. Running his hands over Schaeffer's pecs to tweak the reddened nipples, Ren said, "I thought about what you looked like naked the moment I saw you."

"Shit," Schaeffer cursed and fumbled at the button tab of Ren's jeans. A moan ripped from Ren at the brush of fingers against his zipper. "Same."

"Bed," he choked out and stripped off his clothes, flinging them into the darkness. Schaeffer joined him, and soon they were rolling together in a hot tangle of legs and arms. Schaeffer was hard and huge, and Ren's ass clenched at the thought of having all that power inside him.

Their lips met again, their kisses slow and lingering, learning each other's taste. Schaeffer grasped their cocks in his big hand, and Ren arched up into all that rough, delicious friction.

"So fucking good," he rasped, and Schaeffer kissed along his cheek and jaw, licking a path of wet fire to his ear. "So long. Want this. Want you."

"You're incredible," Schaeffer whispered. "I can't believe I'm here with you." His hand remained busy, fingers dancing along their shafts, then picking up the pace, stroking fast and furious.

"All of me," he groaned. "Oh God, that's good. So good." His hips bucked, and his heart pounded frantically. "Schaeffer, fuck, oh God," he screamed out his climax, spurting sticky wetness between them.

He opened his eyes to see Schaeffer panting, lips thinned in a snarl, sweat rolling down his face as his hand continued to work his dick. Ren joined him, and at his touch, Schaeffer's eyes rolled back in his head, and he pumped out endless amounts of hot come, coating their hands.

They lay together, hearts pounding in tandem. Schaeffer moved first, kissing his cheek and rubbing him. Ren hummed his pleasure and played with the thick hair under his fingers.

"That was perfect. I'm kind of not mad about the flight being canceled."

Schaeffer's chuckle was warm, and he held Ren close. "I'm not disagreeing. Sure beats a cramped seat and a bag of peanuts."

Ren murmured in Schaeffer's ear, "How about we take

a shower? I'd really like to get clean and touch you all over." Schaeffer's dick twitched against Ren's thigh, and Ren smiled into Schaeffer's cheek. "I feel you liking that idea."

"I do," he replied in that deep, smooth voice. "I think you're going to like it too."

Half-hard again, Ren rolled off the bed and walked to the bathroom. "I can't wait." After infrequent, furtive sex in a tent, Ren couldn't think of a better way to spend a snowed-in night, and he intended to take full advantage of whatever Schaeffer wanted to give him.

CHAPTER TWO

At the sight of Ren's beautiful, round ass disappearing from sight, Schaeffer blinked and rubbed his hands over his face.

I hope this isn't a dream. The sound of the taps squealing as the shower turned on answered his question.

He jumped out of bed and picked his way through the scattered clothing. When he entered the bathroom, Ren already occupied the small tub shower. He pulled aside the curtain.

"I'm waiting." A bright grin shone from his deeply suntanned face, and Schaeffer was again, as he was at the airport, caught up in Ren's lively face and beautiful green eyes.

"It's kind of narrow for two." Dubious as he was, Schaeffer stepped into the tub, and Ren shut the curtain and slipped an arm around his waist. Instantly hard, Schaeffer pushed his hips into Ren's as the hot water cascaded down their bodies.

"I like tight spaces," Ren breathed into his ear, causing goose bumps over his body. "I can feel everything that way." Ren's fingers brushed between his ass cheeks and rested there.

"E-everything?" Schaeffer shivered.

"*Mmm*." Ren licked and sucked at his neck, while those wicked fingers teased his hole. "All of you."

"I-I like it." Schaeffer palmed their dicks, but Ren pushed his hand away.

"I have plans for that. First, let's wash up."

Schaeffer took the bottle from Ren, poured the body gel over his chest, and sudsed up. "You really like being clean."

"After almost eighteen months of living in sand and dirt, yeah. I'm gonna take as many showers as I can get."

He splayed his hands over Ren's broad chest and shoulders, rubbing the woodsy-smelling bubbles all over. "What do you do, and where were you?"

"I'm a wildlife photographer. I was in the Serengeti, following the rare Eastern Black Rhino. It's critically endangered, so I was lucky to get to see one."

"Wow. That's incredible. You must have amazing stories and pictures."

Ren let the spray shoot over his face, then gave the space over to him. "It was an experience I'll never forget, but it can get very lonely."

His brows shot up. "You were by yourself?"

"In the beginning I had a guide helping me locate the rhinos, but that was only for a couple of months. I-I'm alone."

Sensing a story but not knowing Ren well enough to ask, Schaeffer refrained, instead washing his hair and rinsing off. He stepped out first and grabbed a towel, which gave him the chance to admire Ren's strong flanks and the flex and bunch of his muscles. Ren caught him staring, and a slow smile broke over his face.

"Like what you see?"

He did. Eight long months had passed since his last hookup. It was after a flight from JFK to Denver. The Denver pilots had planned a night out, but for Schaeffer, who kept his sexuality a secret from his coworkers, it was a night to let loose and be himself. He'd found a gay bar far out of town and met someone on the dance floor. They'd hooked up in the man's car in the parking lot. It was getting harder and harder, year after year, to keep ducking the flight attendants' not-so-subtle hints that they'd love to hang out or hook up. Many of the captains and first officers also had wives who wanted to set him up with their friends.

Despite the strides made in the airline industry, not even seven percent of commercial pilots identified as queer, and there were many, *many* times in the flight deck when homophobic comments disguised as jokes ran rampant. He kept his mouth shut because the military had taught him not to make waves.

In Schaeffer's opinion, there was a reason why a private life was called…private. What he did in his bedroom was for him and him alone.

"I do like it." He hooked a finger into the towel Ren had draped around his waist and pulled it off, revealing his rapidly stiffening cock. "So much that I don't want you covering it up."

A flare of heat rose in Ren's eyes, and his lips parted. "No?" He gripped his shaft and thumbed the wide crown. "Why?"

Schaeffer sank to his knees and was so eager to taste Ren, he swallowed him down without breathing. Ren's clean scent surrounded him, and Schaeffer held on to his thick thigh muscles as he licked and sucked, bobbing his head rapidly. He swirled his tongue over the head, swallowing the bittersweet tang of his precome.

Soon, in that tiny bathroom with the bad lighting, he had to reach out to shut the door, hoping Ren's cries of pleasure didn't bring security knocking. God, he wanted to fuck this man. He wanted to burn the wild, ferocious sight of him in his memory. He wanted to keep the taste of him on his tongue. The rest of the world dropped away, and the floor tilted beneath him, leaving Schaeffer grasping for the only reality in his world.

Ren.

Who, from his groans and sighs, was rapidly approaching another intense orgasm. He pulled off.

"Hey. What the fuck, no," Ren cursed as Schaeffer rose to his feet.

"It's too soon." With a wry expression, he pointed to his own raging hard-on. "I want inside you."

A dark, sensual smile curled Ren's lips, and he ran his hands over Schaeffer's throat and neck before taking his mouth in a hot, needy kiss.

"What're we waiting for?"

Following Ren out of the bathroom—again, that fabulous ass like a beacon calling him home—he watched him stop at his backpack and take something out. Ren turned around with a grin.

"Supplies."

His desire rising to a fever pitch, Schaeffer met Ren on the bed and rolled him underneath, reveling in the rough feel of hair sliding against his skin. God, he'd missed this. So damn much.

"You always come prepared?"

"I've been away for the past year and a half, and I'm going on vacation. You think I'm not going to want some… company along the way?"

But Schaeffer didn't want to hear about future men Ren might be with, when Ren was naked and under him at the present. He stopped him from talking with a harsh kiss that left them both gasping for air. Schaeffer tore the condom wrapper and rolled it onto his aching dick, then slicked himself up.

"You're with me now." His fingers delved inside Ren, working him only for a few seconds before he withdrew and replaced them with his cock. Ren's eyes flew open and locked with his. "Tonight you're mine."

Chest heaving, Ren moaned as Schaeffer filled him inch by inch. Schaeffer's hips started pistoning frantically, and he barely felt the stinging scratches Ren clawed into his shoulders. The soft heat of Ren's passage clasped him tight. He was falling, flying, soaring. Ren's shaft poked him in the stomach, and he reached and grasped it.

"Fuck, yeah." Ren throbbed in his hand and came, trickling through his fingers at the same time he hit his climax. He drove deep one last time, lost his breath, and collapsed.

"Schaeffer?" Ren murmured.

"Mmph? Oh, sorry." He eased out slowly and got rid of the condom, then lay flat. Ren left him, and Schaeffer heard the water run. A minute later, Ren returned and slid under the covers next to him. "Not another shower?"

"No, but I haven't spent the night in a regular bed in years. I want to be clean."

"How did you get into photographing endangered wildlife?"

Like him, Ren stretched out to stare at the ceiling. "When I was a kid, my favorite place was the zoo. As often as I could, I'd take the train up to the Bronx Zoo. There's something so amazing about those big creatures, you know? And losing them to hunters and poaching, plus civilization encroaching on their territory, makes me so fucking angry. Once they become extinct, they're gone forever."

"I never thought about it much, but yeah. That's wrong." With Ren so passionate about the cause, he understood.

"Worse than wrong. Any loss of species upsets the ecosystem, and that has a negative effect on the civilization around it. Everyone's heard of the dodo bird and the passenger pigeon, but there are so many animals in the world that are dying off—the snow leopard, tigers, monk seals, rhinos, not to mention birds, insects, fish…it's a long and unfortunately growing list."

"And you're photographing all of them?"

"Gonna try." Stretching, Ren turned on his side. "I grew up in the foster system, and the only place I felt at home was with these animals." He pushed a hank of wet hair from obscuring his eyes. "Maybe it's because no one seems to care if they live or die either."

A shiver ran through Schaeffer and his fingers trailed a path down Ren's arm. "Hey. Right now I'm really glad you're here."

"Yeah? Me too."

They lay for a while, his hands still busy touching Ren. It wasn't often he had the luxury of time with a partner after sex, and he was enjoying the moment.

"So what's your story?" Ren asked.

His fingers ceased stroking. "What do you mean, my story?"

"What do you do for a living?" A deep dimple creased his cheek. "Pick up guys in the airport and have incredible sex with them?"

He forced himself to remain calm. "I think that's considered prostitution," he answered with a frown. "I'm not a hooker, in case you're worried."

Ren shifted to sitting upright. "I didn't think so. I was joking." He slid a bare foot up his shin. "I'm sorry. I guess I'm out of practice at making small talk."

The tension drained from Schaeffer. "No, don't apologize." In a way it did hit a little too close to home, considering his past sex life of "get it and forget it."

"I'm an airline pilot."

Ren's jaw dropped. "You're shitting me."

"No. I started out in the Air Force. I always loved flying and started taking lessons when I was sixteen. Went to college and followed all the channels to get into an officers' school so I could fly. I had to give them a ten-year commitment, but I was ready. I wanted it. After that, I signed on for ten more years. That's when I went to Afghanistan."

Concerned, understanding eyes met his. "Was it as bad as what we saw on TV?"

"Worse," he whispered. "I—it's like nothing I've ever seen before or since. Or ever want to." His eyes burned hot with unshed, threatening tears. Tears he'd been holding inside since everything happened. "I-I ended up with a medical discharge, but after a few months, I knew I couldn't sit around for the rest of my life. So I applied to be a pilot with Red White and Blue Airlines."

"And you get to fly for free anywhere you want? Were you supposed to be flying tonight?"

"No, I was a deadhead."

"Huh?" Ren's brow puckered with confusion.

He explained, "An employee of the airline who gets to ride on a flight that has empty seats. We don't pay for them, and we're called deadheads. I was lucky enough to have gotten a seat on that flight to California. When it was canceled, I was lucky to find you."

"Interesting." Ren eyed him with speculation. "How is it? Being a gay pilot? Are your peers supportive?"

His hands tightened on the sheets. "I'm really exhausted. Maybe we should talk more in the morning."

But Ren wasn't finished. "They aren't, are they? Do they give you a lot of grief?"

He fixed his gaze on his lap. "No, they don't know. Only my family."

"You've never told anyone?" Ren seemed shocked.

His mouth twisted in a horrible, fake smile. "Imagine me, twenty years ago, telling one of my superior officers I was gay. The old Don't Ask, Don't Tell was a joke." He shrugged. "When I joined the Air Force, I was twenty-one, right out of college. Anyway, after my medical discharge, I did what a lot of ex-military pilots do—I became a commercial pilot. I've been flying for four years now."

"I imagine it's hard to have relationships."

"It is. And even harder when you're not home for long."

Ren propped up on his elbow. "*Hmm.* With all the flying I've done, it's something I've never thought about. What're your hours?"

"I get about two weeks off a month, but because I'm not senior in years, I usually work weekends. And since I don't have a family, I'm okay with it. Let the parents have time with their kids. I don't have that issue."

They lay silently next to each other, and Schaeffer wondered why he'd unburdened himself. He'd had hotel quickies before, but it usually didn't go beyond sex and an awkward goodbye, knowing they'd never see each other again. He watched as Ren left the bed to peer out of the window.

"Still coming down. Mind if I turn on the light? I want to check my phone and see if there're any updates about tomorrow."

"Yeah, sure, go ahead."

He blinked and rubbed his eyes when Ren switched on the lamp. The sight of their clothes flung to the far corners of the room was a reminder of how lust-crazed they'd been upon entering. Ren scrolled through his phone, then placed it on the nightstand and turned off the light.

"Nothing. I'm not even sure they'll be taking off tomorrow." With a sigh, he returned to the bed, sliding his bare legs in between Schaeffer's. "Guess we might be stuck together longer than we thought." A smile curved his lips.

"I hope that won't be a problem."

Getting an entire night with this man was a bonus Schaeffer couldn't have anticipated, and he planned on taking full advantage. "I think I can deal with it if you can." He reached for Ren to pull him close, already feeling his desire rising.

"I can. Hopefully I have enough condoms."

Schaeffer nibbled on the strong cords of Ren's neck. "Guess there's only one way to find out." Their lips met, Ren's mouth open, hot, and wet, and Schaeffer fell into the kiss.

Schaeffer had no idea where he found the stamina, but they had sex twice more that night. Maybe it was his prolonged abstinence, as he'd been flying without long layovers, and when he had the time off, all he wanted was to sleep. But Ren made him insatiable. The second Schaeffer touched him, he wanted him. And lucky for him, Ren was equally needy.

At three a.m., Ren needed to make a run to the lobby to see if he could find what they needed. Schaeffer waited in bed, and Ren reentered the room. He held up six small packets.

"I feel like a high school kid sneaking out to do all the bad, wrong things. Lucky for us, the bathroom had one of those old machines."

Schaeffer eyed them. "I hope they're not expired. God knows the last time that machine was used."

Ren fell out laughing. "Are you kidding? Expiration dates are a year from now. They had three different kinds to choose from. All sizes, colors, and tastes." He put the pile of foil wrappers on the nightstand. "And you bet your sweet ass I wasn't the only one there looking." His eyes twinkled, and Schaeffer laughed.

"Well, there isn't room service and the cable is spotty because of the weather, so what else is there to do?"

Ren smirked. "Got that right." He got naked and climbed into bed, but at the moment, Schaeffer was more interested in talking than having sex. When Ren started kissing him, he put a hand to his face. "We should slow down. Otherwise, we could run out, and then we'll be stuck."

Ren settled against the headboard. "I guess you're right. We could watch television." He found the remote and switched it on, and as Schaeffer had suspected, the satellite wasn't working and all they had was snow and the pay-per-view. Ren snorted and shut it off.

"I'm not gonna pay to watch straight porn."

Schaeffer chuckled. "How about you tell me more about your travels? What other animals have you photographed?"

Ren studied his hands. "Quite a lot, but I think the snow leopard was my favorite. They're so beautiful and elusive. It was one of my first freelance assignments, and it took me three months before I sighted my girl. I named her Windy. I knew she was there from tracks in the snow, but she'd just had her litter and was extremely protective and wary."

"I've only seen them on television shows, but it looks like they survive only in very remote places and harsh conditions."

"It was the most isolated location I'd ever been to. High in the mountains of East Asia—Mongolia. They face the scourge of human population growth, as well as infrastructure development linking China to Europe. These transportation corridors, as they're called, are running directly through their territory. And then there are the farms. Even though it's illegal to hunt and kill snow leopards, that doesn't stop the farmers from shooting them when they come after their livestock."

The love for his work and the animals he photographed shone from Ren's eyes, and Schaeffer was caught up in his passionate words. "That's an incredible story."

"I'm lucky. My job is more than a means to pay my bills. It's part of my life."

The edge of a heartbreakingly sad smile touched Ren's lips, and Schaeffer wondered at the rest of the story. Why would a man so full of life cut himself off from the rest of the world for months and months?

"Didn't you…wasn't it lonely? I know I said it already, but that sounded like you were in the middle of nowhere."

"It was what I needed at the time."

Why, dammit? Schaeffer wanted to know why a man like Ren—charming, funny, and sexy as hell—needed that solitude. He could suggest making some coffee and getting to know each other better instead of slapping their bodies together again. The friction it created was heart-stopping, but eventually they had to come up for air. And the way it looked outside, they'd be here for a while.

Then he heard the sound of deep, easy breathing next to him. Ren's eyes were closed, and his chest rose and fell steadily.

Guess his answers would have to wait.

CHAPTER THREE

He wasn't asleep.

How could he rest with all the ugly memories running through his mind like a pinball dinging the corners of a machine? Schaeffer's questions and the emotions they'd dragged to the surface had him wishing he could leave the room and never return.

It had all gone so well up to that point. He hadn't laughed and enjoyed being with another person as much since the trip with his brothers, Chris and Kevin. His foster brothers. His only family. All gone in a split second. What else could he do but hide away from the life that had taken everything from him?

Running away, immersing himself in those windswept nights and the brutal cold forcing him to focus on his survival, hadn't helped. His thoughts had been consumed with his devastating loss as he'd waited out a raging blizzard. The weather calmed and he'd walked out into the world filled with nothing but endless white, he'd contemplated chucking it all—the job…life…walking off into the mountains and disappearing for good. He was an insignificant speck. Who would notice?

Then he'd spotted her. The snow leopard with her cubs. The most beautiful sight he'd ever seen, bringing tears to his eyes that froze on his lashes, temporarily blinding him, but he didn't care. He'd retraced his steps into his shed, retrieved his camera, and taken the pictures that changed his mindset and life forever. Beauty existed everywhere, and without him to show the world, no one would know. Her plight, and that of all of those in jeopardy, rested in the hands of people like him. People willing to take the risk to prove that yes, if a tree fell in the forest and no one was around, there was a sound. It was the sound of a future, gasping for air.

She'd never know it, but his leopard saved him, giving him hope when he'd believed he had nothing left of his heart.

He continued his deep breathing and eventually, he must've fallen asleep for real. He opened his eyes and the digital clock glowed 3:11. And as always, once awake, he couldn't fall back asleep, so, leaving Schaeffer huddled under the covers, he padded to the bathroom and made sure to close the door so the toilet flush wouldn't wake him. He tiptoed out, retrieved his knapsack and cursed, realizing he didn't have a toothbrush or toothpaste. He'd put that in his checked luggage, and God knew when or if he'd ever see it again. Thankful for the small bottle of hotel mouthwash, he rinsed his mouth. Better than nothing.

He returned to the room and stood in front of the coffeemaker, dying for a cup but hesitant to wake up Schaeffer. He checked outside. The snow had stopped, and all was silent. A glance at the bed found Schaeffer sitting up, those gray eyes still hazy with sleep but no less beautiful.

"Did I wake you? I'm sorry. It stopped snowing."

"No, you didn't. I guess I sensed you weren't in bed any longer, and I wondered if you'd left."

Puzzled, he sat on the edge of the bed. "Leave? Why would I?"

Schaeffer broke eye contact and lifted a shoulder. "It's how it goes. I meet someone, we have sex, and they leave."

Damn, it broke his heart to think of Schaeffer being left. While he'd never had a relationship, he knew a few guys in the city whom he could call and have a good time. Not like what he'd had with Schaeffer, but Ren chalked up the explosive intensity to it being his first time after a long dry spell. Things were bound to get down and dirty. Everything felt better when you hadn't had it for a while.

"Where would I go?" Ren leaned in close and kissed Schaeffer, intending it to be quick and fun, but he lingered, enjoying the softness of his lips. Schaeffer's breathing grew heavier, he pressed harder and was rewarded with a moan and the touch of his tongue.

"I don't know, maybe the airport to see what's going on? I know you're anxious to get to California."

All this was said in short gasps because it seemed Ren couldn't stop kissing Schaeffer in between his words.

"I'm anxious to get you inside me." He slipped in next to Schaeffer, and without preamble, took his cock into his mouth. Schaeffer's cries turned to pleas, and Ren gave him one final lick before letting him go.

"What the fuck?" he panted, eyes glazed and dark with hunger.

"I need this." Ren reached over to get the condom, then rolled it over Schaeffer's heavy erection. With Schaeffer holding his hips steady, Ren rose on his knees and sank onto his shaft. "Oh, yeah. God, so good. You're killing me."

Schaeffer grabbed him around the neck and rose up to meet him with a crushing kiss. Ren had missed this. The burning sense of being filled to the point of splitting in half and falling apart. Hot, messy kisses and strong arms holding him tight. They rose and fell in perfect rhythm as if they'd known each other for years, not mere hours. They came almost simultaneously, Ren holding his dick while Schaeffer's fingers dug into his hips, giving him purchase as he thrust up inside him.

Legs wobbly and still a bit fuzzy at the edges, Ren climbed off Schaeffer and fell onto the bed, breathing heavily. Schaeffer left him to use the bathroom, and a moment later Ren's phone buzzed. He scrambled to get it, and when he saw the notification, called out to Schaeffer, "They got me on a flight leaving at seven thirty this morning. Check your messages."

Schaeffer stuck his head out of the bathroom. "Okay."

Ren accepted the booking and waited for Schaeffer to tell him if he was on the same flight. Hopefully, they could switch seats with one of the passengers sitting next to them so they could be together.

"No. I'm not leaving until Wednesday, and even that could change." His smile was contemplative. "It's because of what I told you. They need to take care of the paying customers first."

Dammit. Determined not to let the mood sour, Ren rolled out of bed and pulled Schaeffer into the shower. "Guess we'd better make good use of the time we have left."

Decidedly shaky-legged from having Schaeffer in him more than out for the past twelve hours, Ren walked slower than usual as they approached the restaurant.

"I'm starving," Ren said. "I hope they have food left."

"I do too. That burger last night was good, but it's only

a memory now."

It was early enough that it only took ten minutes to be seated. Schaeffer warned him that the flight might be delayed again, so he would be wise to order more than he could eat and take it with him. Taking his advice, he decided on a full pancake breakfast with eggs and bacon to eat in, and a turkey and Swiss sandwich to take for later.

Schaeffer had a cheese omelet, bacon, and home fries, and got himself a few Danishes and three muffins to take with him.

Ren chewed his bacon. "Feeling the need for a sugar rush?"

He shrugged. "Once you leave, I'll just pick at these until I get to the airport, whenever that might be. I hate eating alone."

Inexplicably saddened by the thought that at this time tomorrow they wouldn't be together, but not knowing what to say, Ren nodded and stuffed more pancake into his mouth. It wasn't as if he could tell Schaeffer he'd stay and wait. He didn't have endless time off. His next assignment was one he'd been relishing since he'd received it—an attempt to photograph the endangered Sierra Nevada red fox, a creature essential for the local ecosystem.

"Schaeffer, you got caught up in this mess too?" a deep voice came from behind him.

Ren set his fork on the plate and met Schaeffer's startled expression. Recalling Schaeffer wasn't out, Ren gave him a tiny nod, as if to say he remembered, and the slight panic in Schaeffer's eyes receded.

"Frank, yeah, kind of. I wasn't working. I was supposed to be flying out to California to see my family."

"You want to pick up a flight? Jessop, who was on the seven thirty, can't make it. He skidded off the thruway on his way in to work, and he's in the hospital. If you're interested…" Frank glanced at Ren for the first time. "Sorry.

Didn't mean to interrupt your breakfast."

"It's okay, we're almost done," Schaeffer responded quickly. "Ren, this is Franklin Conners. He was the captain on my first flight when I joined RWB Airlines."

"Nice to meet you." Frank inclined his head and gave him an impersonal smile, which Ren returned. Frank then focused on Schaeffer. "What do you say? If you log on to NAVBLUE, I'm sure you can name your route. I hear they're desperate. Half the crews are out because of the weather."

Ren's eyes flicked up from his plate to find Schaeffer's gaze on him. He raised his brows and chomped on a piece of bacon.

"Maybe I will."

"Well, okay. I'd better go. I'm due out on the twelve o'clock to Dallas."

"It's so early." Schaeffer checked his watch. "What're you going to do over there all day?"

Frank's expression turned conspiratorial. "I'm not going to the terminal. You know Teresa, one of the new flight attendants? Gorgeous redhead with a great ass. I'm meeting her upstairs." He winked. "She couldn't sleep."

Schaeffer's hand tightened on his fork. "Uh…you and Bridget got a divorce? You never told me."

"Nah. But I'm here, and so's Teresa, and what Bridget don't know won't hurt her. Know what I mean? Want me to see if she has a friend?"

"Ah, no thanks." Schaeffer looked extremely uncomfortable, and Ren wished this blowhard would leave.

Frank eyed Ren. "I'm sure Teresa could hook you up as well. There are lots of bored ladies around, looking for some fun."

Ren had never hidden who he was and he wouldn't start now, but he didn't have to make Schaeffer uncomfortable either. "Thanks, but I'm sort of with someone at the moment."

Not a truth but not a lie.

"All right. Talk to you, Schaeffer."

Chuckling, he walked away, and Ren winced.

"So this is one of your esteemed colleagues who'd look down on you for who you are, yet he's a cheating, lying SOB."

"I don't know about him. He's never said anything homophobic to me." Schaeffer toyed with his eggs. "I really hate hearing shit like that. I met his wife a few years ago. She's very sweet. They have four kids at home. What's wrong with these people that they can't keep it in their pants?"

Staring off into the crowd of diners, Ren shrugged. "I guess they do it because they can? He's probably been cheating on her for years."

Dispiritedly, Schaeffer forked more eggs into his mouth and chewed. "It's just sad. Some people would give everything for what they have, and they're busy throwing it all away."

"Do you want that? Marriage and kids?"

Schaeffer's smile was a combination of sorrowful and sweet. "First I'd like to be able to go out on a date without worrying. I can't even think that far ahead about the other stuff."

"At least we had some time together last night." He grinned in an attempt to lighten the mood.

"And don't forget earlier."

Relieved that the vibe had turned more positive, Ren nonchalantly stuffed some more pancakes into his mouth. "The day is young."

Schaeffer picked up the pace and cleaned off his plate. "Check, please."

Ren finished his coffee and tossed a bunch of bills onto the table. "We don't need to wait." He rose to his feet, and Schaeffer followed at his heels but stopped him before they made it to the elevator banks.

"I have to check and see if the room is still available for today, and change the reservation to my name, in case I don't get onto your flight. Hang on a second."

Ren waited, watching Schaeffer talk to the front-desk clerk and make the necessary arrangements. Funny how Schaeffer had become so familiar, so fast. Stuffing his wallet into his pocket, Schaeffer retraced his steps to where Ren stood.

"All set?" he asked.

"Yeah. No trouble at all." Schaeffer hit the elevator button.

In the haven of their room, instead of the hot, frantic sex they'd had, they spent their time kissing and touching, learning every inch of their bodies; using their lips, tongues, and hands as if they knew that because their time together was coming to an end, they wanted to soak in each other's scent…taste…touch. For him, there was no better feeling in the world than the harsh rasp of a lover's body as it played against the dichotomy of soft lips and velvet-smooth tongue.

He trailed his hand along the strong curve of Schaeffer's back and placed a kiss at his nape. "I'm going to shower."

A noise drew him to the window instead, and nose to the glass, he peered outside.

"Look," he said, pointing out the window. "Planes are already taking off."

According to the news he'd read on his phone, the total snowfall was about twenty inches, but with the temperature rising, it had begun to melt. It would take a long time until cars could be dug out and the streets plowed, but the airport was busy clearing the runways.

Schaeffer joined him, and Ren leaned into his broad chest. They were of similar height and build and fit together perfectly. It had been so long for him without the touch of another, Ren found himself greedy for it and wanted Schaeffer's arms around him all the time. *Damn*. Since when had he become such a needy bastard? Who cares, he decided, his brain fuzzy with lust, and hummed with pleasure at the touch of Schaeffer's lips on his neck.

"Of course. Getting the runways operational is top priority. They have to get the world moving again." One final kiss, and then Schaeffer left him. "I'm going to log in now and see if I can get on that flight to Santa Ana this morning."

Ren watched him as he returned to the bed. "How does that work? Don't you have a set plane you have to fly?"

Head bent over his laptop, Schaeffer's fingers flew over the keys. "Nope. We have to bid on the flights we want. Senior pilots will usually get first choice, and they have their favorite routes."

"You're not senior? I thought you were the captain."

"No. I'm a first officer. Four years in still makes me pretty new, so I have some time to go. But I'm fine with it. I'm learning a lot. It's a hell of a lot different than an Air Force jet, for sure."

"I can only imagine." He watched and waited as Schaeffer input his information, and within two minutes, a big smile burst over Schaeffer's face. "Got it." He closed the lid. "I might not be your seatmate, but I will be traveling with you."

"Is there a mile-high club for pilots?" he joked, but Schaeffer didn't join him.

"That's almost impossible. Frank is pretty much an anomaly. Most pilots are happily married and not fooling around with flight attendants. We're all there to do a job."

The last thing he wanted was to insult Schaeffer. "Hey, I didn't mean anything by it—just me being silly. I'm sure you're the utmost in professional conduct."

"I try. Honestly, I rarely come out of the flight deck. The captain is the one who'll step out to take a break and chat."

Ren frowned. "So what you're saying is that once we

get to the airport, it's pretty much goodbye." A pang hit his heart, but he was resigned. Tomorrows were never promised. A lesson he'd learned in the hardest way possible.

"Yeah. I have protocols to follow."

"I get it." He thought for a moment. "Maybe we can share a ride when we land?"

"My brother is picking me up. I haven't been able to see him or my niece and nephew in a while."

"What does he do?"

"Corporate risk management."

"And he's older?"

"Only by two years, but he never lets me forget it." A flash of humor glimmered in Schaeffer's eyes. "He's forty-seven, but don't tell him that. He's fighting it every step of the way and looks damn good. Better than me."

Raising his brows, Ren gave Schaeffer, who now reclined on the bed, an appreciative once-over. "I'm not complaining. You look and feel pretty damn good to me."

Bright red crept up Schaeffer's neck. "Same."

Ren strolled to his side. "We still have a little time until we have to leave."

His gaze hot, Schaeffer kicked off the covers. "Let's stop wasting time."

"Have everything?" Schaeffer asked him.

"Yeah. The most important things are my cameras, and I have them in here." He tilted his head toward the hard rolling case behind him. "The other stuff is no big deal—just some clothes and incidentals."

"Okay. We'd better get going. I'm sure the hotel shuttle to the airport is gonna be crowded, and it's always better to be early than late."

"I'm with you." He waited behind Schaeffer for him to open the hotel room door.

Instead, Schaeffer turned and cupped his cheek. "I wish…I wish I could say goodbye the proper way, in public, but I-I can't."

"I get it."

As if pained, Schaeffer's lips twisted in a grimace. "I wish I did." His thumb played along Ren's cheek, and he sighed. "But anyway, I wanted to be able to do this, one last time."

Like coming home, Schaeffer's lips tasted sweet and hot, and Ren rested his hands on Schaeffer's hips as they kissed. Schaeffer held his head steady and slipped his tongue in Ren's mouth, and Ren sucked it briefly. He released Schaeffer with a painful sigh.

"If you don't stop, we'll miss our plane."

Those storm-cloud-gray eyes filled with regret and something else Ren couldn't determine. "I'm not sure it wouldn't be worth it."

But Ren knew. There was no mention of future get-togethers while they were both in California. Once they landed, he'd be off to enjoy the beach for two weeks before he headed to his next work assignment, while Schaeffer would enjoy his family vacation, then return to the city and the skies.

"I know it would be. But we each have our obligations and our reasons. It was great getting to know you." He kissed Schaeffer again, memorizing the mouth he'd initially believed to be hard and unforgiving. Now he intimately knew how soft and tender those lips could be. "We'd better go."

Once on the crowded shuttle, there was little more to say and no privacy to say it. When they disembarked, he felt one last squeeze on his arm. Then Schaeffer walked away. Head hanging, Ren checked in with the agent to make sure his luggage had been rerouted correctly, sent a prayer because he knew it most likely had not, and made his way to security. It was a little better but still not great even with TSA PreCheck, and by the time he got a cup of coffee and found the gate, he'd had enough of people-ing. Of course there were no seats, so he parked his ass on the floor by the window to wait. Out of the corner of his eye he saw the flight crew approach and sipped from his cup. He immediately spotted Schaeffer and tracked him as he joked with the crew and greeted the gate agents. With a swipe of his ID tag, he disappeared down the jet bridge and was gone.

Ren sighed and finished his coffee.

"Good morning, ladies and gentlemen. We will now begin boarding..."

With a grunt, he rose, and though he was near the rear of the plane and in a middle seat, he elected to stand, knowing he'd be squashed in between God knew who for the six-hour duration of the flight. To his surprise, he heard his name called and approached the ticket agent.

"I'm Renaldo Stewart."

"Mr. Stewart, you've been upgraded to business class." She handed him his new ticket.

"I have? How?"

"Many people either didn't show or elected to take an alternate airline, so a few seats for our elite customers became available for upgrades."

He always forgot that with all the traveling he did, he'd accumulated hundreds of thousands of miles and held a pretty high status. That sort of thing barely mattered to him.

"Thank you very much."

"Thank you for your loyalty and for flying with RWB Airlines. You can board with group one now."

It was a long way from where he'd started, scrounging for enough money to make the subway fare from Brooklyn to the Bronx Zoo.

As he entered the plane, he peeked into the flight deck and recognized the back of Schaeffer's head. Even though they weren't communicating, warmth settled in his chest. With a sigh, he lowered himself into the more spacious seat, complete with pillow, blanket, and water bottle. Pleasurably achy and exhausted from the hours of uninhibited sex, he closed his eyes and was asleep before the flight attendants gave the safety lecture.

CHAPTER FOUR

Schaeffer had never worked with Captain Ron Vance before, and he liked the confidence the man had shown when they'd hit a rough patch of turbulence over Flagstaff.

"Thirty years flying these jets, Schaeffer. And I like the long-haul flights."

"How come?"

"Gives me a chance to rest a bit. All those less-than-three-hour jump flights get harder as you get older."

"How much longer are you planning on flying?"

A wistful expression crossed Vance's face. "Only two more years. My wife and I want time to enjoy our grandchildren." With the plane flying on automatic, Vance showed him pictures. "That's my son and daughter-in-law and their three little ones." He scrolled to the next screen. "And my daughter and her wife have one on the way."

Schaeffer blinked. "That's wonderful. Congratulations." The ease with which Vance introduced his daughter and daughter-in-law made him hope that if he came out, people would be as accepting.

Vance took the controls again. "The important thing is being there for the people who mean the most."

"I agree. I'm on my way to visit my family. My brother and sister-in-law are barbecuing, and my father is a huge Lakers fan, so we'll be watching the games. And of course, my niece and nephew will want to go to the beach."

"Sounds like a nice vacation." Vance nodded with approval. They were now flying over Lake Havasu. Only about an hour or so to go. "You're not married, are you?"

"No, sir."

"No need to sir me. Ron was a good enough name for my father, and it works for me."

"Just my Air Force training. Hard to break."

"Got a special someone?"

He thought of Ren sitting on the plane, less than one hundred feet away from him, but it might as well have been one hundred thousand miles.

"Not really. I haven't been able to make a connection last."

Vance's eyes brimmed with sympathy. "Trust me, I understand. It's not easy. It takes a lot of work when you're away so much. But for that special person, you'll want to put in the overtime. Now take the controls, please. Have to hit the head and get a snack."

The vista all the way to Southern California spread out in front of him, and he smiled to himself, imagining his father puttering around the backyard deck, getting the grill ready for him. The radio crackled.

"Flight One Six Five, you're on course for SNA."

He answered. "Flight One Six Five. Affirmative."

Hand on the instruments, he adjusted the speed and watched for the usual wind at the mountains as they passed over Palm Springs. Vance returned, and Schaeffer left the flight deck to use the bathroom. Afterward, as he listened to the flight attendants talking about their plans that night in Newport Beach, he couldn't help but take a peek through the cabin. Ren wasn't in first class—he was in business and not visible. Yes, he'd checked the manifest.

"Want to come to the beach with us, Schaeffer?" one of the attendants asked. "Supposedly, it's going to be almost eighty degrees. We were thinking of boogie boarding."

"Sorry. I'm all booked up with family time."

"Even in the evening?" Her smile was enticing. "We could take a ride to LA."

"Maybe next time. I'd better get back. Prepare for landing."

He buckled into his seat and listened to Vance make the announcement that they were beginning their descent and give the weather in Southern California. Vance's hands were deft and sure on the instruments while Schaeffer assisted with air traffic control. The flight attendants did their usual prepare-for-landing speech, and within fifteen minutes, they glided onto the runway and taxied down the tarmac. When the plane stopped, he and Vance unbuckled their seat belts. The jet bridge attached to the door, and they gathered their personal items in preparation to leave.

"Pleasure flying with you, Schaeffer. And thanks for filling in for Jessop. Word is he'll be okay. Some bruised ribs, a broken nose, and possible concussion. He'll be out for a few weeks."

"Ouch." He winced. "That's going to hurt like hell."

"Yep, but he got lucky." Vance rose and rolled his shoulders. "All right. Let's go make nice with the passengers so we can get out of here."

Both stood in the door to the flight deck with the flight attendants, wishing everyone a good stay in sunny Southern California. At the sight of Ren walking toward him, his heart beat faster. He wished…God, he wished things could be different, wished he could be more courageous and free. Wished for the impossible. Their eyes met.

"I hope you had a good flight," he said.

"I slept, since I didn't get much rest the night before." God, he hoped his cheeks weren't red.

"Have a nice stay."

And then he was gone.

It took almost twenty minutes for the plane to empty out and for them to file all their paperwork. Now that Ren had left, he was anxious to see his family and texted his father and brother in their group chat that he'd landed.

Anson couldn't make it. Waiting outside. Move your butt.

Laughing and now lighthearted, he quickened his pace. If he couldn't keep a relationship, at least he had a loving family. From the bits and pieces Ren had let slip of his childhood, he didn't have either.

John Wayne Airport was the perfect, low-key place to land—you walked outside, and palm trees surrounded you. Unlike the hustlers and honking horns outside of JFK and LaGuardia, an orderly line of cars awaited to pick up passengers. The area was small enough that he spotted his father immediately in the new Jeep he'd leased. At the sound of the horn, he raised a hand and hurried over.

"Thanks, Dad. I'm sorry you had to get up so early. I could've taken an Uber."

"Pfft. And pay all that money?"

"Dad. It's ten minutes away. You could've stayed in bed."

"I haven't seen you in months. You think I'm sleeping when I know you're coming? Anson took Kendra's car to the shop—it wouldn't start this morning. She took the kids to school. They didn't want to go. They're so excited you're coming."

A swell of emotion tightened his throat. As much as he loved living in New York City, he missed his family and looked forward to having a week to do nothing but soak in the good times with them.

They pulled out of the airport onto MacArthur Boulevard, and within minutes, merged onto the 55 Freeway. He yawned, and his father sent him a sharp look.

"You okay? Not getting burned out, are you?"

"No, just tired."

"You didn't sleep much at the hotel? Too busy watching the snow fall?" Cackling, his father left the 55 and joined the traffic on the 5 Freeway, and soon they were passing the familiar sights of Tustin—the high school and its football field. Schaeffer had been a star running back, and more importantly, it was where he had his first kiss with another boy, Johnny DeMarco, under the bleachers. They'd meet in the park after hanging out with their friends, and they'd trade quick, explosive blowjobs. The fear of exposure had lurked around every tree or bush they'd hidden behind, but their desire was too strong to resist. They continued until graduation, when Schaeffer went to UC Riverside, and Johnny entered UC Irvine. Last he'd heard, Johnny was an accountant in Newport Beach and married to a former pageant queen. They had four kids.

"Not really." Too busy having sex with the most intriguing man he'd ever met. "I never sleep well in hotel rooms."

"Here we are."

They pulled into the driveway of his father's modest three-bedroom, two-bath ranch. A large tree provided shade across the front bay window. With the real estate market booming, he'd benefited from the rising home prices, and as a former contractor, was able to update and modernize the property.

Schaeffer took his carry-on into the house and walked through the open and airy living area. Sliding glass doors provided a direct view to the backyard deck and the sparkling pool.

"I'll be out there this afternoon, once I take a nap," he threw over his shoulder.

"Take as long as you need. Anson and Kendra won't be here until the kids get out of school—probably about four."

"No way I'll sleep that late. We'll have lunch."

His old bed with its navy comforter and fluffy white pillows beckoned, so he kicked off his shoes, and without even undressing, lay down and closed his eyes.

A pounding on the door woke him, and before he had a chance to blink, it slammed open and his niece and nephew hurtled inside and threw themselves onto the bed with him.

"Time to get up," his brother announced.

"Uncle Schaeffer, I got an A on my spelling test," Scotty yelled at top volume. In his ear.

"And I painted you a picture, see?" Mini chattered. A crayon drawing of a lopsided plane flying into some palm trees was thrust in his face. Mini's real name was Claire, but she was such an exact duplicate of her mother, they all called her Kendra's mini-me, which she'd shortened to Mini herself.

"Beautiful, honey." He kissed the top of her head. "And go you, Scotty. That's great. Your father couldn't spell 'cat' at your age." He snickered and ducked the stuffed football Anson threw at his head.

"Listen, you gonna sleep the whole day away, you lazy bum?"

He rose from the bed to give Anson a hug.

"Good to see you too. I was up earlier. Just taking a predinner nap. Where's your better half?" Holding a clinging

Mini in one arm, he gave her another hug, and set her on her feet.

"She's with Dad, getting the food ready and pouring her glass of wine."

"After a day teaching young kids, she deserves the whole bottle." He slung an arm around Anson's shoulders while Scotty ran ahead shouting for his mother who, as Anson had predicted, stood at the large island with a glass of white wine. When she saw him, she put it down and held out her arms.

"Get over here, you big lug."

He kissed her and laughed. "Love you too."

Her gaze traveled from him to his father and Anson, who were taking out the fruit-and-cheese platter and beer from the refrigerator.

"All my guys in one place at the same time? I'm the happiest girl in the world."

He accepted a bottle from his brother. "Thanks. You're looking gorgeous as usual."

"And you're still tired, even though Dad said you conked out right after he brought you home this morning and took a second nap. You working too hard? Or was it just the jet lag catching up with you?"

"You do look at little ragged." His brother frowned. "Seriously. You okay?"

"I'm fine." He took a slug of beer, unwilling to say more. "Kids look great." They were playing outside. You'd never know a man in his seventies lived in the house, considering the backyard had a swing set, trampoline, and pool.

Anson's face softened. "Still having nightmares?"

"I'm fine," he answered quickly. His stomach growled, and the slight tension swirling around them broke. "Hey, I'm hungry. Isn't it dinnertime?"

His father picked up the plate of burger patties, and Anson took the hot dogs. "Let's get it on. Can you get the corn and buns out of the fridge?"

"Sure thing." He slid out the ears and handed the buns to Kendra. "Do I spy homemade coleslaw, potato, *and* macaroni salad?"

"All for you. Everyone needs to come home to a meal filled with love." Kendra waited until he closed the refrigerator door. "And speaking of love, I know you don't talk about it much, but are you seeing anyone? Living in New York, you must have the opportunity to meet so many men. Is there anyone special?" His brows rose, and she met that with a shrug. "Hey, I waited a few minutes before asking."

He hugged her again. "I love you."

He was one of the lucky ones. When he came out, his father and Anson supported him without hesitation. They understood why he kept it a secret while he was in the military, but since he was discharged, they'd begun to question his reasons for living a dateless, loveless life.

"You know how hard it is with my schedule."

Kendra's pretty brown eyes grew steely, and he braced himself. She might be ten years younger than Anson, only one hundred pounds and five-foot nothing, but woe to the person who ignored her with a smile or a nod and thought to dismiss her. It was the joke of the family how she'd brushed Anson off the first time he asked her out, saying, *"What does a white boy from Orange County want with a Black girl from LA?"*

Apparently, everything. After the conference where they'd met—Kendra had been one of the waitresses in the restaurant where Anson ate breakfast and dinner every night at his conference—Anson had returned home and told them he'd met the woman he was going to marry. Each weekend, he'd drive up to see her to prove he had more in mind than a brief fling.

In a year, that prediction came true, and at their wedding in his father's house, Schaeffer had never seen his brother happier.

Kendra was getting her college degree, and after their marriage, she received her master's in teaching. She and Anson were as fiercely in love all these years later as they were on their wedding day.

"I'd agree with you, except that so many pilots are married or have a steady someone. Besides, you have a great pension from the military. You don't need to kill yourself. Take some Schaeffer time."

He hugged her. "I plan to do just that with all of you at the beach this weekend."

"That's not what I mean and you know it, but you've only been here a few hours, so I'll hold off on the nagging for a day or two." Her generous lips kicked up in a grin. "We'd better get out there, or the men will be screaming for their side dishes. I had to keep your brother from dipping into the potato salad all last night as I was making it."

Laughing, he followed her outside but couldn't help wondering where Ren was spending the night, wishing he too could have a loving family to welcome him home.

CHAPTER FIVE

Four days on the beach can help revitalize even the most wounded soul.

Toes in the sand, Ren lifted his face to the sky and breathed in the salty air. It had been an unusually warm week in Southern California, and at night in his Airbnb he watched the news stories of another snowstorm back east and raised a bottle of beer to the set.

"Better you than me, folks. Not gonna lie."

He'd rented a car, and the first day, too wound up to sleep, drove the Pacific Coast Highway up to Rancho Palos Verdes and spent the day hiking, soaking in the sweeping views from the different vantage points.

After that, he'd returned to Newport Beach, bought beach towels, a ton of food, more sunscreen, and had spent hours on the sand. Every day he brought one thermos of coffee and one of water, a bag full of fruit and some sandwiches, a portable battery for his phone and, of course, his cameras.

Early morning walks had gifted him with whale sightings far out in the ocean and dolphins a bit closer to shore. He'd caught tons of pelicans flying overhead and was thinking of taking a ride to La Jolla to photograph the lolling seals on the beach.

But for now, he was enjoying this Saturday, and even though the beach was filling up, he didn't mind. At some point, he'd have to get used to humanity versus wildlife again.

A small crowd began to gather at the shoreline, and he rose to his feet as well. Following the horizon to where people were pointing, he could make out the spray of water and the large gray bulk lifting out of the water.

"Whale," he heard someone call out, and he grabbed his camera and raced to the ocean.

He stood along with everyone else, and lucky for him, with his professional equipment, he was able to zoom and focus on the glittering water. Having perfected the art of waiting motionless, he remained still and was rewarded when, after three minutes, the majestic bulk heaved itself up. His rapid-fire shutter captured the moment, and his lips curved in a smile as he continued to shoot.

"Uncle Schaeffer, Uncle Schaeffer, did you see? Was that a whale?" Excited children's voices carried in the air.

He froze, and forgetting about the whale, turned around, but with his camera on such high zoom, only saw blurry images. After he adjusted, he spotted Schaeffer, a little girl bouncing on his shoulders, face animated and bright. A young boy was standing in front of him, pointing.

God, he looked…perfect. Broad shoulders he remembered pinning him down to the bed, his chest gleaming with sweat and sunscreen, his hair lying in messy, damp waves over his brow. A slight sunburn reddened his nose.

Without thinking, he snapped a slew of pictures. Schaeffer, perhaps sensing someone staring, faced him and pushed his sunglasses over the top of his head, revealing those beautiful gray eyes, now cold with anger. Ren lowered the camera and raised his brows. He wasn't sure if Schaeffer would acknowledge him, especially with his family at his side.

A range of emotions flickered over Schaeffer's face, the anger changing to disbelief and shock. Then came what Ren had hoped for—a smile. The child slid from his arms until her feet touched the sand, and Schaeffer took both her and her brother by the hand and whispered in their ears. They nodded and ran off. Ren glanced over and saw a man and woman sitting under an umbrella on chairs over a large blanket spread on the sand, probably Schaeffer's brother and sister-in-law.

Schaeffer approached him. "I thought it was some creeper taking pictures of kids, but it's you."

"In the flesh." He laughed, and as Schaeffer drew near, he lowered his voice. "Although I know you're used to seeing me with less on."

That cute blush tinged Schaeffer's cheeks. "What I see looks pretty damn good," he murmured. "How've you been? Where are you staying?"

"I rented a house nearby. So far it's been great. Beach every day. Filling my soul with fresh sea air. It's been a while since I've spent any time near the ocean."

"You've come to the right place."

Their gazes locked, and Ren wondered if Schaeffer was remembering their time together and the naked abandon they'd shared in the dingy room. "How—how're you doing? You look great. You're here with your family?" He tipped his head toward them.

"Yeah, my brother, Anson, and his wife, Kendra. Mini and Scotty are my niece and nephew." Schaeffer licked his lips. "Would you…do you want to come meet them?"

"I wouldn't want to interrupt your family time."

"It's okay." Schaeffer gave him that grin he remembered from New York, and his heart performed strange gymnastics. "Because out of the corner of my eye I see them coming over, so it looks like you're trapped, whether you like it or not." He leaned in close. "Don't worry. You've faced down rhinos and leopards."

Ren set his baseball cap more firmly on his head. "Yeah, but they don't ask questions," he muttered.

"Hi. I'm Kendra, Schaeffer's sister-in-law. Do you two know each other?" Big brown eyes focused on him, and her face brightened. Her hair was done in braids to her shoulders, and a visor shaded her eyes.

"Nice and subtle, Kendra. Have you ever seen me talking to someone else on the beach before? Yes, we do."

"He's got you there, babe." His brother snickered. "I'm Anson, the older, wiser brother."

"Good to meet you both. I'm Ren."

"Do you know each other from the city?" Kendra asked, holding on to the little girl's hand. The boy was running to and from the sand to the shoreline.

"We met in New York during the snowstorm. Kept each other company watching the departures board." Ren figured that was the safest answer to give.

"I'm glad you two didn't have to be alone." She eyed him. "Are you here with anyone?"

He enjoyed her indirect questions. "No. I rented an Airbnb nearby, and I'm doing nothing but enjoying the beautiful, warm weather."

"That's great. We're in Tustin."

"Nice area."

Anson and Schaeffer exchanged looks as if they were used to this. Ren's lips twitched as Kendra continued.

"Schaeffer is staying with his father, so it's not too far. You know, in case you two want to see each other."

"Kendra, you want to make dinner reservations for us?"

Schaeffer interjected. "Or maybe buy our movie tickets?" Clearly annoyed, Schaeffer folded his arms.

Unfazed, she shrugged. "I'm simply stating facts. If Ren isn't familiar with the area, he might not know." The little girl joined her brother, racing around on the sand.

"Thanks, Kendra. I'm somewhat familiar with Orange County. But I know Schaeffer was really looking forward to spending time with you all, so I don't want to intrude."

"You wouldn't be," Schaeffer murmured, and that funny dance in his chest began again. "I've spent every night this week with them and my father. Today he announced he's watching the Lakers game and staying put. And those two"—he pointed at Kendra and Anson, who were trying not to grin and failing miserably—"they've got their date night. The kids both have sleepovers at their friends'." He raised a brow. "I'm free."

This was a much different Schaeffer than he'd left at the airport. There, in public, he'd been slightly uptight, only sharing that beautiful smile with him in the privacy of the room and their bed. Here, with his family, he was light and free. Ren was glad Schaeffer had a safe place to be himself with people who loved him. Ren didn't have that concern. Those who'd mattered most to him were gone. Anyone else's acceptance of his sexuality didn't matter one damn bit.

"I guess we could do something, if you'd like."

"I'd like," Schaeffer said softly, and for the first time since he'd arrived in California, Ren wished the day at the beach was over and it was nighttime. Schaeffer pulled out his phone. "Give me your address, and I'll come to you. We can decide what we want to do when I get there."

Trust me. I know what we're going to be doing. I haven't stopped thinking about you and our time at that hotel.

He finished reciting his address just as the kids came running back. "We're hungry. I want lunch," Scotty demanded.

"Ice cream. I want ice cream." Mini ran around them in circles.

"Kids." Anson fixed them with a frown, and they stopped jumping like rabbits. "Calm down and try not to act like wild animals in front of Uncle Schaeffer's friend."

Ren chuckled. "Trust me, I've seen the real thing, and they're no match for a lion cub."

"Who're you?" Mini asked.

"My name's Ren."

"Are you Uncle Schaeffer's friend?"

He met Schaeffer's eyes. "Yeah. I am."

At six thirty that evening, the doorbell rang, and Ren's nerves kicked into overdrive. He laughed at his foolishness. *You spent almost two days naked with this man. What're you worried about?*

He opened the door and almost swallowed his tongue. The evening had cooled off, and Schaeffer wore a blue button-down tucked into charcoal jeans and looked so damn gorgeous. A touch of silver glimmered in the dark hair at his temples, and those beautiful eyes glittered.

Get a grip. He's just a guy.

But what a guy.

"Come on in."

"Thanks."

As he passed by, Ren inhaled the scent of his aftershave and wanted to end the evening smelling like Schaeffer. He rolled his eyes at his own stupidity.

Schaeffer stood in the living room. "Nice place."

"It's good for what I need. A place to sleep. A deck to grill on when I'm in the mood to make something, and it overlooks the water."

"Beautiful view." Schaeffer wandered around. "Beats the hell out of my apartment in Queens."

"You live there because of the proximity to the airports?"

"Yeah." He settled on the sofa. It was covered in natural linen slipcovers, providing a perfect backdrop for Schaeffer, whose gleaming eyes and sun-burnished skin were a vision of pure masculinity. "Where's your place in the city?"

"I-I don't have one. I keep my stuff in storage. Since I'm away so much, it never made sense to buy or rent." He ran a hand over the club chair. "It doesn't mean much to me. Growing up in foster care, I never had permanency, so I guess that's why I've got no problem living the nomadic life. Didn't make sense to get too attached because people always left." He shrugged. "What do you feel like eating?"

A slow grin crept over Schaeffer's face. "I had an idea—"

"Sounds dangerous," he joked.

"Says the man who's slept surrounded by wild animals," Schaeffer bantered right back, and Ren laughed, enjoying himself more than he had with any other man. "My idea is to do a New York versus California taste test."

"Of what?"

"How about burgers?"

Ren's eyes lit up as Schaeffer's smile broadened. "Oooh, like In-N-Out versus Shake Shack."

"Yep, you know it."

"I dunno, man, last I remember, Shake Shack's fries got it going on."

"Guess we'll have to see. There's one of each nearby. We could order Shake Shack and In-N-Out and bring them here to do the testing." Schaeffer rose to his feet, and they walked to the door.

"I like that. Burgers for dinner and cake for dessert." He winked, and Schaeffer blushed but took Ren's face between his hands and kissed him hard and deep, leaving him breathless and shaking when he released him.

"I've been dying to do that since the beach this afternoon." Schaeffer tugged on his lip, and Ren wanted to rub up against him like a big cat and mark him as his own.

"Let's get those burgers," Ren said and almost didn't recognize his own voice, rough with a combination of longing and desperation.

"I'd rather eat you." Schaeffer's possessive growl sent tingles down his spine.

Ren ran his nose along Schaeffer's cheek, feeling him tremble, loving that he could make this steady man lose control. "Later. That's a promise."

Schaeffer drove, and Ren couldn't get enough of staring at those strong hands on the wheel. Knowing they directed a two-hundred-ton jet at thousands of feet in the air was a big fucking turn-on. Now he understood the enticement of a man in a power position who held your life in his hands.

Jesus, he was becoming a slut for this pilot, and he was not unhappy about it.

They stopped first at In-N-Out, and he jumped out of the car. "I'll go get it." Without waiting for Schaeffer, he ran inside to get their food. He was afraid if he didn't, he'd suggest pulling behind the dumpsters in the parking lot for a quickie, he was that turned-on. He'd spent much of his late teens exploring his sexuality in parks and empty lots in the city. There was always a place for two horny guys to get it on.

The line was predictably long but when it was his turn he ordered their Double-Doubles with everything, plus two orders of fries—one regular and one Animal Style. When he brought it to the car, Schaeffer made an attempt to grab for it once he slid inside, but Ren put the seat belt on and held the food out of reach.

"Come on. Just one little taste. A fry? Please?" He fluttered his lashes, but Ren snorted.

"You'll have to do better than that. I know you can."

Schaeffer blushed. "Shake Shack isn't far. Let's go pick it up and head back to your place."

Schaeffer drove to Shake Shack and went inside to pick up the food while Ren sat and thought about having Schaeffer in his bed. Would he stay the night? Did he want him to? While his body responded with a hell yeah, Ren knew this wasn't about to go anywhere, considering this nomadic life he'd chosen. For the first time, regret swirled inside him.

"That was simple," Schaeffer declared as he settled into the driver's seat. "Online ordering is a lifesaver." Dark brows drew together. "Everything okay? You look way too serious."

Ren shook himself out of his weird vibe. He had this gorgeous man next to him, whom he really liked. Even outside of sex. Time to enjoy it for as long as it lasted.

"I'm good. And I'll be even better once we get to my house." They drove off and hit the PCH, following the trail of cars. At the red light, Ren shifted closer and whispered, "How do you feel about naked french-fry eating?"

"What the hell. Jesus." Schaeffer's smoldering eyes met his, only to have the car behind him lay on the horn and beep at him incessantly. "Calm the fuck down," he grumbled and shot Ren a wicked smile before accelerating. "You're in so much trouble."

Ren stretched his arms overhead and didn't miss Schaeffer's quick ogle of his abs. "Promise?"

They returned as the sun was setting, and watched the orange-streaked sky turn to a blue-hued violet. Ren went inside and brought out two beers, then gestured toward the table.

"Let's eat out here. It's too pretty not to enjoy."

"And you like being outdoors."

He slid the burgers and fries out of the bags and onto the table. "I do. Now. Should we do a blind test?"

Schaeffer shrugged. "Why not?"

"Good. You first." He pulled out a bandanna and brandished it. "Let me blindfold you."

Those dark brows rose high. "Blindfold?"

Giving him no chance to protest further, Ren tied it over his eyes and murmured in his ear, "Don't worry. I'll be gentle."

Schaeffer turned his head and missed Ren's mouth, lips landing on his cheek. "For now."

Ren tore off a piece from each burger and fed them to Schaeffer, his fingers teasing along the outline of his lips. "Good?"

"*Mmm*. Yeah. Although I think you taste better."

"Guess you'll have to find out later." He whipped off the bandanna and handed it to Schaeffer. "My turn."

Schaeffer tied it over his eyes, cutting off his visual sense, so he relied on what he could hear—even movement in the air had a certain sound and feel to it. A bit of burger touched his mouth, and he opened wide. Schaeffer slipped in the bite, and Ren chewed slowly. Finished, he licked Schaeffer's fingertips, which had remained resting on his lips. "So good."

"Next," Schaeffer growled in that husky voice Ren remembered from their time together in the hotel. Obedient, he parted his lips again and fed from Schaeffer's hand. His tongue swiped up the bits of cheese, onion, and ketchup, and he hummed his pleasure.

"All done," Schaeffer purred. "Which one did you like better?"

He couldn't care less anymore and reached behind to take off the bandanna, but Schaeffer's hand stopped him.

"Keep it on. Let's go inside."

Heart banging at a furious pace, he rose, and with Schaeffer's arm around him, proceeded with careful steps into the bungalow.

Schaeffer kept a firm hold on his waist. Ren reached

out with a hand, and Schaeffer took it and placed it on his chest. Frantic pounding played under his palm.

"Feel that. Feel how much I want you."

He pushed Schaeffer's hand to his own breastbone, and they stood listening to the music of their blood, beating hot and fast through their veins.

Schaeffer's breath was ragged against Ren's cheek. "I haven't been able to stop thinking about our time together. I wasn't ready for it to be over."

Ren heard what he couldn't see. The break and crash of the ocean waves. The growing tension between them, rising like a living creature with a life and mind of its own. One that couldn't be stopped even if they tried.

Schaeffer popped the tab of his jeans and tugged, but he batted the long fingers away. "I'll help. I can do this with my eyes closed." Within a few seconds he was naked and could smell Schaeffer's desire in the air.

He was pushed to the bed and remained still, nerves tingling, every hair on his body raised. "You're staring at me, aren't you?"

"I like to look at things of beauty." A warm, wet tongue licked a path from behind his knee to the swell of his ass, and he moaned, legs falling apart. "And you're fucking gorgeous." Kisses pressed to his inner thigh, the jut of his hip bone, avoiding his straining cock.

"I was thinking the same thing. Even though I'm blindfolded, I know what I'm seeing. That sexy swirl of chest hair…strong, hairy calves that feel so good rubbing on mine…a gorgeous dick I want in my ass."

Trusting Schaeffer as he had no other man, ever, Ren lay waiting for Schaeffer's next move. A hand to each knee spread him wide. Ren trembled.

"Not yet." Schaeffer played his tongue along the cleft, the tip of his tongue tickling the rim of his hole. "God, you look and taste like a miracle. One I thought I'd never witness again."

Ren clawed at the bed as Schaeffer's pointed tongue drove deep and firm into his hole. In the dark, the sounds of his gasping and Schaeffer's hungry attack on his body were amplified. So…vibrant and alive. Ren grabbed his dick and rubbed his erection at a furious pace. His toes curled, his head thrashed, and he entered the point of no return. At that moment, Schaeffer pulled out of him, but he was too far gone. He stiffened and came, his cock jerking and jerking, and Schaeffer licked his belly.

"My favorite dessert."

Pliant and boneless, his head still whirling, Ren made an attempt to move his hand. "Condoms in the night table."

He heard the slide and shut of the drawer, and his ass clenched and pulsed with a need so intense, it was a relief to feel the stretch and burn when Schaeffer pushed inside him. He needed this, needed Schaeffer to fill him and make him come alive.

"Jesus, you're everything." Schaeffer ripped off the bandanna and crushed his mouth over Ren's.

Delirious with desire pouring through him like those rolling ocean waves, Ren sucked Schaeffer's tongue, digging his hands into Schaeffer's hair to anchor him in place. His softened dick twitched and filled. "Fuck, you drive me wild." Ren's ankles hooked over the small of Schaeffer's back, sending him deep into his welcoming body. He was split in half yet made whole.

"Oh God," Schaeffer moaned and bit at Ren's lips as he thrust harder and faster. The bed creaked and protested, but Schaeffer drove in until he groaned and came, the hot come filling the condom. "God, Ren," he sighed and buried his face in Ren's neck.

"Yeah," Ren whispered. "I know."

They held each other a moment longer, unwilling to break the spell of perfect pleasure that had been woven around them. Schaeffer kissed his shoulder, then moved out of him. He got rid of the condom and returned to the bed, where he put his head on Ren's chest. Ren felt the curve of his lips against his cooling skin.

"Your heart is pounding." Schaeffer pressed his lips to the place.

"Guess that's what you do to me."

They lay together a few minutes more.

"We never did decide which burgers were the best." Schaeffer laughed.

"We could do breakfast sandwiches in the morning to make up for it." Ren carded his fingers through Schaeffer's thick, dark hair. "Stay with me tonight?"

CHAPTER SIX

He should leave. He had his dad's car—and his dad tended to wake up early—and also, Schaeffer didn't feel like explaining who Ren was when he wasn't quite sure himself. Plus, Anson and Kendra were doing brunch at their house for his first Sunday morning home. But his limbs were heavy, and Ren was warm, and he had no desire to move.

"I'd like that."

"Good. Because I was only asking for show. I wasn't planning on letting you go."

He glanced up at Ren. His heart did a funny loop, and a sudden urge to hold Ren tight and ask him not to leave him...*ever*, struck him and he blinked.

"I'm your prisoner, huh?"

Ren smiled, and Schaeffer settled in and closed his eyes.

He awoke, sitting straight up in bed, sweating and shaking. Ren was by his side, his hand massaging his back.

"Are you okay? You had a bad dream, I think."

He knew. It was the same dream that had plagued him for years—finding his mother dead, watching his best friend's jet explode in the air, and in both instances, him helpless to do anything but stand and watch.

"It—it's okay. Must be the greasy burgers. Gave me indigestion." He climbed out of bed, washed his face with cold water, and directed a stern scowl at the mirror.

Get it together.

Ren had remained in bed, and Schaeffer rejoined him, anxious to put the nightmare behind him.

"Everything okay?"

"Yeah," he lied. "I'm fine."

When it was apparent neither of them could sleep, they showered and went on the deck to gather the remains of their dinner. He made a face at the soggy fries and tossed them into the trash can in the kitchen. "That's a crime. And now I want fries."

Ren checked his phone. "Everything is closed for delivery. We'll have to wait for breakfast." Something must've shown on his face because Ren cocked his head. "What's wrong?"

"Ahh, well, my brother was planning on this big bagel thing tomorrow morning. But it's no big deal."

Ren's smile was strained. "If you want to go…I'll understand."

"I said I'm staying. It's not until noon." Unwilling to have any tension between them, he waved at Ren. "Can we sit?"

Ren shrugged and followed him to the couch.

Schaeffer stretched out his legs. "My family supports me, and if Kendra had her way, she'd be hooking me up with every man she suspected was gay. I'm not keeping you a dirty secret, if that's what you're thinking." His phone chirped, and he ignored it, but it continued. Over and over. "I'm sorry. I need to see what's going on." He checked his texts, rolled his eyes and held it between them so Ren could read the screen. "Case in point. Look at the texts my brother is sending."

How was your date?

Don't worry, brunch isn't until 12:30. Maybe you'll get lucky. Winky emoji.

Why don't you invite Ren tomorrow? Kendra's idea.

"No shit. Of course it's Kendra's idea," he mumbled.

Ren's lips twitched. "They're a handful, huh?"

"That's one way to put it," he muttered, then nudged Ren's knee with his. "Why don't you?"

"Why don't I what?"

"Come to brunch with me. You've already met Kendra and Anson. My dad would love to hear your travel stories."

"I-I dunno. It's a family thing."

"And? You were invited by the family."

Ren stared at his hands, lines of regret etched in his face. "When I was a foster kid, I used to watch all the shows with these perfect parents and their perfect children living their perfect lives. I knew it was bullshit, but I was hooked, you know? I guess you want what you know you can't have."

"Were you ever adopted?"

"Nah." He lifted a shoulder. "I had about five foster homes. They were okay."

"You turned out pretty good, far as I can see." He couldn't imagine not having his family there. "Did you… did you ever try and find your parents? Are they around?"

A corner of Ren's mouth kicked up. "I never knew who my father was. My mother left me with a neighbor.…Later I learned that she was killed by a guy she'd spent the night with. ACS took over and put me in foster care. I was four years old, and no one ever came to find me."

Schaeffer put an arm over his shoulders and pulled him close. "I'm sorry."

"Not your fault. I'm one of a thousand stories—millions, in fact."

Something struck him. "You mentioned brothers at one point. They were foster brothers?"

"Yeah. To me, like actual brothers. Chris and Kevin. They were being raised by their grandmother, and when she passed away, they went into the system. Chris was seven and Kevin was nine when they came to live in my foster home. I was fourteen."

"So you became the big brother."

His expressionless face transformed into one of grief and anger. "I don't really want to get into it. I think you should go home. That way you won't have to worry about being late or anything."

"That's nice," Schaeffer said mildly. "You're reneging on your invitation? You don't want me to stay?"

"I'm not the best company right now. Talking about the past does that."

"Then we'll stop and concentrate on the present. Like later tonight and brunch tomorrow." His grin was bright, and Ren eyed him with burning eyes.

"You don't give up, do you?"

"Not when I want something bad enough." He kissed Ren's damp hair and smelled the coconut shampoo they'd used. "Or someone. I have to fly home next week, and I don't know what your work schedule is like. But now that I know where you are, I'd love to spend as much time together as we can." He rubbed Ren's cheek with his own, enjoying the rough scrape of his late-night scruff. "Come with me tomorrow. We're not a television family. No one's perfect."

"Maybe. I can tell you when we wake up, right?"

"Sure."

They went to bed, and as Ren began to kiss him,

Schaeffer held him closer.

Nobody's perfect. Except I think you may be perfect for me.

On the car ride to Anson and Kendra's, Schaeffer sensed Ren's increasing nervousness. After getting off the freeway and about two blocks from the house, he pulled over to the side and shut off the engine.

"Okay, what? You look like you're going to throw up."

Ren rubbed his face. "I've never met anyone's family. I don't date—there's never been the time or opportunity. Or interest. And kids…what if I screw up and say the wrong thing?"

He lifted a shoulder. "I guess we take you out in the backyard and shoot you. Come on, Ren. You're being silly. You saw them. They're regular people. Like me."

"Yeah, I know I'm being ridiculous. And you said they like doughnuts?" They'd stood in line for close to an hour, but the wait was worth it. Seaside was the top spot for doughnuts in the area, and Schaeffer knew how much his family loved them but rarely had the time to make the drive out to the beach to get them.

He laughed and leaned over to kiss Ren. "They're gonna love them. Watch."

He was right, of course. The moment they stepped into the house and everyone saw the box, the kids were dancing around Ren and Anson gave him a high five.

"My man. Seaside's? This is the best. I keep meaning to go, but I'm too tired after I come home to make the drive."

"Told ya," he whispered into Ren's ear and was rewarded with a grateful smile.

"I figured what's a little sugar amongst friends?" Ren joked.

"How about we all go outside?" Kendra moved toward the glass sliders at the rear of the house. It had a similarly open yet cozy feel as his father's home, which made sense as Kendra had decorated both. "I have bagels and lox and all the trimmings, plus pitchers of mimosas. If you'd rather have something else, Ren, let me know."

"That all sounds delicious. Thank you for having me on such short notice."

"Are you kidding?" Anson hooted. "She's been waiting for the day Schaeffer brought someone to meet the family."

Ren met his eye, and Schaeffer winked.

The adults settled at the big table under the umbrella while the kids ran about the yard and played on the swings and slide. Anson poured their father a glass, then Kendra. "You two are on your own."

He poured a mimosa for Ren and one for himself. His dad took a sip and set the glass on the table.

"You and Schaeffer met in the city during the snowstorm?" he inquired.

"That's right, sir."

His dad waved a hand at Ren. "No one calls me sir unless they want to borrow money from me." He pretended to frown and peered at Ren. "You don't wanna hit me up for a loan, do you?"

"No, not at all," Ren answered, laughing and shaking his head.

"Good. Call me Walter. What do you do? Are you a pilot as well, or do you work for the airline?"

"No. I'm a wildlife photographer."

Kendra's lips made an O. "Really? Wow. That sounds amazing. We always watch the nature channels with the kids. What have you photographed? Have you been in magazines?"

Schaeffer settled into his chair and watched Ren's inhibitions fade over meeting the family. He became animated, recounting the stories of his wildest photography experiences, and Schaeffer could once again feel the passion he had for his job.

"Before the gray wolf was removed from the endangered species list, I was on assignment in Minnesota. In January. And let me tell you, it was cold. I was tired and ready to pack it in, having accomplished only one brief sighting that wouldn't be good enough for my needs. I was walking to my vehicle when I spotted a snowy owl and decided to take some pictures. He took off in a hurry, and a creepy feeling came over me. I turned slowly and came face-to-face with a gray wolf. He stood between my vehicle and me, and I had to figure out how to get the hell out of there."

Kendra sat enthralled while Anson and their father made their bagel sandwiches and listened.

"Damn. What did you do?" He couldn't imagine staring into the eyes of a predator. Their teeth looked huge even at the zoo. And that was at a distance.

"Not much at first, except snap a whole bunch of shots with my camera. He was pretty young, and I think he didn't know what to make of me either. I knew enough not to make sudden moves. Then I remembered I had several hunks of beef jerky in my pocket. I'd keep them to eat while waiting for that perfect shot, 'cause it can take hours or days sometimes. Maybe that's what he smelled. I slowly took them from my jacket, and he didn't look angry or growl. Only interested. Maybe he wasn't that hungry, but I didn't know what else to do."

"Oh my God, Ren, you're killing me," Kendra gasped, and Anson cackled.

"Babe. He's here, so obviously he made it out."

"You be quiet." Exasperated, she shushed him. "Don't kill the mood. Go ahead, Ren. Please finish."

Schaeffer couldn't stop smiling and had to duck his head and gulp his drink. Ren, who had an instinctual flair for the dramatic, continued.

"I wanted to get him far away from me. As always, I'd studied the animals I went to photograph prior to the assignment and was counting on their similarities to dogs in chasing things tossed. Not that they're dogs, but you get my point. So I did a Hail Mary with that beef jerky and threw that sucker as far as I could. Sure enough, he took off after it, and I ran to my Rover and sped out of there like a bat out of hell. I thought the assignment was a failure, but I had several wildlife magazines vying for pictures of both the owl and the wolf."

"Ren photographs rare and endangered creatures. When we met in New York City he was on a layover from Tanzania, where he'd been for almost two years, tracking and hoping to photograph black rhinos. It's because of his work that we get to see the rarest creatures on earth." Hearing himself, he realized he sounded like a proud spouse or boyfriend, and shut up.

Too late. His father, brother, and Kendra gazed at him—Kendra sporting a self-satisfied smirk, while Anson didn't bother to hide his shit-eating grin. Ren drank his mimosa.

"I try to find them in the wild, living naturally. Sometimes I get lucky and spot them at the beginning. Other times, like with this rhino species, it took months. They can be elusive, but when I do see them, it's like no other feeling in the world."

"How long are you here for?" His dad took a bite of his bagel.

"I have a week and a half left before I have to go up north."

"What's there?" his dad asked.

"The Sierra Nevada red fox. Usually, I prefer to stay as close to the ground as possible and leave the high inclines to those who know what they're doing, but occasionally I have to brave that kind of terrain. And the Sierra Nevada red fox is one of our country's most rare animals. There are almost none left—conservationists think perhaps twenty in total. I'm hoping it won't take months. Others have tried and failed because it's so elusive."

Again, he watched his father's thoughtful, serious expression. "Is this normal? You disappearing for months or years, even?"

Ren had taken a bite of his bagel and chewed it with deliberation. "I'm not disappearing. I'm working. This is what I do for a living."

"And your family is okay with not seeing you for all that time?"

Anson glared at their father across the table while Kendra put on a bright face. "I think that's enough serious talk on a beautiful Sunday afternoon. Why don't—"

"No, Kendra." Ren's voice was kind but firm. "It's all right. I don't mind answering. I don't have any family, Walter, so that's not a problem for me. But it sounds like it might be one for you?"

"Dad," Schaeffer stepped in. "Ren doesn't owe you, me, or anyone else an explanation for doing what he does."

His father remained unperturbed. "I never said he did. But if you're going to be involved with someone and they're never around…" He shrugged, leaving the question in the air.

Ren stated quietly, "But we're not in a relationship. Schaeffer and I are enjoying each other's company while we're in the same city."

"That's right, Dad." He forced a smile. "It's nothing serious."

"Coulda fooled me, but what do I know anymore?"

Sensing the tension, Anson raised his glass. "How about a toast to new friends?"

"That sounds perfect to me," Kendra seemed eager to

add.

Schaeffer knew what they were trying to do and pressed his thigh to Ren's. He raised his glass with everyone else.

Later in the afternoon, his father left the heat of the backyard to watch the Lakers play, but the four of them remained outside to watch the kids swim. Kendra had changed into a bathing suit and was in the pool with them.

Anson's brows pulled together. "Ren, don't let our father make you feel uncomfortable. He's old-fashioned and thinks everyone should be married, have kids, and a regular nine-to-five. Of course I want my brother happy, but that's for him to decide, not his family. You and Schaeffer do what you want, how you want. If it brings you together eventually, that's great, and if not, *c'est la vie*."

"Thanks, Anson. I think Schaeffer and I are doing just fine."

Around four, Schaeffer decided that family time was nice but he wanted more alone time with Ren. Kendra had gotten the kids out of the pool and into the bath, and his father remained immersed in the game.

"I think we'll head out. I know you have an early start tomorrow."

In the middle of loading the dishwasher, Anson tipped his head toward the door. "Don't make excuses on my account. I wouldn't want to be hanging out with us either if I could be alone with a date. Not that we aren't fascinating…" He laughed at his own joke, and Schaeffer loved his easy acceptance. "Ren, it was great meeting you, and I hope we can see you again before you or Schaeffer have to leave."

"Thanks. I feel the same. Tell Kendra—"

"Tell Kendra what?" she asked, walking into the living area. "Are you leaving already?"

"Already," Schaeffer joked. "Any longer, and you'd have to charge us rent. I'll see you during the week. Thanks, honey."

Kendra hugged him. "Don't you let your father make you feel bad. Ren is great."

She gave Ren a big hug. "I loved getting to know you. Don't be a stranger."

"Subtle, Kendra." He sighed and rolled his eyes while Ren took it in stride.

"Thank you for having me to your family day. It was great getting to know you."

With Ren at his side, they ventured into the den.

"Dad, we're leaving."

His father lifted himself from the recliner and offered his hand to Ren. "I hope I didn't make you uncomfortable, and if I did, I apologize. They're always telling me I'm stuck in the last century."

"That's not such a bad thing. For many reasons. And no offense taken. Whatever happens, I'm grateful for Schaeffer's friendship. I think that's the most important thing."

"I like that. And I agree."

They shook, and then he hugged his father. "Talk to you later."

His father squeezed his shoulder. "I'll see you when I see you."

They spoke about inconsequential things on the car ride to Ren's place—how the bagels compared to the New York City ones—poorly, they both concluded—the continued population growth in Southern California, and how glad they were not to be caught up in the cold and snow back east.

Once inside, Ren tugged his hand. "Let's sit."

A sense of dread trickled through him as he followed Ren to the couch. Was this the end? Had all the talk about relationships and family and permanence been too much pressure for someone who'd always lived on the fly?

Sitting next to each other, Schaeffer itched to hold Ren but waited patiently for him to begin.

"I had a really nice time. Your family obviously loves

you very much, and they're incredibly warm and generous."

"They liked you as well."

In their time together, he hadn't seen Ren this flustered, and Schaeffer's heart sank. He might not be a master of dating and relationships, but he could sense an "It's not you, it's me" speech coming. "I'm hearing a 'but.'"

Guilt flashed in Ren's eyes. "Yeah, well…I like spending time with you. You're an incredible lover. The whole time we were at your brother's, all I wanted to do was drag you off somewhere so we could be alone."

"We're alone now, yet I'm getting the feeling you're ready to tell me goodbye."

Ren's hands balled into fists. "I'm a nomad. I don't know the first thing about relationships. I don't even have a place to call my own. I grew up in turmoil, without roots. I don't know what it means to sit over a dinner table every night with the same person, or do these weekly family things. My life is on the road, wherever they send me, and I've loved it."

With each word Ren spoke, Schaeffer's heart shriveled a bit until he couldn't take it any longer. "Stop. I get the point. It's okay if you just want to hook up and walk away. I mean…this was all a chance meeting anyway. It was never supposed to happen."

Those clear green eyes gazing at him shone with fear and confusion, and yet deep within he saw a spark of something. Hope.

"What if it was?" Ren asked. "What if we tried to make this work? Somehow."

Maybe the mimosas were stronger than he'd thought. Schaeffer grabbed his shoulders. "What're you talking about?" Hope that had lived tightly wound in his heart unraveled before him like a shining thread of gold.

"I don't want to say goodbye."

CHAPTER SEVEN

Schaeffer's stunned face had him instantly regretting his words.

"I-I'm sorry. I shouldn't have said anything," he mumbled. God, could he have been any more off base?

"No. Stop." Face bright, Schaeffer pulled him closer. "I don't want to let you go either."

Their lips touched, and Ren lost himself in the hot, velvet sweep of Schaeffer's tongue in his mouth. Shedding their clothes along the way, they stumbled into the bedroom, naked and panting.

"I want *you*, Ren. Not a figment of my imagination. Not someone I can find who reminds me of you. And if I have to exist for weeks with only the memory of you until I see you again, I'll deal with it." Schaeffer's hands roamed over his quivering flesh, and Ren melted from the words. "Because the dream of having you is better than the reality of anyone else. I want you."

"Take me." Ren pulled Schaeffer over him. "Take everything you can from me."

"I'll give you everything I have." Schaeffer grabbed the lube and condom and sank two fingers into his ass. Pleasure washed over Ren, and he grabbed on to the curve of Schaeffer's biceps.

"Now."

Another kiss, this time a lingering one when they parted. Ren ached with an emptiness only Schaeffer could succeed in filling. Schaeffer breached his hole and Ren urged him on.

"Everything, more. I need it all."

"I don't want it over too quickly."

It'll never be over. Perfection doesn't fade. It lasts forever.

"Please, please." He arched his hips, the angle forcing Schaeffer deeper, and a wildness sprang into Schaeffer's eyes, turning them almost inky black as his arousal grew. He growled, then thrust hard, pummeling Ren into the bed until all he could do was hang on to Schaeffer's sweat-slicked shoulders and give himself up to the building storm within.

His cock lay hard and red between them, the friction from the brush of Schaeffer's taut abs tantalizing but not nearly enough. Edgy and trembling, Ren teetered on the brink of stepping off a cliff but not yet being ready for the fall.

Schaeffer captured his lips, and their tongues played, rubbed and slid. "I've never met anyone like you. I've never wanted anyone like you." His hips flexed in short, hard pumps. "And I don't want to let you go."

Schaeffer consumed him. His hand grasped Ren's dick, his tongue plunged into his mouth, and he buried his huge, hard shaft to the root.

"Don't…oh God, don't stop. Don't leave me like this." He bowed up tight and screamed as the most powerful orgasm of his life ripped through him, scattering him to pieces.

"Ren, Ren…" Schaeffer pinned his arms above his head and ravaged his mouth. Bodies merged, their mouths locked, his breath became Ren's and their hearts raced in tandem. Several more thrusts, and Schaeffer came. Ren felt him throbbing and pulsing in the condom.

"Am I alive?" Schaeffer's lips moved against his neck, and he mustered the strength to chuckle.

"I don't know, but if not, it was a hell of a way to go."

A warm, wet tongue licked his neck up to his ear. "I'm alive, and I'm not going anywhere."

He stroked the curve of Schaeffer's ass. "Even if you did, I'd track you down. A skill I've perfected over the years. There's no escaping me now."

Schaeffer's lips curved in a smile.

The next morning, Ren got up early as always and made coffee. Watching the sun rise over the water from his deck was a pleasure he'd never tire of. He sipped, then set his cup on the wooden railing and picked up his camera. Coming in early for feeding, varied birds flew and hovered over the water. He sighted a booby—rarely seen in Southern California. Pulse spiking, he took shot after shot, until it flew too far to capture even with his high-powered lens. He put the camera on the table next to him and heard the door sliding open. Strong arms encircled his waist.

"What was that you were so caught up in taking pictures of?" Schaeffer asked in between neck kisses. "I could've watched you in action for hours, the way you positioned yourself and moved to get the right angle. It's fascinating."

Being a loner, he rarely had the opportunity to discuss

the mechanics of his work, and it was a pleasure to meet someone, even a layman like Schaeffer, who recognized how it happened behind the scenes. "A tropical booby."

Schaeffer's laughter rumbled through him. "You're kidding. That's its name? Poor bird."

"*Mmm.*" He tilted his head to give Schaeffer easier access. "I doubt he cares. And it's incredibly rare to see one this far north. They're native to Central and South America, so I got lucky." He turned so they faced each other. "In more ways than one." Schaeffer's face burned red. Considering all the intimacy they'd shared with each other over the past few days, it was sweet to see. "How'd you sleep?"

"Like a baby. You're very warm."

"No need for an electric blanket."

"I could use all that body heat back in New York." Schaeffer rubbed their bristly cheeks together. "I look forward to when you come to visit."

"Listen," Ren began, and watched the shutters fall over Schaeffer's eyes. "I'm not saying I don't want to try this. But I don't often know how long my assignments will take. It all depends on the perfect shot, or what I'm hired for. Sometimes it's a year in the life; other times, the magazine is looking for something specific, like an updated photograph."

"I understand."

"Do you? What I'm trying to say is I can't tell you, 'I'll be there on Tuesday, June third.' "

Schaeffer cupped his jaw in that big, capable hand. "I don't care when. As long as I know you're coming, I'll be ready for you."

"How is this fair to you? Keeping you hanging around ready to jump for me, whenever."

"When you're used to nothing, you recognize something special." Schaeffer silenced him with a kiss. "It's my choice. And I choose you."

He struggled to hold on to the hope that there was a

possibility instead of the reality that this was doomed before it could start.

Inside the house, Schaeffer rummaged through the refrigerator. "Eggs? I can make those."

"Yeah, sure. There's bacon too."

"Of course."

Soon the house smelled like home cooking, and Ren recalled with startling clarity the last morning with Chris and Kevin and how they'd teased him about his lack of kitchen skills when he'd burned the toast and their eggs stuck to the pan.

"What's wrong?" At the stove, Schaeffer frowned. "You look like you've seen a ghost."

Immediately, he smoothed out his features. "Nothing. It's all good. Guess I'm hungry."

"Well, get your plate because breakfast is ready."

They sat facing each other, and Ren took a bite. "These are good."

Schaeffer grinned. "That's the extent of my culinary expertise. I refuse to do delivery three meals a day, so I taught myself to make the bare minimum." He picked up a rasher of bacon. "It's not much, but it's something."

"Beats my pathetic cooking. I'm more of an open-the-can-and-dump-it-in-a-pot cook. I wish I could cook, but I'm never in one place long enough to learn."

They ate until their plates were cleaned.

"Can I ask you something?" He didn't want to bring the mood down, but he was curious about Schaeffer's family.

Schaeffer wiped his mouth. "Sure."

"What happened to your mother?"

Schaeffer paled. "Heart attack. My dad left for work that morning, and she took us to school. I was eleven. Anson was thirteen." He pinched his eyes, and Ren's pulse spiked as he waited for him to continue, sensing Schaeffer's unresolved trauma from the devastation in his expression.

"I'd gone to a friend's house, and when I returned home and walked inside…she was lying on the floor. The ME said it must've happened during the morning."

"Jesus," Ren sucked in his breath. "That's…I'm sorry."

"My father walked around in a daze afterward. We moved out here a year later. My aunt lived in Tustin and helped as much as she could, but my father got it together and dedicated himself to making sure we grew up knowing we could count on him for everything. I don't really remember much about that time. Grief has a way of blocking memories and pain."

"I don't know about that," Ren responded without thinking.

"Something *you* want to talk about?"

Forcing a smile, he picked up his plate and rose to his feet. "Nope. Let's put these in the dishwasher and go out and enjoy the day."

Schaeffer narrowed his eyes as he joined him. "Where to?"

"I was thinking of taking a drive to Laguna…maybe farther—to La Jolla, even."

"I have to return my father's Jeep first." He loaded the machine, added detergent, and pushed the button.

"No problem. I'll follow you to his house, and then we'll go in my car." He swatted Schaeffer on his rear. "You can pick up some things since you'll be staying here."

"Bossy, aren't you?" Schaeffer's good mood had returned, and his lips curved upward.

"As long as it gets me what I want. You, with me."

It was dark by the time they returned from their outing.

Along the way, they'd had a change of plans and decided to visit the San Diego Zoo. Ren hadn't been in years and was anxious to see their Southern White Rhinos. Back at the house, Schaeffer set the bag with the gifts he'd bought for Scotty and Mini on the kitchen counter and dropped the weekend bag with his clothing to the floor.

Ren plopped onto the couch with his camera to view all the pictures he'd taken. Schaeffer kicked off his sneakers, grabbed them each a beer, and joined him.

"You can set it on the table, thanks. Look at these." He held the camera between them. "Aren't they beautiful? Do you know there are only two wild white rhinos left in the world? They're both female, so the breeding initiatives were done by artificial insemination. The miracle of modern science."

"Yeah, that's pretty amazing." He wiggled his toes. "One thing I can always count on after visiting the zoo is my feet killing me."

"Sounds like someone needs a foot massage." He wiggled his fingers. "Lucky for you, I learned from some of the best in the business when I was in Tibet." He took Schaeffer's feet in his hands. "Lie down."

"Being bossy again, huh?" But Schaeffer listened and stretched out, giving him his bare feet.

It took Ren only a few moments to recall what he'd learned, and he began to press and stroke the special points in certain spots that he was taught would release tension as well as chemicals in the brain. One look at Schaeffer's blissful face, and he knew he hadn't forgotten.

After a few minutes, Schaeffer cracked open an eye. "Tibet, huh? Is there any place you haven't been?"

"Probably." He grinned. "All I know is, I've had a ton of tetanus shots and vaccines for every type of virus out there. You should see my passport." He pushed hard on a pressure point.

Schaeffer groaned, and a deep flush rose on his face. "Oh God, that feels almost as good as sex."

"One day I'll get some oil and give you a full-body Ku Nye massage."

"I have no idea what that is, but if it involves you rubbing oil all over me, I'm in."

About to suggest something deliciously dirty, his phone buzzed. Peering at the screen, he saw that it was his editor.

"I gotta take this. It's work-related."

Schaeffer swung those long legs off his lap. "I'm gonna go in the bedroom and turn on the TV."

He nodded and answered the call. "Hey, Samuel."

"Ren, nice to have you back on the grid."

"Damn good to be back, too."

"I'll bet." He chuckled. "I remember those days when I traveled so much, I had no idea where I was sometimes when I woke up."

Samuel Binder was a world-renowned photographer and editor of one of the premier wildlife magazines, whom Ren had met by happenstance almost eight years earlier. Ren had been hiking in the Adirondacks, looking for whatever he could find to take photos of. He worked at a camera store in the city and convinced them to let him frame his wildlife photos and put them up in the store, reasoning that he could sell more cameras and equipment if he could point to the quality of the photos they took. Along the way, he'd gotten several sales and had soon developed a small following of people asking him if he could take pictures of their pets. Not what he aspired to, but it paid the rent.

He and Samuel had both stumbled upon a scattering of the increasingly rare spruce grouse, and after spending the day taking copious amounts of photographs, Samuel invited him to dinner. Not knowing who Samuel was at the time, Ren figured it might be a hookup, but he soon discovered Samuel wasn't interested in him for anything other than his prowess with his camera.

When Ren showed him his shots and what he'd been putting together as the beginning of a portfolio, Samuel offered him a job as a roving wildlife photographer for *Nature's Beauty*, a highly respected photographic magazine of endangered and threatened species. Ren jumped on it and never looked back. He was known for his willingness to take on almost any assignment, no matter the risk or how long he'd have to spend waiting. Over the years, Samuel had become more than his boss—he'd been a friend and confidant. A role model.

Ren said, "Right now, I'm enjoying lying my head down in a nice bed with clean sheets and the ability to order my food with the push of a button."

"I know you are. And those shots you sent last week are stupendous. There's one we're considering for the cover."

"That's awesome." A cover shot meant exposure, and according to his contract, more money for him. A win-win. "It was a long, hard journey, but I'll never forget it."

"And now you're off to the mountains to search for a fox. I remember those days. I must say I'm glad it's you now and not me."

"I am. Next week, though. Don't rush my time off, please."

"Feeling a little burned out?"

Was he? Or was it something else? He listened to Schaeffer in the bedroom, laughing at something he watched on television, and Ren wished he was in there with him.

"No. Not burned out. I love what I do, you know that. It's a special high getting that perfect shot of something rare and beautiful, even if it's a tarantula."

"I don't know why, but I sense something's different. Anything you want to tell me?"

Damn. Who knew Samuel was so intuitive?

"Nah. You haven't talked to me in a while, is all. By

the way, how's the weather?" A cackle escaped him. "Has it stopped snowing?"

"Shut up," Samuel answered good-naturedly. "It's the winter. Soon it will be spring and gorgeous upstate. Maybe you'll want to come home for a while?"

"A new assignment?" His pulse quickened. The East Coast meant possible time with Schaeffer.

"In a way. See if you can wrap up your fox in the next two or three months, and then I have something for you to look at."

"What? You've piqued my curiosity."

"Exactly why I'm not going to say a thing until you get here."

"You always were a devious bastard," he pretend-grumbled. "Not even a hint?"

"Something different than your usual is all I'm going to say."

"Which of course tells me nothing."

Schaeffer appeared and entered the kitchen, where he opened the freezer and took out a pint of coffee ice cream and one of fudge brownie. He disappeared into the bedroom, and Ren had visions of naked ice cream eating.

"Okay, Samuel. I've got to go. I'll call you before I head into the mountains."

"Do that. Good luck."

"Thanks." He tossed the phone onto the couch and ran into the kitchen to grab the hot fudge and a canister of whipped cream from the fridge.

"Don't start without me," he yelled, racing into the bedroom. Schaeffer had the pint of brownie ice cream next to Ren's side while he held the coffee.

"Everything okay?"

"Yeah. Just my editor." He opened the whipped cream and shot it directly into his mouth. "Want some?"

"I want you."

"You can have both."

Schaeffer pounced on him, and as they kissed, Ren wondered how he was going to be able to walk away and leave all this behind.

CHAPTER EIGHT

Heart racing, Schaeffer bolted upright in bed, gasping for breath. Sweat poured down his face, and he trembled.

Fuck.

Another nightmare of epic proportions, almost as bad as when he'd first been discharged from the Air Force. He knew why. Stress brought them on. His vacation was over, and Ren was heading to his next assignment. Last night had been their final time together before saying goodbye this afternoon.

"What's wrong?" Ren asked, his voice sleepy, and Schaeffer forced himself to smile and lie down, snuggling in close and tangling their legs together.

"Nothing. Just, uh, thought of something I forgot to do. It's no big deal."

Ren rubbed their noses together. "You know what I've learned about you this week?"

"No," he murmured, his desire rising. "Do I snore?"

Ren's lips touched his ear. "You are the worst liar in the history of lying liars."

His eyes flew open, and he gazed into Ren's solemn face. "What're you talking about?" he sputtered.

"Schaeffer. We've spent every night for the past week and a half together. You had a nightmare the first time we spent the night together, and now it's our last. You think I don't know when something's bothering you? You know you can tell me anything. No judgment." Ren kissed him. "You've been inside me. There's nothing more intimate than that."

"I—it's nothing important."

"Right. It only woke you up at three a.m., a panting, sweaty mess. Come on."

It was Ren's palm laid to his cheek that broke him, but instead of answering, he tossed the covers off. "I'll be right back." He swung his legs over the side of the bed and forced himself not to run to the bathroom, where he splashed cold water over his face. He returned to the bed, but Ren hadn't moved. "I get nightmares. Not often, but they come in times of stress."

"Have you always had them?"

He hung his head. "No. They started after my mom died. Over the years they lessened in number and severity but resurfaced after my first flying mission in Afghanistan. We were shot at and escaped, but it hit home how vulnerable we were."

"And you didn't say anything to anyone? Your commanding officer?"

He snorted. "No, William—Buddy—Belson wasn't the type to confide in. 'Man up,' he'd yell in our faces if we complained or fell behind. I was too afraid to say anything, fearing they'd start digging deeper and discover I was gay. The nightmares went away after a couple of weeks, and I thought everything was fine."

"Until now?"

Schaeffer pinched his eyes shut. "Until several years later. We were on a mission and came under fire, and my closest friend died when his plane was hit."

Ren's smile was tender as he ran those long fingers over his face. "You could've been killed too."

"But I wasn't. I'm alive, and Steve died. Christ, it was horrible."

"I can't imagine." Ren hugged him. "I'm here for you."

But you're leaving. Maybe for good.

For a minute, Schaeffer clung to those strong arms, knowing this might be the last morning they shared together, and then, self-conscious, he let go. Discreetly, he wiped at his eyes.

"I'm fine, really."

"Are you? Tell me you've seen a therapist. The military must have people."

He rose from the bed to pace. "Yeah. Of course. After it happened, I was pretty much a wreck, and they gave me a medical discharge. I came home—here. I saw someone every week. He helped me enough to be able to get into the flight deck and fly and learn to love it again. But every once in a while, something sets it off."

"Now it's me." Ren drooped. "I'm sorry. I wish—"

He stopped midstride and ran to the bed. "No. It's not you. None of it has anything to do with you. Let's look at the bright side."

"Which is?" Ren asked, doubt clouding his face.

He tugged Ren up to standing and held him, but this time there was no fear or desperation in their embrace.

"That we've had the best time together. We're not alone anymore." He ran the back of his hand over Ren's cheek. "You…have become very special to me."

Ren's eyes glowed, and he placed a hand over his and held it steady. "Yeah? Funny. You're special to me too."

Schaeffer's heart pounded. He'd laughed at Anson when he'd come home after his conference and couldn't stop talking about Kendra, figuring it would die down after a month or two. After all, she wasn't the first woman Anson had been involved with. But she was the last. Meeting Kendra had changed him from a hard-drinking, different-woman-every-weekend type to a dedicated, devoted husband and family man.

Now with Ren and the days and nights they'd spent together, he understood.

"Let's go to bed."

They slipped under the covers, and as had become their habit over their week together, he lay with Ren pressed to his chest, their legs entwined. The nervous tension drained from him, and he closed his eyes.

They awoke curled around each other. Schaeffer kissed Ren, his lips more urgent with each passing moment.

"One last time. I need you."

"Oh God," Ren cried out as Schaeffer pushed inside him.

He couldn't stop watching Ren beneath him. The pure sensuality of his face at his climax was a work of art, and one Schaeffer would carry with him during the long nights they were apart. Ren held him close and bit his shoulder, then kissed away the sting.

"I'm going to miss you," Schaeffer whispered.

Ren kissed him softly. "I am too. So damn much."

After that, there was nothing left to say.

It was a subdued afternoon at his father's house—even the kids stayed with them rather than play in the yard. He and Ren had spent several evenings with Anson and Kendra, and Schaeffer loved how seamlessly Ren had merged into their lives. Ren had photographed the kids separately and the family all together, and brought the pictures as a farewell gift. He handed them to Kendra, and when she saw them, she burst into tears.

"We don't want you to go."

Anson held the photos. "I know you normally don't take pictures of humans, but since these two can act like little wild animals sometimes, it's appropriate," he joked. "I'm shocked you got them to stand still for the family shots. Thanks, Ren. They're amazing, and we'll treasure them."

"Next time you can take more pictures, and we can see how they've grown." Kendra sniffed and ran her fingers over the glass of the frames. "Because there's going to be a next time."

Schaeffer alternated between loving how his family accepted Ren and wondering how long it would take for that to come to pass. Ren had told him the assignment was one he'd attempted several times with little success, as the fox was so infrequently seen. He was determined to stay as long as it took to get that coveted shot.

It didn't seem fair for the weather to be so beautiful—endless, cloud-free skies of a rich cerulean blue—when his heart was heavy. Soon both would be in the air, the distance widening between them...

Beer bottle in hand, his father cleared his throat. "Listen. I wanna say I'm sorry if in the beginning I didn't act all gung-ho about the two of you. I was wrong. I haven't seen

Schaeffer so happy in years, so I'm guessing whatever you've decided is right for the both of you."

Schaeffer glanced at Ren. "Thanks, Dad. That means a lot to me. We're figuring it out, but we know this is what we want."

Solemn-faced, Ren nodded. "I don't know much of anything about relationships, but I know Schaeffer is the best man I've ever met. I'd be a fool to walk away."

"On that I'll agree with you," his dad said and held his bottle aloft. "Safe travels, and until we meet again."

"You're always welcome here, Ren, if you need a place to stay." Kendra hugged him. "I know what it's like not to have family, so consider us yours."

Kendra herself came from a single-parent household, and her childhood had been spent avoiding her mother's drug addiction and abusive boyfriends until she was old enough to move out on her own. Her mother had refused all of Kendra's attempts to leave and get clean, and she died from an overdose. Kendra was only twenty at the time.

Kendra, with her kindness, had managed to get Ren to open up a bit about his past—not everything, but enough that they could bond over their lack of family and stability growing up.

Schaeffer's heart swelled at how Ren's natural warmth and joy in life had grown in their days together. What had started out as pure sex in that ugly hotel room at the airport had been merely a cover for how desperately both of them wanted—needed—someone to hold on to.

Ren checked his watch. "I hate to say it, but I've got a plane to catch."

They all walked with them to the front, and Schaeffer unlocked his father's Jeep. "I'll be back later."

A final round of hugs, and they were off.

"I hate thinking of you heading off by yourself into the mountains. Seems so lonely." He entered the freeway toward the airport.

Ren's eyes grew pensive. "I'm used to it, remember? It's my job."

And Schaeffer wanted to say, *Yes, but it doesn't have to be.* But he didn't think he had that right. After all, what could he offer Ren? To share his bed in the tiny rental apartment in Queens? Go to out-of-the-way restaurants because he was too afraid of running into people he knew? Mentally, he continued to question himself as they drew closer and closer to the airport.

"Is everything okay?" Ren put a hand on his thigh. "I know this sucks, but we talked about it, and I thought we came to a good compromise."

Schaeffer pulled into the parking lot. "We did, and it is. I'm just looking at the reality of not having you tonight. I don't like it."

Ren leaned over and kissed him. "Only in body. I'll be with you in spirit. And in other ways."

He parked, and they walked into the airport. Ren stayed outside the security gates with him, but Schaeffer couldn't stand prolonging the departure. "I'll miss you. Let me know when you get there. My flight doesn't leave until five thirty-eight tomorrow morning."

"So precise. Just like a pilot." Ren smiled into his eyes. "I'll see you."

"No goodbye?"

Ren frowned. "Not to you. That's what you say when it's over."

He kissed Ren, memorizing his taste and the feel of those sweet, soft lips. "Okay. Then we'll never say goodbye."

One last hug and Ren was walking away, heading through the TSA PreCheck line and then security. Schaeffer kept him in sight, watching as he turned the corner…and then he was gone.

Schaeffer left the airport, feeling as though his heart

still walked with Ren. A piece of him was missing, and he knew he wouldn't be whole until they were together again. Like a robot, he found the car, paid the parking, and returned home. Everyone was in the backyard, watching the kids in the pool, but he wasn't in the mood and wandered a bit in the kitchen and living room. Needing a minute alone, he decided to go to his old room. On the bed he found a large envelope with his name in Ren's handwriting. Heart pounding, he opened it and slid out a slew of pictures Ren had taken of him during their time together. There were ones of him with Anson, Kendra, and the kids, and with his father. Several of him sleeping. A few when he was sneaking ice cream from the fridge or flipping their burgers at the grill.

All of them were candid, with him unaware of Ren's camera. Some of the two of them he did remember, Ren having set the timer for them to pose together. One especially he couldn't stop staring at—it was taken during sunset on the deck, Ren behind him, chin resting on his shoulder, holding him as they gazed into the camera.

"Dammit," he cursed and wiped at his eyes. "He's not dead. Just away. He'll be back, probably sooner than later. You're being a sappy jerk."

Careful so as not to bend them, he returned the photos to the envelope and finished packing up the room. He washed his face, placed a smile on his lips, and stopped at the refrigerator to grab a beer before joining the rest of his family outside.

"Ren's flight take off on time?" his dad asked.

"Yep." He drank down half his beer in a few swallows.

"You really like him, don'tcha?"

He met his father's curious eyes, and his throat tightened. "Yeah. I do. A lot."

"You in love with him?"

Anson and Kendra were in the pool with the kids, and their shrieks of laughter rose in the air.

"It's a little quick for that. There's still so much about him I don't know. And stuff I haven't told him either."

"You mean about the nightmares and your discharge?"

Schaeffer finished his beer. "I mentioned it."

Shooting him a dark look from underneath his brows, his father huffed out a breath. "And he's got plenty of shit he's dealt with, I've gathered."

"I'm assuming. He grew up in pretty harsh circumstances." There was little doubt in his mind that the conditions of Ren's childhood—losing his mother at such a young age, then bouncing around between foster homes—were the main contributors to his inability to form lasting attachments. Plus, he hadn't yet talked about his foster brothers. There was still so much to discuss.

"But he made something of himself." his father's approval was evident. "He's a fighter."

"Yeah. Obviously. But at a cost. His job requires long stretches of isolation. That has to be harsh on him."

"He seems to be able to handle it."

"Maybe." Schaeffer had his doubts. But the one thing he was certain of was how much he was going to miss Ren in the months to come.

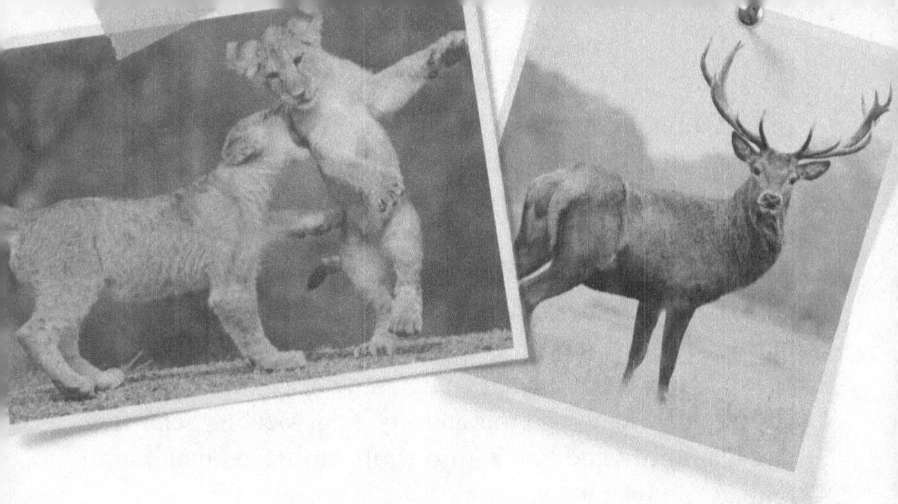

CHAPTER NINE

"No, Samuel. I don't mind. You tell me where to go, and I'll be there."

Before he'd had a chance to find his gate, he'd received a text from Samuel.

"I know it's a pain in the ass, but I figured with you being in the States and on the West Coast already…it's been years since we did a spread on the condor."

"Big Sur, huh? I can deal with that."

A loud chuckle filled his ear. "I'm sure you can. I haven't been there in years, but I remember it's one of the most beautiful spots in the country."

"It is. But also not the most accessible by plane. My best bet is to rent a car here and drive."

"Okay, you handle it, and I'll talk to you when you have something for me."

"All right. Bye."

Ren reversed course and headed to the rental car area.

In half an hour, he was zipping along the 405. With more than an eight-hour drive ahead of him, he had plenty of opportunity to ponder what happened in the past week with Schaeffer.

Aside from the obvious physical attraction, he'd never enjoyed simply being with anyone more. Their senses of humor meshed, and there was never any awkwardness between them. He'd been content and happy with his life. He'd thought he wasn't missing anything. Meeting Schaeffer and his family and being so warmly embraced made him realize…maybe he was.

The simple touch of someone's hand. Shared laughter. A kiss to his cheek. Feet tangling with his under cool sheets. Listening to a racing heartbeat after lovemaking so astonishing and perfect, it would be impossible to recreate. Except every time with Schaeffer was turning out to be like that.

Traffic slowed as he reached LA, and he decided the smart thing to do was stop for the evening and start fresh in the morning. It had been over five years since he'd been in the area, and he found a small hotel near Santa Monica. After gorging himself on street tacos, he took his cameras and walked along the pier. People passed him on all sides, and with the sun preparing to set, he headed to the sand and the shoreline to capture the fiery rays.

"Cool equipment."

He finished his shot and turned to see a man around twenty-five, with shaggy blond hair and matching scruff, wearing board shorts in a bright neon green and black. He sported tattoos all over his chest.

"Thanks."

"You a photographer?" The guy rubbed his chest and flexed. It took everything Ren had not to laugh.

"Yes."

"That's cool, dude."

"So you've said."

"I was wondering…me and my band have a gig nearby. We're pretty hot, not gonna lie, and always get a good crowd."

"That's nice." The conversation was getting more painful by the second, and Ren wished he were back in Newport Beach with Schaeffer.

"I was wondering if you might wanna come watch?"

Ren suppressed a grin. Was he trying to come on to him?

"I don't know…"

"You could take some pictures of us performing. Might be good for your career."

Ordinarily Ren would say no and walk away. Not to mention, he was tired after an emotional day of leaving Schaeffer. He could use a bed and pillow. But now that he was alone, the thought of sitting alone in a small hotel room, staring at the walls, wasn't the pleasure he'd once thought. Calling Schaeffer might make him appear pathetic and needy to hear his voice. Which he was, but only he needed to know that.

"Yeah, I could do that. Give me the details."

The guy's face lit up. "Really? Awesome, dude. Here's the club. Show starts at nine thirty, but you can come at eight thirty, get a drink and watch us set up and do sound checks and take some pictures. Tell them at the door that Zack sent you."

"Okay, Zack. I'm Ren. See you then."

"Cool, bro."

Ren wondered if his vocabulary consisted of more than twenty words but shrugged it off. Zack seemed harmless and nice. It wouldn't hurt to spend a few hours listening to some cover band and taking their picture. Anything to stave off the loneliness of not having Schaeffer at his side.

At eight forty-five, he walked into the dimly lit club, his sneakers sticking to the residue of missed beer pongs and Jell-O shots on the floor. The band was setting up onstage, and he took some distance shots, as well as one of each member of the band, which consisted of Zack, a drummer, and a bass player. Zack was the lead, standing at the mic and strumming his electric guitar. Ren sat at a small table in the middle of the bar and took a few more casual photographs. After a few minutes of the band doing their sound checks, Zack set his guitar down and approached him.

"Dude, you made it."

"I said I would."

"Yeah, well, my friends thought I was scamming them and making up some bullshit story."

The club filled up, and the show started. The band—Deep Dive—wasn't half bad, and Zack had a decent voice. They played a bunch of '80s metal, then some punk and pop tunes. Drinking his beer, Ren was glad he'd come, if for no other reason than he needed to start socializing with people, and it was better than sitting in his hotel room, watching some crappy television show.

At the end of their set and after they'd performed two encores, Ren was satisfied he'd taken enough pictures. Zack and his bandmates made their rounds of the tables, saying hello to people they obviously knew, and Ren watched several guys and women flirt with Zack. He soaked up the fawning of his groupies.

Zack flung himself into a chair next to him. "Whadja think?"

"You were good. I enjoyed it."

"Thanks. You get our pictures?"

"Yeah, of course." He shifted closer to Zack to show the digital gallery. Instead of focusing on the camera window, Zack shifted nearer and whispered in his ear, "Why don't you show me later? Come to my place."

His lips on Ren's ear felt wrong…foreign, and Ren drew away from his touch. "Sorry. I can't."

He almost laughed at the affronted expression on Zack's face. "You're kidding."

Ren finished his beer. "I'm with someone. But thanks anyway. If you give me your email, I'll send you the pictures. No charge, even."

"Why not, though? We could have a great time. Hang out, smoke some weed…"

"I told you," Ren said, impatience creeping into his voice. "I'm with someone." There wasn't a single thing Zack could do to convince Ren to go home with him.

"So? He's not here. He don't have to know."

No. Schaeffer wouldn't ever have to know. But Ren would. And there was no way in hell he'd screw up what was happening between them, even though he didn't exactly know what it was.

He rose to his feet. "Listen. Do you want the pictures or not? I gotta go." This separation was stupid. Maybe if he got to his room before midnight, he could still catch Schaeffer awake.

"Yeah, sure." Zack's thundercloud expression deepened. He recited his email, and Ren took it down in his phone. He left some money for the beer and a tip and left.

It wasn't a far walk to his hotel, and the weather was a typical Southern California evening—warm but with low humidity and a gentle breeze that brought the scent of the ocean to the pedestrians strolling the boardwalk.

On impulse, he found an entrance to the sand, took off his sneakers, and walked to the shoreline. He took out his phone, captured a picture of the moon, and texted Schaeffer after sending it.

Change of plans. I'm on my way to Big Sur to find the California condor.

Schaeffer answered immediately.

Looks like Santa Monica, not Big Sur. And that moon is beautiful.

Ignoring the fact that he'd get sand all over his jeans, Ren sat and dug his toes in.

It is, isn't it? I wish we could share it together. I stopped here for the night. I know it sounds weird since we barely know each other, but it feels strange being without you.

Schaeffer didn't respond for a moment, and Ren wondered if he'd scared him off with his serious talk about missing him. Then a request for FaceTime popped up, and he hit the screen. Schaeffer's face appeared.

"Hey. See where I am?" He turned the phone, and Ren had a view of the sky and the moon. Schaeffer refocused on him again. "I'm lying outside on the chaise. Now we can truly share it."

He laughed. "You're a total romantic."

"Says the man who sent me a picture of the moon. I would've thought you'd be asleep by now."

"Funny story about that." He relayed what happened, starting from when he met Zack on the beach to when he left him at the bar.

"I'd be disappointed too if you said no to me."

"That wouldn't happen. I had no desire to be with him, not after the week we just had."

"Do you have any idea how long it will be until you'll be back east?"

He wished he had a firm answer, but he didn't want to lead Schaeffer on. "No. If I get lucky and see the condors quickly, which isn't unthinkable, I still have to go find those foxes. So it could be anywhere from a month to… who knows?" Terrible as he felt saying it, Ren wanted to be up-front with Schaeffer. "I know we said we wanted to make it work between us—"

"Are you having second thoughts?" Schaeffer broke in, his voice quiet.

"No, not at all." He gripped the phone. "I'm telling you about what happened tonight because I've always heard from Samuel—the editor in chief of the magazine I work for—that there shouldn't be secrets between people in a relationship. I don't want to be with anyone else, but if my schedule makes it hard for you…" He lifted a shoulder. "I don't want you to feel trapped if you meet someone else."

"Me?" Schaeffer's voice rose in disbelief. "You think I would want someone other than you?"

"I mean…I hope not. I'm sure as hell not looking, but I'm asking you to put your life on hold when we've only known each other a week. That's crazy fast. Isn't it?" He didn't know why, but he wanted Schaeffer to tell him no. It would mean this was more. But more…what, Ren couldn't say.

Schaeffer rubbed his chin. "Yeah, it is. But what happened between us…it's totally out of character for me. You're so much more than a hookup or someone random." His voice dropped and the surf continued to roll with a *shushing* sound, but Ren heard each word as if Schaeffer sat there beside him on that moonlit evening. "I haven't been able to get you out of my mind."

A wave of relief crashed over him, leaving Ren even more connected to Schaeffer than when he'd left him that afternoon. "I haven't either."

Schaeffer's face lit up. "I'm so glad I got a chance to talk with you instead of a text. I was wondering where you were tonight and what you were doing."

"Where I am is away from you, and what I'm doing is wishing I wasn't."

Schaeffer brought his face close to the phone. "I wish

you were here too. But I know you have a job that takes you away from home and family. You made that clear." His smile was gentle. "I don't have to like it, but I'd be happy if you called if you had the chance and let me know what's happening with you. Or, because where you go most likely won't have cell service, I can email you. Just to let you know I'm thinking about you."

"I'd like that. I want to hear about your life. I want to know everything about you."

Schaeffer laughed. "I'm pretty boring. Not sure there's much I can say."

Ren remained serious. "Let me be the judge of that."

CHAPTER TEN

"I can't believe it's been almost a month already since you got to Big Sur. Did you finally get your condor pictures?"

Schaeffer stretched out on his bed. It was two a.m., and he'd come in less than two hours ago from San Francisco. He had visions of doing nothing but sleeping the day away, but at the ringing of a FaceTime request, he woke up pretty damn quickly. A call that early could only be bad news.

Turns out, it was anything but.

Scruffy-cheeked and yawning, Ren rubbed his eyes. "Finally, yeah, tonight. Nice sunset ones, where the fiery sky gave great contrast with those massive wingspans. Soon as I finished, I packed up and headed to the hotel."

"And you called me? You didn't want to sleep?" Schaeffer teased.

"Not really." A smile softened the rough edges of Ren's weary face. "I'd rather talk to you." His voice was as gentle and sweet as a spring breeze.

Even from behind a screen, vulnerability glimmered from those beautiful eyes, and Schaeffer's heart pounded. What was happening here? He wanted to pack his bags and fly cross-country to wherever Ren was, if only to be able to taste the breath on his lips and soak in the heat of his skin. He wished he could reach through the phone and touch his face.

"Me too."

"I guess this is the next best thing, since we can't be together."

"I wish there was a way to make that possible." Was he hoping Ren would tell him to come and visit, wherever he'd be next? Schaeffer couldn't be sure he wouldn't get on a flight and go. He held back a yawn.

"You look like you need sleep more than I do." Ren frowned. "Did you have a late flight? Shit. I'm sorry I disturbed you."

"I can sleep later. It's the best wake-up I could have, aside from the real thing next to me."

The harsh lines on Ren's face smoothed. "You have no idea how bad I wish that could happen. Much as I love my job and I'm stoked to try and get a photo of the fox, I'd rather be heading to the airport and flying to you. I already let Samuel know I'm done here, and once I catch some sleep, I have close to a six-hour drive to Mono Creek. I'd rather set up while there's still light."

His spirits fell. "Damn. Well…maybe you can call me when you get there?"

Ren nodded and yawned again. "Yeah. If there's service, I'll make sure to call or text you. Meanwhile, this conversation's been all about me. What's new with you? Work okay?"

He shrugged. "Same shit. I have time off, since I did a long-haul, so I'll catch up on sleep and things at home." He lowered his gaze to the bed.

"Hey, what's wrong?" Ren peered closer. "Are you sure you're all right?"

"Yeah, of course. What could be wrong?" A loaded question, but he wasn't about to dump his silly problems on Ren when they had so little time together. "It's just jet lag. We get it too."

A line bisected Ren's forehead. "Okay…well, take care of yourself, and I'll let you know where I am as soon as I can."

"Good. Have a safe trip, and I'll talk to you."

"Talk to you soon."

The screen went dark, and he lay down, pillow wrapped halfway around his head. It was hard, knowing Ren was going to be almost unreachable for who knew how long. The past weeks hadn't been as easy as he'd made it out to be, but he'd be damned if he'd spend his all-too-infrequent time with Ren concentrating on his issues. Yeah, the nightmares had returned, but he was dealing with it. His burning eyes fluttered shut.

It was a beautiful morning, and he wished he could stay in bed. His mother knocked twice on his bedroom door.

"Hurry up, sleepyhead. I'm making pancakes for breakfast, and you know your brother will eat them all if you don't come quickly."

At those words, he jumped up and dressed in a minute, barely putting a brush to his hair, or teeth. He skidded into the kitchen, and as she'd said, Anson already sat at the table with a pile of pancakes swimming in syrup.

"He didn't take them all, did he?"

"I should've. Lazy butt."

"Don't talk to your brother like that," his mother scolded. "I have yours right here, sweetheart." She set the plate in front of him, and when she turned her back, he stuck out his tongue at Anson.

It was a half day, and he'd forgotten to ask if he could

go to Charlie Summer's house to play. Charlie had a pool and the newest video games, and he always had the cool kids over. For the first time, he'd invited Schaeffer, and he couldn't wait to go. After he shoved all the pancakes into his mouth, he grabbed his backpack.

"Can I go to Charlie Summer's after school? It's a half day. There's plenty of time later on to do homework."

"I've never met his mother. You know I don't like you going to strangers' houses."

"C'mon, Mom. I'm not a baby."

"You should've told me yesterday after you came home from school. I could've called her. I'm sorry, but no."

"That's stupid. You're not being fair." He stomped out of the kitchen. "We don't have cool things to play with here."

"Schaeffer." His father's stern voice stopped him. "Don't talk to your mother like that."

"She's so mean," he yelled. "She never lets me have any fun. I'm going to Charlie's and you can't stop me."

Without waiting for a response, he ran out to the school bus.

After school, he went to Charlie's house—his mother didn't show up or call to tell him to leave, he figured she'd chew him out at home—and enjoyed swimming and playing video games.

"Mom?" he yelled when he came into the house around four thirty. Charlie's mother had invited him to stay for dinner, but knowing his mother was already angry with him for disobeying her, he didn't want to push his luck.

"Please don't be mad," he called out. She always had the radio on to some pop music station, but now the house was strangely silent. Anson had little-league practice and wouldn't be home until six.

He dropped his bag and walked into the kitchen.

"Mommy," he screamed, seeing her lying on the floor. "Mommy."

He shot straight up in bed, his eyes swollen, face wet. "I'm sorry, Mom. I didn't mean it." For years after, the vision of her lying crumpled on the floor remained so vivid in his mind, he was afraid to close his eyes.

After the funeral, at his aunt's urging, his father had put him and Anson in therapy. It took a year before he could sleep through the night without waking up crying. The nightmares had died down during high school and college, and he'd relished their disappearance. He could finally get on with his life. Sleep was so important to a pilot's ability to fly, he knew he'd be compromised if he didn't get enough rest.

Upon Steve's death, they'd returned with a vengeance.

"Get a grip," he chastised himself. "It's not your fault. None of it is." He pulled the covers over his head again, hoping to block out the world. "It's not your fault." Exhaustion overwhelmed him, and he closed his eyes.

Late-morning sun was flooding his tiny bedroom when he next awoke. He picked up his phone to see it was a few minutes until eleven, and he groaned and stretched. Coming off a coast-to-coast was always the hardest, but he knew how to push his way through it—get up and out of bed. It was the only way to reacclimate to the time.

Showered, dressed, and feeling more human, he decided to go out for a late breakfast. If he didn't leave the apartment, he'd stay inside all day and vegetate. Not that a day on the couch doing nothing but watching television didn't sound like heaven, but from experience it would end up being three days of doing simply that. He grabbed his car keys and wallet and left.

The diner on Union Turnpike was bustling even for a weekday, but within five minutes he was seated at a table for two and given a menu, water, and coffee. He sipped and let the warmth travel through him.

"Schaeffer?"

He glanced up. "Yes?" A man stood opposite him.

Salt-and-pepper hair and dressed in jeans and a T-shirt. Schaeffer searched his memory. Should he know this man? Was he one of his random hookups? Something about him looked familiar. Guilty at not remembering his name, he pretended jet lag. "I'm sorry, I'm still half-asleep. I got in from San Francisco early this morning, and my brain isn't fully firing."

"I understand. It's been a long time." Warmth filled his brown eyes. "I'm Andy. Andy Tavares. We worked together once, about two and a half years ago. I was at the airport early today too, coming in from LA. I thought I'd sleep all day, but we know that never works out, so I figured maybe a trip to the diner and having a dozen cups of coffee might help." He waited, and Schaeffer knew he should invite Andy to join him.

"I feel you. Want to sit with me? If you're not meeting anyone."

"Thanks, no, I'm not." He took a seat. "It's hard to maintain a social life when you're leaving every few days. As you know."

The server stopped by, took their order, and poured Andy his coffee. After he left, they sat for a moment in a slightly awkward silence.

"How long have you worked for RWB?" Schaeffer asked, figuring it was an easy segue into conversation.

Andy sipped his coffee. "Ahh, that's good. About eighteen years." At Schaeffer's raised brows, he chuckled. "Yeah, I'm an old-timer. I went to college, tried my hand at retail for a while but found it boring, then figured that since I love to travel and talk to people, why not get paid for it? Most flight attendants are eager young things in their twenties, looking for the excitement of travel. I hate to tell them it's more about dealing with people and their personalities. And their messes." He snickered. "Because, man, people get messy up in the sky."

"I bet you have stories. I miss most of it, being cooped up in the flight deck."

"Which means you have your own cross to bear. Some of the captains are a piece of work." For a split second, their eyes met, before Andy took another sip of coffee.

The struggle was real because damn, Schaeffer wanted to know what Andy was insinuating but didn't want to act as if he were all about the gossip. Even if he was.

"Oh?" That seemed like a response that wasn't discouraging yet showed enough interest that would—he hoped—allow Andy to continue. And Andy did.

"When I first started, male flight attendants were few and far between. As poorly as the captains—and I'm sorry to say, first officers as well—treated the female flight attendants, us male 'air waitresses,' as they liked to call us, were treated even worse."

Not surprising from what Schaeffer had heard, but that was secondhand. He hadn't spoken in depth with any flight attendants.

"How so?"

Andy gazed into the distance as if remembering. "They'd ask us why we didn't get a real-man's job, or if we'd rather wear a dress like the other attendants, or they'd call us *sweetheart* with a wink. Little sly comments about how the view wasn't as pretty now as it used to be, or how the gays were ruining it for everyone."

Having flown hundreds of flights over the past four years, Schaeffer didn't dispute Andy's words. He'd heard almost as many disparaging remarks about the male flight attendants as sexist comments about the female ones.

"And you've never felt comfortable to say anything or complain to your union or the NGPA?" The National Gay Pilots Association was a worldwide advocacy group supporting the LGBTQIA flying community. There were times over the years that Schaeffer had considered joining, but his tours in the military had engrained such a fear of disclosure that he shelved the idea, putting it off for another day.

"Back then, they didn't have as much of an impact. They were just starting out."

"True. But you still shouldn't have to put up with bullshit like that. Besides, not every male flight attendant is gay."

"That's not even the point." Andy frowned. "Of course not. Some pilots—not the majority, because most are fine—but there are a bunch who are very old-school, super conservative, and would prefer to have women serve them with a smile and tight skirt."

"Yeah, I get it. I've worked with a bunch of them. I try to shut it down if they start ranting about something, but I'm not always successful."

During cross-country flights, members of the crew were particularly susceptible to being trapped with someone who used them as their sounding board to vent all their complaints. Schaeffer had learned more about people's marital issues, infidelities, and other family dynamics than he'd ever wanted. Not to mention their political and religious views, which was always a hard-pass topic for him.

"Well, you know it's hard. Pilots think they're God."

He winced. "Not all of us."

Andy's grin was rueful. "Yeah, sorry, that was obnoxious. For the record, I've never heard anyone say a bad thing about you."

Schaeffer flashed a grin. "Glad to hear."

Their food arrived, and they spent a few minutes eating. Andy set his fork on his plate of eggs and bacon. "So what's your story? Where were you up until four years ago?"

In the middle of chewing his pancake, Schaeffer gave himself time to decide how much to reveal. "I was in the military, flying intelligence missions in Afghanistan. After I was discharged, I needed to do something and didn't want to give up flying, so I followed in the footsteps of so many other retired military pilots. I trained first on single engines, then moved up to the 737s and Airbuses. That makes the airline happy—they can use me for standby, in case someone cancels."

"I'll bet. How was it in the military?"

It was his turn for the memories to hit. And they hit hard. "I wanted to do it, but I was never happier to leave."

"How come?" Andy asked, buttering his toast.

"All the death and destruction got to me," he answered simply. "I'd had a couple of close calls, but when my best friend was shot down in front of me…" He blinked, and to his mortification, his voice wobbled. He stopped to take a deep breath. "I knew I couldn't do it anymore. If I wasn't at one hundred percent, I wasn't doing my job."

Mental health issues were still talked about in hushed tones in the military. Upon notifying his superior officers that he was having nightmares after Steve was killed, instead of treatment being offered, he was told to get it together and tough it out. He tried, but when his lack of sleep resulted in sluggish response time, Schaeffer knew it was time to call it quits. He unilaterally sought treatment from a psychologist. He wouldn't risk it and have someone lose their life because of him. It devastated him to leave, but it was the right thing to do.

"That's rough." Andy sounded nothing but sympathetic. "I can't imagine."

"No one should. And despite all the headway the military has made in providing mental health care, not enough people are benefiting because it's still seen as a weakness, even though I know better now. I was talked about for seeing a shrink, and it makes me so damn angry because shit like that discourages people who need the help from getting it because they're afraid. I was granted a medical discharge." He forced a smile. "And here I am."

Why he'd decided to open up about his past to Andy, a virtual stranger, he had no clue. Maybe he sensed no judgment. Andy's brown eyes remained warm and filled with compassion.

"Thanks for sharing with me. I'm sure a lot of people who need help don't get it because of the stigma. Not to mention how they treat their gay men and women. I'm not surprised so many veterans have psychological problems. I'm glad you got help."

Schaeffer finished his pancakes, wondering if what Andy had said was true. Had therapy helped? His doctor had thought so, but if true, why did he still feel so damn guilty?

When the check came, over his protest, Andy grabbed it. "Hey, I barged in on your peaceful morning. The least I can do is buy you breakfast."

"All right, but I owe you one."

"How about dinner tonight? Eight o'clock?"

Why not? Better than sitting at home with takeout.

"Yeah, sure. How about pizza? We could do Paul Michael's."

"Sounds good."

Schaeffer picked up his coffee cup. "I'm going to finish my coffee, but I'll see you then."

Andy nodded, and after slipping his wallet into his jeans pocket, walked away. Schaeffer sent Ren a text.

Having dinner with a flight attendant who's been with the airline almost twenty years. Interesting perspectives.

He didn't expect an answer, nor did he receive one. Ren was either driving or sleeping, but he thought it would be nice to let him know how he was spending his day. Upon returning home, he cleaned out his refrigerator, went through his mail, and took a nap.

Steve's jet was on fire, the flames surrounding him. Schaeffer watched it spin down to earth and crash. Through the blaze, he saw his mother's face.

"I love you, Schaeffer. Try to be happy."

"Mom," he cried out. "I love you."

He woke up panting and shaking, covered in sweat. His head pounded, and he wanted nothing more than to stay under the covers. But having dealt with these nightmares for so long, he knew they would stay with him until he channeled his energy into something else to take his mind away from them.

Deciding a shower would do the trick, he first checked his messages, and found one from Ren.

Enjoy yourself tonight but not too much.

Impossible. You're not here.

He climbed out of the bed and went to take a shower.

At eight that evening he walked into the restaurant and spotted Andy at a table for two.

"Hey, I hope you weren't waiting long. I had to find a place to park."

"No. I just got here a few minutes ago, myself."

"Can I get you gentlemen something to drink?" A server waited by their table.

"A glass of Chardonnay for me," Schaeffer answered. He'd popped some Advil to quash the post-nightmare headache, and the dull ache had receded.

"I'll have a Pinot Grigio," Andy said.

She withdrew, and a little nervous, Schaeffer drank from his water glass. Having dinner with a man wasn't something he normally did. Usually his hookups at home were quick and hurried and anonymous, at a bar or club in the city. If he wanted something more than a blowjob, he'd wait until a layover, where he'd have a hotel room to himself.

"Everything okay?" Andy's brows pulled together. "You look like something's bothering you."

He pasted a smile on his lips. "Nope. All good. What did you end up doing after breakfast?"

"Sleeping." Andy laughed, and he joined in, his nerves

evaporating. It was silly to be concerned that Andy would think this was more than simply a friendly dinner.

"I was a little better. I got rid of the food that died in my fridge, paid my bills, then took a nap."

"Guess you're more organized than me."

The server returned with their drinks, and they each ordered their own personal pizza—Schaeffer had mushrooms and sausage, and Andy pepperoni.

"So where are you off to next?" Andy swirled his wine.

"I think Chicago, Dallas, St. Louis, and Charlotte." He shrugged. "It all looks the same at this point."

"Yeah. A hotel room is a hotel room. Unless you're sharing it with someone."

"I guess." The conversation felt as if Andy was dancing around the question of whether Schaeffer was gay or not. "I mostly just catch up on sleep or watch movies."

"You don't do nights out with the crew?"

He sipped his wine. "Not really. I'm not much of a party person. I'll FaceTime with my family in California and catch up with them."

"So I guess I shouldn't suggest going out to a club after dinner?"

He met Andy's gaze. "Uh, no. Sorry."

"Understood. I just want you to know that I find you very attractive, and if you're interested, I'd like to take you out sometime."

Shit.

"I-I'm not—"

"Out, yeah, I know. I could see that, but we could be discreet."

Double shit.

While he'd never deny his sexuality, how the hell could he get out of this? Andy seemed like a nice person, but Schaeffer wasn't about to reveal that side of his personal life to a stranger, nor did he want to screw up what he and

Ren were working on. He laced his slightly shaky fingers together.

"I'm sorry, Andy. I don't want to give you the wrong impression and have you waste your time. I'm not interested in anything other than friendship."

Before Andy could answer, their food arrived. The pizzas were placed in the center of the table between them, but neither made a move to eat. Andy's brow furrowed, and he studied Schaeffer with intent, dark eyes.

"Okay. I hope I didn't make you uncomfortable."

"No. Not at all."

"We can be friends, though, right?"

Schaeffer smiled, relieved the conversation had turned around. "Yeah. I'd like that."

They finished their dinner, Schaeffer paid the bill, and Andy insisted on leaving the tip. Their cars weren't parked far from each other, and they arrived at his first.

"This is mine." He stopped by his Jeep. "Thanks for the evening."

"I enjoyed it. Pizza was good, and the company was even better." He stuck out his hand. "I'll see you. Hopefully one day we can work together. It would be nice to fly with a friend."

Schaeffer took it. "I'm all for that."

He watched Andy walk away, then climbed into the Jeep and drove home.

In the four years he'd worked for RWB, Schaeffer had pretty much kept to himself. Pilots rarely worked with the same people unless you were senior enough to make special requests. He came home after his shifts and caught up on sleep and his bills. Flying so much didn't leave time for friendships, and his decision to not be out at work left him uneasy. Not a week went by without someone suggesting going out, either at home or on a layover. Meeting Ren had staved off the loneliness for a while, but dammit, he missed him like crazy. He craved Ren's smiles and longed to touch his face.

It was after ten when he turned the lights on in his apartment. He tossed his clothes into the hamper and settled on the couch to watch the news and scroll through his messages. A surge of happiness jumped through him at an email from Ren.

Hope you're having a nice dinner. I've got a room at a motel near the campground and picked up food at a supermarket. The roads are pretty wild here, and there's still snow. I'm storing my extra stuff, then heading out to set up the blind I'll be living in until I get my shot. Talk soon.

Ren attached a photo of himself. His sunglasses were perched on his head, and his hair was sun-streaked and slightly shaggy. Memories rushed through him—holding Ren and kissing him to wakefulness so they could make love. Ren's rough fingers sliding down the curve of his back, rendering him weak at their touch.

An ache shot through his heart, and he pressed his hand to his chest. He'd never missed a lover before, and the pain of their separation was proving harder than he'd ever imagined.

"Dammit, Ren. I miss the hell out of you. You'd better get that picture soon."

But he knew that as much as it hurt not to have Ren with him physically, not having Ren in his life would be much worse.

CHAPTER ELEVEN

Things were different this time.

Ren crouched in his blind, a telephoto lens peeking out, and prepared for another long wait to see if any of the foxes would show up. When he'd arrived three months earlier, he'd spoken to the park rangers on his way in, and they hadn't seen any foxes in the area, but from experience, Ren knew that meant little. Years could go by without a sighting, but they were there. He'd seen their scat and footprints, and during his daily hikes had found fur clinging to the underbrush. If he could get this shot, it would be one of the pinnacles of his career.

Six months ago, he would've bought enough supplies and prepped for a minimum yearlong stay. It would be the only thing on his mind.

Six months ago, he hadn't met Schaeffer.

God, he missed him.

Schaeffer wasn't the first man he'd spent his off time

with. He'd never professed to a life of celibacy, and in his travels throughout the world, he'd been with Ernesto while in the Alps, photographing the Italian wolf; and with Emil in Norway, who'd helped him locate the Steppe Eagle. Mingati, a Maasai man who'd offered to guide him through the Serengeti in his search for the rhino, had occasionally sneaked into his tent. Homosexuality was illegal in Tanzania and many other African states, so their times had been hurried and few.

But those encounters had been nothing more than a way to pass the long days and nights he'd sat alone, watching and waiting for the perfect shot. He'd said goodbye, and there was never a second thought after they parted ways.

The first day after leaving Schaeffer, he'd wanted to turn around and drive right back to Orange County. A quick call to him had only made the distance harder, but after ending the conversation, he'd laughed. Seemed he had his first crush. How cute. That didn't stop him from scrolling through all the pictures they'd taken.

Cell signal was spotty at best anytime in the park, so whenever he could, he grabbed the time to text Schaeffer. Schaeffer would text him on his way to or from a flight or on a layover. After all these months, they'd gotten used to it, but that didn't mean he had to like it.

Twigs snapped outside his blind, and he poked his head out at the approaching footsteps. It was Dex, one of the rangers he'd introduced himself to when he'd arrived. He'd seen the ranger vehicles make their pass-throughs as they traversed the grounds, monitoring the campers.

"Hey, Ren, how's it going?"

Dex was big and brawny, with short brown hair, a trimmed beard, and wore aviators over his eyes.

Probably a lot better if you didn't interrupt me, he wanted to say but refrained, knowing he should stay in their good graces. Deciding it was time for a break, he stepped out of the blind and stretched.

"Okay. Nothing new. Have you seen anything?"

"The foxes? Nah. I've been here four years, and I think I might've seen them once, but even then, can't be sure. Bobcats, bears, and deer, more likely."

That he knew. He'd gotten some nice insect, wildlife, and flower photos he could sell, apart from what he was paid by the magazine. It was a decent side hustle that brought in extra money. He slapped at the mosquitos. Dex laughed.

"Run outta bug spray?"

"Almost. Guess I'll have to bring another can with me tomorrow."

"Man." Dex peered around the small space. "You don't take a break, do you?"

"Not if I want to get what I came for so I don't have to do this for a year…or even another month if I can help it."

Dex removed his aviators, blue eyes curious. "Anxious to get home? Got a girl waiting for you?"

Ren, who'd pulled out his phone to check for cell signal but found none, met Dex's gaze. "I have someone special."

"Well, that don't mean you can't enjoy yourself. There's a restaurant past the ranger station—about a mile from the showers? The Creekside Inn. Lots of people get together there in the evening for a drink and something to eat. Better than the fast-food places farther away or the canned crap you've been eating."

"I gotta stay here—"

"One night away ain't gonna kill you. You got those remote cameras, I'm sure." Dex replaced his sunglasses. "Think about it. Gotta be lonely sitting here all day long. See ya."

He mulled over Dex's words after the ranger drove off. Was Dex sending him some kind of signal? He wasn't about to fuck things up with Schaeffer for some random screw. They hadn't said the word *exclusive* to each other, but he knew, without it needing to be said, that Schaeffer wasn't hooking up with anyone. And neither would he.

But it would be nice to take a break and have a conversation with someone other than the voices in his head and eat a fresh meal. And yes, technically, he could set up his cameras for automatic recording, but he'd always prided himself on taking those extra steps to get the shots he wanted, which was why he kept an air mattress in the extra-large blind he'd bought and hiked to the ranger station to take showers and use their bathroom.

Still…

"One night won't make a difference. And if I get a video of the little fucker, so be it." The perfect photo no longer seemed that important when he had the perfect man waiting at home for him.

Mind made up, he settled in for the remainder of the afternoon.

At seven thirty that evening, he pushed open the door of the Creekside Inn, which was indeed filled with campers and locals, as Dex had told him it would be. The food smelled delicious, and he couldn't wait to sit and order. The tables were all full, but there were several open seats at the bar. As soon as he sat his ass down, he heard Dex call out, "Ren, you made it. Damn, I woulda sworn you were gonna stay up there with the critters."

The bartender set a coaster and a dish of pretzels in front of him. "What'll it be?"

Dex answered for him. "Get him anything he wants, Willy. It's on me."

Not wishing to be beholden, Ren protested. "Thanks,

Dex, but you don't have to."

The man Dex was with snickered. "Don't look a gift beer in the mouth. If you don't want it, I'll drink it."

"All right, then. Just a Stella if you've got it." Ren dipped his head to Dex. "Appreciate it."

They came over to his spot at the bar, and Dex sat next to him while the other man remained standing. "I didn't think you'd come. This is Mike, also a ranger, and another unmarried soul."

"But always looking. Nice to meet you, Ren. You're the photographer? We get a lot of your type here."

"I'm sure you do. It's beautiful and pretty much untouched. Not many people know about this spot."

Dex took a swig of his beer. "And we like to keep it that way."

He understood. Areas like this in the US were rare, and people spoiled them with their loud voices, trampling feet, and trash, not to mention the stupid things they did to get the perfect picture to post on their social media accounts.

He raised his bottle. "Here's to protecting our parks."

"So how'd you decide to come to this area?" Dex asked.

Ren chuckled. "I wasn't in the mood to mountain-climb. I know the foxes have been seen around Lassen National Park more often, but it's higher elevation and more remote than here." He waved over to the bartender. "Can I order food at the bar?"

"Yup."

Seemed Willy wasn't as chatty as the rangers.

"A cheeseburger with everything and fries, please."

"You got it."

"Set us up with some wings too, Willy," Mike demanded. He directed a question to him. "Where you from, Ren?"

"Originally New York, but I've been traveling all over for so long, I don't really have a place, except my storage unit in the city."

"Never been to New York, but I imagine it's pretty different than here."

He busted out laughing. "You could say that again. But you get used to it."

Dex scratched his head. "Don't think I could. I need my wide-open spaces and quiet time."

"For that you'd need to go upstate or to the beach."

He wrinkled his nose. "No, thanks. I got everything I need right here."

Mike elbowed him. " 'Cept a wife. Ain't had no luck finding that."

Dex drank the rest of his beer. "Nope."

"Speaking of the ladies, if you'll excuse me, I see Miranda, and I owe her a dance."

Ren watched as Mike approached a dark-haired woman. They kissed and walked to the small dance floor. Mike wrapped his arm around her waist, and she laid her head on his chest.

"They look pretty friendly."

"Those two have been on and off for years."

Ren noticed Mike's hand drifting lower to rub Miranda's bottom and winced. He didn't like seeing that, but she reached up and kissed him, so it appeared she didn't mind.

"Looks like they're on right now." His cheeseburger and fries came, and he doused them in ketchup and took a big, satisfying bite.

"So it does. You live with your girlfriend?"

Ren finished chewing. "No girlfriend—that's not my thing. And like I told you, I don't even have a place right now. I came to California after spending over a year away, and I rented a house by the beach for a while. I stopped at Big Sur before coming here."

"I see."

Ren imagined it had to be hard in this tight-knit community to be a gay man. They didn't exactly give off the love-is-love vibe here, but maybe he was wrong.

He finished his burger, and Dex had a few wings. Ren figured he'd test his theory. "No one you see you'd like to dance with? Lots of nice-looking young women I've seen making eyes at you."

Dex wiped his hands on the napkin. "Yeah? I think it's you."

"Well, they're barking up the wrong tree with me." He downed the rest of his beer and called over to Willy. "Another, please? Put it on my bill too."

" 'K," Willy said, and brought it over a moment later.

"A man of many words," Ren remarked.

Dex set his bottle on the bartop. "I'll be back."

Ren nodded and drank his beer, watching Dex weave his way through the crowd, stopping to say hello or give a smile. The man was young and good-looking, and maybe Ren was wrong in his assumptions, because Dex asked a woman to dance and took her hand. They swayed to the slow song on the dance floor, and she kissed his cheek. Dex pulled her in closer.

Ren finished his beer. "I'm gonna hit up the bathroom."

"No worries," Willy answered.

He returned from the men's room, and Willy had his check ready. Ren handed him the credit card and a nice cash tip.

"Thanks." He pocketed the cash.

"Tell Dex I left." He didn't see him on the dance floor, so he figured he was off with the woman he'd been dancing with.

"Will do."

Outside in the parking lot, he checked if he had cellphone service. Seeing the bars, he texted Schaeffer.

You around?

A rush of excitement shot through him when the message changed from *Delivered* to *Read*.

Yeah. In Dallas. Next flight's in ninety minutes.

He hit Schaeffer's number.

"Hi. I can't believe we're finally able to talk."

"Me neither. How are you? Have you been successful?"

"Not yet. The little bastards are slick. I told my editor I'm giving it another month and then I call it quits."

"Where to next?" Schaeffer asked. "Did Samuel give you another exotic assignment?"

"No, remember? I have to go see him. I'm planning on staying with this gorgeous pilot. Maybe you know him. Broad shoulders, sexy smile, fabulous ass…" He leaned against the wooden railing surrounding the tavern's parking lot.

Schaeffer's quiet rumble of laughter turned his heart upside down. "Funny. I thought that was you. Except for the pilot part." He paused. "I've missed you," he murmured, and the low timbre of his voice sent another ripple of desire through Ren.

"I miss you too. A lot. I can't wait to see you."

Where were these words coming from? He'd never said that to anyone, yet they fell out of his mouth as if it were the most natural thing in the world.

"I know. I have plans for you."

"My only plan is getting naked and in bed with you."

"You must've read my mind," Schaeffer whispered, and Ren heard voices in the background.

"I think we've been on the same wavelength from the beginning."

"I've got to get going. I—it was great hearing your voice."

"Same. I'll let you know when I'm coming. Say hi to your family for me."

Schaeffer chuckled. "Kendra's been bugging me over text. *Where's Ren? Have you heard from him? Tell him hi.*"

He couldn't keep the grin from his face. "Tell her I miss

her and hope to see her soon, even if it's just on FaceTime. Bye, Schaeffer."

"Hey. You forgot," Schaeffer chided.

"So I did. See you soon."

The screen turned black, and he sighed. Hearing Schaeffer's voice didn't quite make up for his absence. Ren climbed into his Jeep and took off down the twisting road. Darkness surrounded him on the drive to the ranger station—he could barely make out the rise of the trees and hoped no small animal darted in front of him. He counted himself lucky to reach the parking lot with no incident. Flashlight in hand, he held the beam in front of him for the trek to his blind. He spied the crowded campsite and turned away, pushing deeper into the grounds. Everything always looked different at night, but it was easier in the brush or desert. The heavy cover of trees could easily send a person in the wrong direction.

Once inside his blind, he checked the cameras but saw nothing of interest on the recording. He put on his sweats, since it got cold at night, and settled in. However, instead of feeling sleepy after the two beers, he was wide awake.

The rustle of branches and shrubs caught his attention. It wasn't unusual for bears to come exploring, and he hoped it would walk on by peacefully. He kept no spare food aside from tins, but bears liked to investigate.

"Ren?"

His pounding heart settled, and he stepped out of the blind. "Dex? What the hell? You scared the crap out of me."

"Sorry. I…uhh…you left, and I didn't know what happened."

"I told Willy to let you know I'd gone."

Dex crossed his arms. "I wanted to see for myself to make sure. You could get hurt on these dark roads."

God, was Dex going to make a move? Ren wanted to save him the embarrassment but didn't know how to extricate himself without it getting awkward.

"I'm okay. I can take care of myself."

"So I gather." Dex sighed. "How do you do it?"

"Do what?"

Dex moved closer. "You know." His gaze shifted to the ground, but then he met Ren's eyes. "You're gay, right? It seems so easy for you."

A wave of pity rolled over Ren, recalling how Schaeffer also had to hide at work. "Hey, listen. Come inside, let's talk."

When they were seated—him in the folding chair and Dex on the air mattress—Ren rubbed his chin. "So you're not out?"

"I could never…yeah. Can you imagine? It's not happening unless I move away. And before you say it, there isn't a shred of doubt in my mind I'd be in trouble if I did come out."

"Why not leave?"

Astonished, Dex stared at him. "Where would I go? My whole family's here, my friends. I've never been anywhere else. And I love it here."

"That woman I saw you dancing with tonight…"

"Amber? Yeah. We went to high school together."

"You looked pretty friendly."

"Some bastard tourist got her pregnant and left her, and now she raises her little boy on her own." He paused. "I—we've been together a few times."

"But?"

"I love her. But it's not the same. The first time I was with a man, I knew….Some guy came for the summer, and we would hook up in his tent at night."

God, he felt sorry for Dex, but he wasn't going to help him on his journey—not in that way, at least. More than ever, he realized that what he had with Schaeffer was special.

"I hope you can figure out the right thing, Dex. It's hard

to live your life the way other people think you should. We're all just figuring it out as we go along."

"But…in the parking lot you were talking to your boyfriend, and it sounded like you already knew the answer."

"You were eavesdropping on me?" Despite his sympathy, Ren grew annoyed at the thought of someone spying on him.

Dex hung his head and rubbed his face. "I'm sorry. I didn't mean to make you uncomfortable. It just…you looked so happy, and I wish I could feel like that."

It was hard to stay angry with someone who was hurting so much. "I know. But somewhere there's a person for you. Trust in yourself, keep looking, and hopefully you'll find them. Now I need to get some rest so I can be up early."

He listened as Dex's footsteps receded, then sank heavily onto the mattress. He'd better find that damn fox soon because hearing Schaeffer's voice again reminded him of everything he was missing. This separation was bullshit.

CHAPTER TWELVE

"Plans for your days off, Schaeffer?"

Captain Lucas Sandusky brought the Airbus A321 to a halt while Schaeffer assisted in the switch-down of the engines. They waited for the jet bridge to be attached, filling in their paperwork as the passengers waited to remove their baggage from the overhead bins.

"Same as always. Catching up on my sleep. Heading out to the beach or maybe a Mets game." He'd been working the most days the airline allowed in a month—twelve to fifteen nights—and was due for a four-day stretch off. Maybe this would be the weekend Ren showed up. He'd called a week earlier, saying he was planning to leave.

"I'm coming to you, so get ready."

And Schaeffer had. Stocked up on food, snacks, ice cream, condoms, and lube, and waited. The times he'd tried to text or call, Ren was out of range, and he'd been unable to complete the call.

Maybe he'd met someone else. Someone exciting and able to share this nomadic lifestyle he craved. They'd only had that one week almost six months ago after the crazy time during the snowstorm. It all seemed so far away now. Was it really feasible for them to have sustained their desire for each other? Schaeffer knew he wanted to see Ren as much as ever, but Ren was the wild card, someone used to freedom, no inhibitions or strings. A man able to be who he was. No hiding. In the dark of night, Schaeffer would awaken and wonder, *Why me?*

"Sounds nice. Better than my weekend." Sandusky cut him a wry smile. "Both sets of grandparents are coming over. It's my daughter's sweet sixteen. First she's having a party at some laser-tag place, then it's back to our house for pool time, pizza, and an ice-cream-sundae bar. My wife's idea."

The captain could pretend all he wanted but from the light in his eyes, Schaeffer could see Sandusky didn't mind too much.

Schaeffer said, "I miss my niece and nephew. They're young, and they grow so fast. It's been months since I visited them, and when we FaceTimed the other week, I swear they looked like they'd grown a foot each."

"I bet." Sandusky finished filling out the log and the administrative report. Schaeffer signed it, and Sandusky rose to his feet. "Okay, let's get outta here."

They opened the door to the flight deck as the flight attendants were notifying the gate agents about wheelchairs. After the requisite niceties to the customers, Schaeffer made his farewells and left.

Eager to put as much distance as he could between himself and the airport, he strode to the garage, paid for his parking, and drove home. Mail had piled up a bit, and he tossed the ads into the recycle bin by the entrance.

When he exited the elevator, he stopped dead. Sitting in front of his door, fast asleep, with several bags piled around him, was Ren. His heart slammed. Hard.

He approached and crouched at Ren's side. "Hey, sleepyhead." He kissed Ren's cheek, scratchy with an almost full growth of beard.

Ren jumped and blinked. "Wha—huh? Jesus, Schaeffer."

Ren reached out, and Schaeffer didn't care that they were out in the hallway where anyone could see them. The most important thing was Ren's breath stuttering against his face and the warmth of his skin to the touch.

"You're here. I can't believe you're here." Schaeffer couldn't stop kissing him. Ren's lips parted, and their tongues met, soft, hot, wet. Ren clung to his shoulders, and Schaeffer pinned him to the door. "You came."

The curve of a smile pressed to his cheek. "I said I would. One rainstorm that washed out the roads for days, two flight delays, an eighteen-hour layover, midair turbulence, and lost underwear." He hugged Schaeffer. "And I'd do it all again. It's you. You bet your sweet ass I came."

Schaeffer stood. "Let's go inside. You look like you need a meal, a shower, and bed. And not in that order." He opened the door and helped Ren in with his bags.

"That all sounds good, but you know what sounds even better?" Ren shut the door and stood waiting. Schaeffer moved closer and ran his hands over Ren's shoulders and arms, over his whole body. He couldn't stop touching Ren.

He's here. He really came.

"What?"

He was so beautiful and perfect standing before him in the flesh, feeling like muscle and bone, heartbeat and joy, pleasure and desire.

"You. Just you."

"You have me."

Their mouths connected, and it was a blur of clothes tossed in every direction and them laughing and tripping over each other to get to the bed. Schaeffer couldn't stop touching Ren or kissing the pulsing vein jumping in his strong, tanned neck.

"I missed you so fucking much. I can't believe you're really here." A harsh groan escaped Schaeffer's lips as Ren grasped his cock with a firm hand and placed a soft kiss to the tip. "So long. It's been so long."

Ren licked the precome from the tip of his erection. "I spent every day thinking of this moment, when I'd taste you and lick every inch of your body."

Schaeffer crawled to the side and grabbed the condoms and lube. "There's more where these came from. I prepared for you."

Ren hovered over him. "There's no way you're prepared for what I want to do to you."

The glow of Ren's startling green eyes stirred something deep inside him. Something wild and uncontrollable. He flipped them over so he was on top, and kissed Ren, nudging his tongue past gasping lips to play and tease inside his mouth. Ren's shaft hit his belly, leaving a sticky streak, and he grinned.

"I can't wait to be inside you."

Ren gripped his hip. "Let's make that happen. I can't wait any longer."

Schaeffer wet his fingers in his mouth, and plunged them into Ren, who hissed, then moaned with pleasure. Schaeffer moved in and out—slowly at first, but Ren worked himself on his hand so he moved faster.

"How's this?" Schaeffer whispered, pulling out abruptly, which earned him a grunt. He sheathed and lubed his dick, and pushed past the rim of Ren's tight muscle. "Or is this better?"

"Nuhhh." Ren's head thrashed side to side, and he clawed first at the bed, then at Schaeffer. "More, come on."

Schaeffer pushed Ren's knees to his chest, bending him almost in half. He thrust hard, his hips flexing and pumping into the tight clasp of soft, hot muscle surrounding his aching shaft. "Oh fuck, Ren, Ren."

"Schaeffer," Ren cried out, and his cock, trapped between their sweaty, rolling bodies, jerked and throbbed, spraying out hot come. He watched as Ren's eyes rolled to the back of his head, and body shaking, he wailed out his climax. His ass clenched in a viselike grip, pulling Schaeffer under with him. Schaeffer's orgasm tore through him, and with a drawn-out sigh, he buried his face in Ren's neck, wishing he never had to move from the bed and Ren's arms.

"Welcome home."

He shifted to roll off, but Ren held him fast. "Don't. I know we're messy and dirty, but I don't give a damn. The months I spent in a fucking tent, all I could think about was you and what this moment would be like. Let me have it a little bit longer."

Schaeffer blinked. Aside from his family, he hadn't thought he mattered to anyone. "I thought about you all the time as well."

"Is it always like this?"

"Like what?" Schaeffer asked, unsure what Ren meant.

"We haven't spent that much time together, but I couldn't wait to see you. All I thought about was what it would be like, with you." He cast his eyes down, a slight blush tinging his cheeks pink. "And it's not only the sex. I missed talking to you. Just…you."

He'd never expected such heartfelt confessions. "I missed seeing your smile when something excites you. But I was worried," he admitted.

"About what?" Ren's gaze met his.

"That it wasn't going to be the same. I imagined that after all the months away, desire would fade and your wanderlust would have you itching to travel."

"What about your desire?" Ren traced his lips with his fingertips.

"My desire is you. That hasn't changed. I want you as much as I did the last time we were together. You being here. With me. It's all I want."

"All those nights sitting alone, I ached for you. From that first time, something in me recognized you as the one I needed to be with. There is nowhere else to be but here with you."

Hearing Ren speak those words, he felt their impact in his chest, and he cupped Ren's cheek. "I still wonder if I'll be enough for you."

"You're more than enough. You're everything." Ren kissed his shoulder. "How many days off did you say you had?"

"Four."

Ren's lips found his. "Let the games begin."

They didn't leave the apartment for the rest of the day or night.

After they'd showered and ordered in a pizza, Ren fell asleep on his shoulder, watching television. Schaeffer led him to bed, tucked him in, and lay watching him until he too fell asleep. At some point in the night they'd returned to their position of choice, and when Schaeffer woke up the next morning, Ren was cuddled into his chest, a leg slipped in between his.

Ren opened his eyes and sighed with pleasure. "So it wasn't a dream. I really am here."

Schaeffer held him tighter. "Yes, it's real. And having you here is my dream." He'd had a nightmare not long after they fell asleep. It hadn't woken Ren up, and Schaeffer had fallen asleep afterward. He wasn't foolish enough to assume they'd disappear simply because Ren had shown up, but that feeling of completeness had returned, and he savored it.

They kissed and made love again, slow and sweet, taking the time to relearn each other, mapping out every inch of skin. Ren left no part of him untouched, and he lay gasping for air after being taken apart piece by piece.

"If this is what being lost in someone is like, don't ever find me."

"I won't have to look," Ren murmured. "You'll be right by my side." With one more kiss, Ren climbed off him.

They cleaned up and got dressed, then sat at his small dining table, eating their bagels.

"Do you want to go to the beach?" he asked Ren. "It's beautiful out, and I know how much you love the water."

Ren's smile was all he needed, and within an hour they'd gathered towels and a blanket for the sand, put water, fruit, and sandwiches in a cooler, and loaded up the car.

"I haven't been to Jones Beach in years," Ren mused and flipped down his aviators, humming to the music on the radio.

Schaeffer grinned. Could life get any better than this moment? Not in his mind.

"And it's going to be even longer. We're not going there. Too crowded."

"So where to?"

"You'll see," was all he said, and Ren shot him a glance but said nothing.

The drive to Long Beach was relatively quick as it was a weekday, but they didn't stop at the main area with the vendors, restaurants, and crowds. They drove past the bustling boardwalk until they reached the end.

"Point Lookout. Quiet and away from the kids and teenagers."

Ren took his hand. "Perfect. Like you."

They found a spot near the water and spread out their

blanket, set up their chairs, and sprayed each other with sunscreen. When they'd settled in, Ren sighed and waved a hand.

"This. This is it. What could be better? I feel like the luckiest man in the world. I'm at the beach, listening to the waves, and I'm with you. The man I care about more than anything."

Schaeffer's heart swelled at his declaration. "I feel the same. Maybe that old saying is right—you know, absence makes the heart grow fonder. There wasn't a night I went to sleep without missing you. As much as I enjoyed being with you in California, having you in my bed after so many months apart…I don't want to let you go."

"I'm here right now. And I'm not going anywhere."

"I wish you didn't have to."

Ren leaned over in his chair and kissed him. "Let's not think about tomorrows. Want to go jump some waves?"

He popped on his Mets cap and rose to his feet. "Last one in…" And sped off with Ren chasing after him.

He had no idea how long they spent in the water, but they exited holding hands and then dried off, with Schaeffer swooping in for a kiss. Ren slung his arm around Schaeffer's neck, and eyes sparkling, laughed into his face.

"Wait until I get you home."

"Promises, promises."

"Schaeffer?"

He froze at the sound of his name. Ren dropped his arm and backed away. Gathering his tumbling thoughts, Schaeffer turned to see a man and a woman.

"It's Ron Vance."

"H-hi. G-good to see you."

Act natural.

"Enjoying some much-needed time off?" Vance's expression was nothing but friendly.

"Y-yeah. I've been working like crazy. Figured a day

at the beach is always good to relax."

"We must be on the same wavelength. This is my wife, Mary Elizabeth." He placed a hand on the waist of the woman at his side, who was wearing a white beach dress and had her gray hair in a ponytail. Her eyes looked kind.

"Hello."

"Nice to meet you. This is my friend Ren."

Ren took a step forward and shook Vance's hand. "Good to meet you."

"You work for the airline as well, Ren?"

"No, I'm a wildlife photographer."

Impressed, Vance nodded. "Now that's one you don't hear every day. You're probably one of the few who's seen more places than us pilots, right, Schaeffer?"

"Considering where he's been, that's for sure."

"Well, we'll let you be. We're here to escape the house. Our daughter-in-law just gave birth, and she and our daughter and the baby are staying with us."

"Congratulations! I remember you saying she was expecting. That's wonderful."

"A little boy," Mary Elizabeth effused. "First one. Our son has three little girls. They didn't know ahead of time, and we're thrilled."

"That's terrific." Schaeffer didn't know what else to say.

"Honey, why don't you go set up the chairs? I'll be right there." Vance tipped his head to where their beach bags were piled on the sand.

"Sure. Nice to meet you two."

Once she was out of earshot, Vance's brow furrowed. "I assume you're afraid I'll say something?"

Schaeffer blinked and licked his lips. "Uh, well…" Ren's touch to his back steadied him.

"You don't have to answer me, Schaeffer. I understand. But I hope you'll listen to what I have to say. I'd never do anything to hurt you—personally or professionally. When our daughter told us she was a lesbian, we worried she'd face hostility. She works in finance, which is still a pretty conservative environment."

"Did she?" Ren asked.

Vance nodded. "It wasn't easy for Alexandra or Lori, her wife. But the most important thing is that they have each other. Jobs can be replaced. People can't. In the long run, that's what matters most. Enjoy your afternoon."

He watched as Vance joined his wife.

Ren laid a hand flat on the base of his spine. "Are you okay?"

He faced Ren. "Yeah. I'm freaking out a little, but…" He met Ren's tender gaze with renewed hope. "Maybe… maybe things are changing."

"Yeah. We can only wish for people to be decent human beings."

Ren lowered himself to the blanket, and Schaeffer joined him. They opened the cooler and took out the sandwiches and fruit. Ren popped some grapes and chewed.

"During this past photo shoot, I met a park ranger. I think I told you. His name's Dex."

"Of course it is," he muttered and rolled his eyes.

Ren snickered. "He's a good guy. Anyway, I had a feeling when he'd stop by my blind every few days to talk that he was looking for more than conversation."

"I'll bet."

"Silly." Ren snorted. "One day I was so sick of my own company and missing you badly, and I ended up going to dinner at the tavern. He was there with another ranger, who started talking about how Dex should find a woman. I left when Dex began dancing with someone. It was that night I called you late. Remember?"

"Oh…yeah. I do. My short layover."

"Uh-huh. I just needed to hear your voice. And of course the phone call wasn't enough, not when I wanted you in front of me, but it was the best I could do."

Words lay between them, never imagined but there, waiting to be said. Schaeffer itched to touch Ren, yet the hesitancy still remained.

"I remember. You were so far away."

"I've been gone on shoots longer, I've told you that. I enjoy my solitude…or I thought I did." Ren chewed his lip. "After our phone call, I went back to the park, checked my cameras, and was settling in for the night when Dex came by."

Schaeffer's heart sank. "Oh?"

Please don't tell me you slept with him. I was faithful. Lonely and faithful.

"Nothing happened, but he confessed how lonely he was and how he couldn't come out. He knew I had someone because he listened to our conversation, and I knew I should've been mad at him, but I couldn't because I felt so damn sorry for him. I think he's going to marry some woman and pretend to live a life he doesn't want. All because he's afraid."

Guilty at his thoughts, Schaeffer sympathized with a man he didn't even know. "I can relate."

"I know." Ren nodded. "And I hate what it's doing to you. It eats me up inside that you feel like you can't be the person you are, because that man is so good, kind, and loving, and he deserves the best. I hate that you don't have it."

Schaeffer brushed the hair off Ren's brow. "I think I do. I have you."

CHAPTER THIRTEEN

"They're going to freak. Whenever I speak to them, they ask about you. I didn't let them know you were coming." Schaeffer opened the laptop and connected to FaceTime, while Ren stayed out of sight as they'd planned.

"Hey, there." Schaeffer waved at the screen.

"Hi. Ooh, don't you look all tan and handsome," Kendra said, and Ren grinned.

"Why, thanks. We had a nice day at the beach."

"We? Who's we?" Kendra's voice squeaked. "Is someone there?"

That was his signal to pop up and wave. "Kendra, hi. Long time no see."

"Oh. My. God. Ren. You're here. I mean there." Kendra was literally hopping up and down. "Anson," she yelled. "Get in here."

"What? What's wrong?" He ran into the kitchen and peered at the computer. "Whoa, my man. Ren, is that you?"

"I'm baaack." Funny how he couldn't stop smiling. The few times he'd met Schaeffer's brother and sister-in-law, they were so warm and accepting, seeing them again was like welcoming old friends.

"When did you get in?" Anson asked.

"Yesterday."

"Oh, yeah?" Anson snickered. "And you're just coming up for air now? You guys been busy, huh?"

Schaeffer turned red. "Shut up, you idiot," he grumbled, and out of the sight of the computer, Ren rubbed his back. Early on, he'd picked up that Schaeffer was an inherently private person, and most likely, there wouldn't be overt displays of affection in public, even with his family. It didn't matter to him. He didn't need to show off his prize after he'd won.

"You're staying for a while, aren't you?" Kendra's steely tone let him know it wasn't exactly a question.

"I don't know what my next assignment is, but I've no plans to leave a minute sooner than I have to."

"I'm so glad to see you two together." She sighed. "It just seems right, if you know what I mean."

Funny thing was, he did. In all their time apart, an uneasiness had settled in his chest, which vanished the moment Schaeffer kissed him.

They glanced at each other and smiled. "Yeah." Ren squeezed Schaeffer's waist. "We're pretty happy too."

"Schaeffer was miserable. Just so you know. A total sad sack for the past few months." Anson threw out that pearl of wisdom, and Schaeffer growled.

"Knock it off. I never claimed I didn't miss him."

"When're you gonna come out for another visit? Both of you?" Kendra asked. "By the way, Ren, if you ever wanted to make a living doing children's photography, you'd make a fortune out here. Those pictures you took of the kids? Every single person who comes here is enthralled with them."

"I think it's easier to photograph migrating herds of antelope than to get children to sit still. I'll stick with the four-legged creatures for now, but I'll always have my camera available for Mini and Scotty. Where are they?"

"Scotty has swim practice, and Mini is at dance."

"About the visit," Schaeffer said, "we're going to have to wait and see because we don't know how long Ren will be able to stay."

"Yeah. I have some meetings with my editors, so hopefully I'll have answers soon."

He was seeing Samuel tomorrow, and Ren was no closer to knowing what it was Samuel wanted to talk about than when Samuel had first dropped his cryptic invitation.

"And hold up," Ren teased. "You two are home with no kids and busy talking to us? What is wrong with this picture? You're getting on our case about coming up for air when you should be locked in the bedroom."

Kendra cackled. "Honey, I'm so tired after dealing with those kids all day that after school is out, all I want is my glass of wine and a foot massage."

"Anson. Give your wife what she wants," Schaeffer ordered.

"Brother, you know I have a plan. Mission activated." He slipped his arms around Kendra's waist and winked at them over the top of her head. "Ren, great to see you again. We'll talk soon. Over and out."

The FaceTime ended, and snickering, Ren closed the laptop. "Someone's about to get lucky." He kissed Schaeffer's neck, the skin quivering under his lips.

"I know. Me." Schaeffer's low, husky laugh rumbled through him, and Ren took his hand and pulled him up.

"I think we're both so damn lucky."

"I know I am."

"Can I ask you something?"

Schaeffer held on to him and nudged his cheek with his

nose. "Anything."

"How come you live here and not with the rest of your family in California? You're all so close. I would think you'd want to be nearer."

The sparkle faded from Schaeffer's eyes, and he hung his head.

"There are many reasons. First, my mother. She's buried here, and if I moved out to California with the rest of my family, who would visit and make sure everything is okay? Maybe it sounds silly, but does that make sense to you?"

"Of course it does." Ren cupped his cheek. "You couldn't leave her alone." His sweet guy wouldn't do that to his mother.

"I tried staying in Orange County initially, but it's pretty conservative, and even though I'm not out at my job, it was easier to find gay people here when I needed to be with someone. It's only been four years that I've lived in New York. And I do visit them every chance I get."

"I'm not criticizing you. Not everyone has to live where their family is. You're obviously close."

Schaeffer smiled. "We are. Remember also how I told you pilots bid on routes and get them by seniority?"

"Yeah."

"Same with domicile—the home base. And when I joined RWB, they were in desperate need of more pilots domiciled in the New York City area. It all has to do with taxes and where a pilot's salary goes the furthest. California borders Nevada, which has no state income tax, so more pilots are domiciled there than in New York City, which doesn't border no-tax states. It's complicated."

"Anything tax-related always is." Taxes were something he had no desire to think about. He paid what his accountant said he owed and hoped the government would leave him alone.

"I understand why my father moved to California—he

was left with two boys, and he needed help from his family. And now…he's lived more of his life there, without her than with her."

Ren understood Schaeffer's father a bit better. He was overprotective because he had no other outlet for his love. "Has he ever had a girlfriend or dated?"

"It took him years after Mom died to go on his first date, and it was a disaster. Anson had just left for college, and I was sixteen and resentful."

Ren smoothed his hair. "That's understandable."

"Maybe. In retrospect, I see how I could've been nicer, but I was a kid and hated seeing him with anyone else. There's never been anyone steady. I know he's gone out a few times, but I don't think it occurred to him to marry again. After my aunt died, he stayed home more and more, and now he's just here for the grandchildren. It makes me sad."

"I suspect he's lonely."

"We don't really talk about it, or about my mother much at all. But I can't forget."

Ren held him closer. "Of course not. She was your mother."

"I'll never forget finding her….I should've come home when she said to. I wish—" He became agitated, and Ren kissed him, hoping to soothe his anxiety.

"Don't. I understand."

How horrible to have that last memory. At least Ren was so young when his mother was killed, he barely remembered her face. And then there was the part of his past he didn't speak of, something even more traumatizing, but he wasn't ready to share. Not yet.

Schaeffer's somber eyes met his. "Yeah. I think you do. Have I told you how glad I am you're here?"

"I am too." Ren pressed soft, gentle kisses to Schaeffer's throat. "All these past months, every night I'd go to sleep hoping you wouldn't find someone before I came back to you."

"I wasn't looking," Schaeffer said. "Why would I?"

"Loneliness."

Schaeffer's hands landed heavily on his shoulders. There was a bit more silver at his temples and lines in his face that hadn't been there six months earlier, but it made him no less handsome.

"Even surrounded by the people I love, I've been lonely my whole life. That day in the hotel room during the snowstorm opened up something inside me I didn't know existed. I'd never been as intimate with anyone. It was just us, and I didn't need anyone else but you."

Ren was caught up in the raw honesty in Schaeffer's gaze. "I feel the same. Meeting you has changed my perspective."

"You here, or even across the country, made it better because just knowing that another person besides my family gives a damn about me…" He blinked, and Ren captured his face between his hands.

"I care. So damn much. More than I ever thought myself capable of. I'd think about watching the sunsets with you, driving down the coast…or just sitting on the deck together, watching the birds flying in the pale early morning sky at sunrise. Loving it all because we get to share those moments. I want those sunrises and sunsets."

"I want that too. With you."

Ren held Schaeffer tight, soaking in his warmth. Those lonely nights of years past were fast becoming nothing but a memory. Schaeffer was his here and now, and for once, Ren looked forward to seeing what the future held.

"You taste like the brightest part of heaven," Schaeffer said. "My own personal shooting star, lighting up my life."

Schaeffer kissed him hard, and Ren clung to him, holding him around his neck, cheek pressed to cheek, as the words flowed from Schaeffer's lips to his. He breathed them in, like a mantra.

"You taste like a dream, but you're not, are you? You're here, and you're everything I've ever wanted."

Prior to meeting Schaeffer, Ren had dismissed as silly and cringey all the love language he'd hear couples use. But now…he liked it. Maybe even loved it.

Maybe…he loved Schaeffer. He'd never loved anyone except his foster brothers, but this was a different emotion. Something bigger. Bolder. Shocking him to a core he once thought dead and desiccated, but now, with Schaeffer watering his soul with joy, life sprang forth.

With Schaeffer's tongue in his mouth, his possessive growls drove all coherent thoughts of life and love from Ren's brain, leaving only want, hunger, and a burning desire.

"You're all I need," he whispered, and Schaeffer smiled against his lips.

The following morning Ren dressed for his meeting with Samuel. Unexpectedly nervous, he changed his shirt twice, which made no sense, since Samuel didn't care what he wore. Schaeffer had offered his car for the drive to Westchester so he wouldn't have to deal with the hassle of the Metro-North.

"Don't forget the registration and insurance card I left for you on the table."

"I won't. I know those troopers are out there." He glanced at his phone before sliding it into his pocket. "I should be back by the afternoon or sooner, depending on what Samuel wants."

"Good. I can get tickets for the ball game. Hot dogs and baseball? What do you say?"

He leaned over and gave Schaeffer a goodbye kiss. "Let's

go, Mets."

It took an hour and forty-five minutes to get to White Plains due to traffic and construction. "Jesus Christ, I'll be a hundred by the time they fix this damn road," Ren grumbled, but he didn't really mind. How could he, when he had so much to be grateful for? He turned up the radio and belted out some AC/DC.

Finally, he reached the low-rise office building in Pleasantville where *Nature's Beauty* had their main offices. Toni, Samuel's wife and coeditor, greeted him with a hug.

"Ren. I was so excited when Samuel said you were coming in today. It's been how long?"

"Over two years. And you haven't changed at all. Still gorgeous." He gave the woman a squeeze. Toni was an old-school nature enthusiast, a botanist and member of the Wildlife Conservation Society.

Toni blushed. "Stop flirting. When are you going to find a man to deal with you?"

"Maybe I have," he teased.

Her jaw dropped, and she put her hands on her hips and glared. "Renaldo Stewart. You did not just say you have a boyfriend and think I'm going to let that pass."

"Damn, Toni. No one's called me Renaldo in forever." He sprawled in the empty chair next to her desk. "And yeah. I met someone." Even the mere thought of Schaeffer set his insides swirling.

"Someone special, from that look on your face. When? How long?"

"We met during the snowstorm that closed JFK about six months ago. Then we ran into each other again when I was on vacation in California. We…connected. I'm staying with him now."

She bit her lip, eyes searching. "It's serious?"

Serious. Such a bland word to describe what he felt for Schaeffer, what he felt like *with* Schaeffer. One single word couldn't encompass the absolute completeness Schaeffer's touch brought him. That gnawing sense of restlessness and craving to escape vanished whenever they were together. Suddenly his life of only one no longer satisfied. He needed Schaeffer to be free.

"I'm not sure what *serious* entails, but he's different from anyone I've ever met. I'm…happy. Very happy with him." A smile broke across his face. Thinking about Schaeffer had him smiling almost all the time.

"I can see that. And that makes me happy. For more than one reason." But despite her words, sadness weighed in her eyes and the frown of her lips.

Not understanding, his brow furrowed. "I'm not following."

Instead of answering, she picked up the phone. "You will. Samuel? Ren is here.…Okay, will do." She placed the handset in the cradle. "Go right in. He's waiting to see you."

Samuel Binder had been a robust hulk of a man, so much so that his doctor had warned him to cut down on the snacking and get back to the outdoors and move a little. When Ren had left for the Serengeti two years earlier, Samuel had joked that the next time Ren saw him, he'd be half the man.

Unfortunately, it proved true, but not for the right reasons. Samuel had lost at least sixty pounds, and his hair had turned completely gray from the thick russet waves Ren remembered. Dark pouches rested under his eyes, and Ren noticed the subtle shaking of his hands.

"Were you planning to tell me?"

Samuel lifted a trembling hand to rub his chin. "Tell you what? That I'm dying?"

A direct hit from a rhino horn couldn't have caused him any more pain than hearing that declaration directly from Samuel's lips, and a painful cry burst from him.

"What—"

"Cancer. I've known for a while. I've managed until now, but it's getting worse. Sit."

Ren lowered himself into the chair by Samuel's desk and waited. "I don't know what to say."

"Nothing *to* say. I've come to terms with it, and I'm doing what I have to do. That's not why I called you to come here."

That was Samuel. Never one to dwell on the negative or allow anyone else to do the same. Curious now, Ren asked, "Oh? What's going on?"

"First off, like I said, the photos from the rhino shoot were spectacular. The one in the watering hole? We're going to do a five-page spread as well as the cover."

An hour ago, he would've been thrilled. Anytime he'd had an entire article and multiple photos instead of a simple photo credit on a single shot, it was a boon to him career-wise. But after hearing about Samuel, he didn't give a shit.

"Great."

"And the candids of the booby you caught in California, we've had a lot of interest from the ornithology community."

"Sure, whatever."

"Renaldo. Stop it."

"Jesus. That's twice in less than ten minutes. First Toni, now you."

Samuel's light-blue eyes hadn't lost their twinkle. "Don't piss Toni off."

"I mean, of course I'm thrilled, really. I know it's helpful for my career, but it's hard to be happy after your news."

"I understand. But I guess it'll make up for the fox pictures."

"Sneaky little fucker," Ren groused. "I know they were there—and the DNA I collected will tell us for certain, at least. I'm sure the few pictures I managed to get were of the little bastard, but unfortunately, they're too blurry."

"Don't be so hard on yourself. It was a crapshoot for

you to even get what you did."

"I know, I know. I wasn't about to sit around for another six months, waiting to see if they'd show up again."

Samuel studied him, those shaky fingers steepled in front of his face. "I'm surprised. Usually when you're stymied, you get even more tenacious and refuse to leave until you get the shot of a lifetime."

"You're right," he admitted. "That was before I met someone. Being with him has made me view my priorities differently."

"I sensed that from things you've said since you've come home. I knew something sounded different when I first talked to you in California." Samuel nodded. "You deserve it."

He grimaced. "Do I? I'm not so sure."

"Still beating yourself up, I see. Thinking you had the ability to save the world."

"Not the world," he lashed out. "Just my brothers. The only two people who cared about me."

Unperturbed by his anger, Samuel looked at him sadly. "Not the only two, you know that. You'll never be able to give all of yourself unless you unburden the pain of their loss in your heart."

"The man I'm with…he's so damn good. So sweet and caring. I'm not sure I know what the hell I'm doing."

"If he cares about you, he'll say what Toni and I always have. What happened upstate couldn't have been prevented. It was a tragedy."

"I promised to always take care of them. But I didn't. I let them down."

"And you think by hiding in the desert or the snow or way up in mountains, you're making it up to them? You're not, Ren. You're only hurting yourself." He paused and took a drink of water while Ren struggled not to reach out and help him hold the shaking water bottle. Samuel might not be able to knock him flat on his ass like he would have if he'd ever attempted that before, but he'd still let him know what he could do with his pity, so Ren kept quiet and silently grieved for the man.

"Which brings me to the reason you're here. Obviously, I can't do this for much longer. I'm tired, my eyes can't handle it, and I have too many damn doctor appointments. I want to know if you'd be willing to step up and be the magazine's photo editor."

Ren blinked. "What—*me*?"

"Well, you would share the duties with Toni and Leroy Hawk, our international editor in chief. This is a team effort."

"But…*me*? I don't know about copy and editorials and placement…"

"Which is what I have staff in place for. But I need you for your vision of that perfect shot. There's no one I trust more to choose the photos for the magazine, and let's face it—they are the main draw. But don't ever tell our writers that." A faint grin kicked his lips up, and Ren's heart squeezed, knowing if he'd had his strength, there'd be a loud belly laugh instead. "No one has what you possess. That genius to know the exact angle of a shot that will capture the critical moment. The golden shot. You're either born with it or you're not. I saw it right away, that first time in the mountains when you showed me your portfolio. You've got *it*."

"What do you need from me?" Ren would do whatever he asked. He owed everything to Samuel and wouldn't let him down.

The water finished, Samuel set the bottle aside and managed a full-blown smile. "It would mean you staying in one place for a while. Here. In the area. I'm thinking that wouldn't be a problem for you now?"

Ren smiled too. "No. It won't."

CHAPTER FOURTEEN

The night was balmy with low humidity, and their seats at Citi Field were great—ten rows behind third base. The Mets were blowing out the Phillies in the third inning, and normally he'd be more into the game, but after the blockbuster news Ren had sprung on him that evening after he'd returned, baseball was the last thing on his mind.

"So, let me get this straight. You're staying put."

Chomping on his foot-long hot dog, Ren couldn't stop smiling. "Yup. No more trips around the world, sleeping in tents, and hiding in the bushes."

It was hard to contain the joy exploding inside him. He wanted nothing more than to grab Ren and hug him, but they were in public.

"You're really going to live here. In New York. I can't believe it. I mean, I feel terrible for the reason, but this is amazing news."

"I know. And I had no idea Samuel was so sick. If I had,

I would've said 'Fuck that fox picture' and come home to spend time with him." Ren slurped down his soda. "My hope is that Samuel goes into remission and all this becomes unnecessary."

Schaeffer gave his shoulder a squeeze. "I hope that too."

"Except for one thing." The crowd roared as the Mets scored again, but they paid no attention. "The staying-here part? That's looking like all kinds of necessary now." His green eyes glowed under the lights, and Schaeffer forgot where they were, the ball game, everything but the two of them as he fell into the fiery passion of Ren's gaze.

"Stay with me," he said softly, but he knew Ren heard him over the cheering of the fans, as his eyes widened. "Move in with me."

"Really?"

"Really. I can't think of anything I'd like better."

Ren leaned against his shoulder, and his lips brushed Ren's hair.

But as Ren stared out onto the field, a haunted expression on his face, Schaeffer knew his mind was not on them moving in together, but on something else.

"I owe everything to Samuel. I told him yes without thinking about things, like getting a place to live, a car…"

"That's what you do for the people in your life you care about. No questions asked. You just do what needs to be done."

"Samuel knew I'd accept," Ren mused. "He gave me the chance to live this life. Without him…" Ren ducked his head, and Schaeffer pretended to be interested in the game but saw him wipe his eyes. Knowing Ren would hate any expression of sympathy, and because Citi Field with its thirty thousand people wasn't exactly the right time and place to have a heart-to-heart, Schaeffer continued as if nothing had happened.

"My lease is up in three months, and I was gonna renew

it, but…maybe we should look for a bigger place? You know it's small, barely big enough for me. And you have all that photography equipment."

"I'd like that." Ren rubbed their cheeks together.

"I like *you.*"

With the Mets leading 14-2 in the sixth, they decided to bail on the game and go home to talk. Schaeffer got them each a beer and sat on one side of the couch, Ren on the other.

Ren said, "I've never lived with anyone before—I mean, aside from foster families." He gazed down at his hands, which, Schaeffer noticed, gripped the bottle.

Whom you never speak of.

"I haven't either," he remarked. "But we get along and agree on most things."

"Yeah." Ren set the untouched bottle on the coffee table. "What're you thinking? One bedroom or two?"

It seemed almost surreal to be having this conversation, yet at the same time, the most normal thing in the world. Being with Ren these past few days had brought into focus how dull and empty his life had been since they'd parted. A life lived without any memories or impact, robotic and motionless. No life at all.

Ren's appearance had quieted the running thread of instability and uncertainty. His presence gave him peace, and that one nightmare aside, he'd slept, but Schaeffer knew from experience it was only temporary. As much as he wanted Ren to live with him, once he did, it would be impossible to hide the nightmares' intensity and frequency.

"Two bedrooms? I imagine you'll want a place for your equipment. Maybe create a darkroom."

Ren's eyes widened. "I hadn't even thought of that. That would be cool. I would love to live near the beach, but with the offices of *Nature's Beauty* in Westchester, it's a hike. And you'd need to be close to the airports so it's easier to get to work."

He rubbed his chin. "*Hmm.* We could compromise and do a halfway, maybe live in Whitestone or College Point? Or Bayside. I don't mind a little commute."

Ren made a face. "That's not near the beach. I'd rather sit for an hour in traffic."

He chuckled. "I don't really care. You pick. I'll go wherever you want. Doesn't matter where we live. We're doing this together."

Ren's eyes turned soft. "We are, aren't we?"

"Yeah. I guess this'll give us a chance to learn about each other."

Ren reached over with his foot. "I know enough. You're gorgeous, kind, sweet, and sexy."

Cheeks hot, Schaeffer rubbed his nape. "Thanks, but I'm not perfect. I have issues, like everyone. I'm sure you do too." He hoped his admission would help Ren open up about his past.

"Yeah, of course, but you know what? The past is where it is for a reason. And it should stay there."

"Sometimes it can't be helped." He frowned, and Ren leaned over and kissed his brow.

"You get this little wrinkle whenever you're thinking hard. It's cute."

"You're deliberately changing the subject." He held Ren by his nape, their foreheads touching. "I'm closer to you than I've been with anyone else. But I know you hold back."

"Don't we all?" Ren murmured. "I'm no different than anyone."

"You are to me."

But his mind raced with troubling thoughts. Would Ren

be interested in dealing with his continuing nightmares? Could he harness Ren's beautiful wild spirit and have him stay in one place?

Ren said, "I guess we'll find out. That's what living together will do. I'll get my computer, and we can start looking."

"God, I never knew apartment hunting was so exhausting." Ren flopped on the couch. They'd left home to meet with the real estate agent at ten that morning, and it was now five in the afternoon.

"You have been out of touch." Schaeffer chuckled. "This is only the first day."

"Oh God," Ren groaned, but then his eyes brightened. "Maybe we'll get lucky and one of the places we saw today will come through."

He joined Ren on the couch and made a face. "You hated all of them. No light, bad exposure, too far from the beach, tiny rooms." He ticked off Ren's objections, and Ren pouted.

"I don't care."

"But I do. Let's not jump at the first thing because it's easy."

Ren pounced, knocking the air out of him. "Why not? I jumped you, and you were easy."

Schaeffer grabbed and held him around the waist. "If I recall, I was damn hard."

"*Mmm*," Ren's husky growl purred in his ear. "And getting harder by the second."

Schaeffer caught the full pout of Ren's lower lip between his teeth for a quick nip followed by a slow kiss. "Yeah. So what're you planning to do about it?"

Ren crushed their mouths together, and desire raced through him like an accelerant through the blood—when his phone buzzed. He ignored it, but it started up again immediately, and he cursed.

"Dammit. I have to get it. It might be important."

"This better be *fucking* important," Ren snarled, just as his phone vibrated with a text as well.

Schaeffer read his message. "It's Bill Parker, the agent. He says he has a place he thinks will be perfect for us and wants us to look at it."

"*Now?*" Ren whined. "My feet are killing me, we haven't eaten dinner, and I was just about to get lucky."

"Hold up, Romeo. It's two blocks from the beach, has an unobstructed view of the ocean, and a wraparound terrace. Two beds, two baths, and within our budget."

"Damn. But it can't wait until tomorrow?"

Ignoring Ren's puppy-dog eyes, Schaeffer grimaced. "He says no. But this is up to you. It's pretty far from where you need to be. It's on Long Island—Long Beach—but…"

"But the beach." Ren jumped to his feet. "I'm good with it." He shoved his feet into his sneakers. "Imagine sitting on the terrace and watching the sun rise or set. Like in California."

It did sound tempting, but Schaeffer was being practical. "Don't forget wintertime when it'll be cold as hell by the water and we won't be using that terrace. Plus, it would mean a wicked-ass long commute for you. I don't want you stuck in traffic every day. That'll make you cranky."

Ren waved off his objection. "Even better for snuggling. Besides, most of my work can be done remotely, so I don't need to go in every day. Maybe twice a month. What I'll be doing is checking the photos and deciding what shots get used. Plus, I don't mind long drives. Even traffic. I just turn up the music. After all, I've got the beach to come home to. And you."

"So the beach comes first, huh?"

"Never." Ren pinched his ass. "You're number one with me."

When they walked inside the unit, Schaeffer instantly knew it was perfect. The large living room windows overlooked the sparkling ocean, and they arrived at the perfect time to get the spectacular glory of the sunset. The kitchen was updated, the bathrooms modern. The larger bedroom had an en suite with a jetted tub, and Ren stuck his head into the smaller second bedroom.

"I could definitely use this as a darkroom, and we can put in a sofa bed, in case your family wants to come for a visit."

Schaeffer planted a kiss on his cheek. "That's sweet of you."

The real estate agent hung out by the breakfast bar while they inspected the apartment. For privacy, he and Ren walked out onto the terrace. The last rays of the sunset gilded Ren's face in profile as he gazed at the waves.

"I love it. What do you think?" Ren turned his back to the railing. "It reminds me of our week in California."

"I think it's beautiful, but I've got some reservations."

"Why? Like what?"

It seemed strange that Ren wouldn't understand. "How can you be sure you're going to be happy with a desk job and not miss traveling all over the world to remote places? You've spent your whole life capturing photos of rare animals—I know that's your passion." He sat on one of the chaise lounges. "I remember your face when you told me about finding your joy again with the snow leopard. I don't want you to lose that lust for life."

Ren's smile was sweet as he joined him and rested a hand on his thigh. "Is that what you think? That living with you will diminish my joy? That my passion is reserved for the wild animals I take pictures of? You're right, I *have* been all over the world. For years I traveled from point to point because I had nothing to come home to. I had to create my own joy because I had no one waiting for me." Ren kissed his cheek, and Schaeffer leaned into his touch. "Now I do. I have you to share that passion with. I rediscovered my lust for life—my love for living—by being with you."

"There are going to be times when you'll be alone here. Sometimes I can work two weeks straight, without coming home, doing overnight layovers."

"As long as I know you're coming home to me, that's all that matters."

They gazed at each other, and Schaeffer held out his hand. "Let's go tell Bill."

After they left the agent with the promise to send in all the paperwork and a reassurance that it was a formality, neither wanted to go home. By unspoken agreement, they strolled the two blocks to the beach, kicked off their sneakers, and hand in hand, walked to the shoreline.

"It's funny," Schaeffer said, staring out at the blue-violet sky as the water lapped at their toes. "We moved to California when I was almost twelve, and everyone thinks it's just beach parties all the time, yet I hardly went there. I was more interested in flying into the sky."

"Another form of escape?" Ren asked.

"Yeah, in retrospect, I guess that's what it was. At the time I didn't realize it or was too young to understand, but I wanted to get as far away from everything as I could—my mother's death, moving away from home and leaving her…realizing I was gay. Flying gave me freedom from the confusion of the life I had waiting for me when my feet touched the ground. I couldn't think about anything else but the sky in front of me and my hands on the controls. I guided my own destiny. I was weightless, all my problems behind me." He took both of Ren's hands in his. "But I learned that no matter how high or far I flew, when I landed, they were always there waiting for me."

He knew he was taking a risk, but life was a risk every day, from the moment you opened your eyes to the time you closed them. He'd risked his life in the Air Force and lost so much. He wouldn't fail again. Not with Ren.

"Whenever you're ready to talk to me, Ren, about anything, I'll always be there to listen."

Ren hung his head. "And if I'm not ready? Ever? I don't know what else I can promise you. Right now, it's nothing more than I've already given. Is that enough? Are you going to walk away and say goodbye?"

Schaeffer took his face between his hands and kissed him, hard at first, then soft, deep and tender, leaving them breathless and shaking.

"We made a promise to each other, and I plan on keeping it. I'll never say goodbye to you."

CHAPTER FIFTEEN

They'd signed the lease for the new place, and Ren had experienced the first extended period of time alone in the apartment when Schaeffer left for a ten-day shift. They spoke every night, and for someone who'd spent most of his life alone, Ren now found himself checking his phone to make sure he wouldn't miss Schaeffer's call.

If he spied something unusual, he wanted to share it with Schaeffer. At night, he buried his face in Schaeffer's pillows and fell asleep wrapped in the scent of his skin. And Schaeffer wasn't just any guy. He was the one.

There was plenty during the days to keep him busy—video meetings with Toni, Samuel, and the editorial staff, plus Hawk from the international team, to bring him up to speed. He acquired renter's and auto insurance, and leased his own car. All the mundane, everyday things in life he didn't have to deal with while trotting around the world. Ren hadn't had a place to call his own since the early days.

Schaeffer was due back tomorrow evening, so Ren knew he had to do what he'd put off. With dread, he got into his car and drove to Calvary Cemetery, stopping on the way at a local florist for two bouquets. It was a journey he made every time he returned to the States, one that always left him scarred.

He parked and tramped through the grounds until he came to their resting place. He put a hand on Chris's headstone first, said a prayer, then kneeled by Kevin's.

"I'm sorry. I know I've said it for the past fifteen years, and I guess I'll be saying it for the next fifty. I promised to take care of you both, and I let you down." His phone buzzed, but he ignored it as he always did when visiting. After several more attempts, it stopped. He laid the flowers at each of his brothers' graves and sat between them, the ever-present guilt swelling in leaps and bounds.

"I've met someone. Crazy story, but it was during a big snowstorm, and we shared a room.... Yeah, I know, but it's not just about *that*. He's special. Like...really special." Sweating, he ran a hand through his hair. "See...Schaeffer is different. I'm different when I'm with him. I'm not the person I was when you knew me—always trying to prove myself. He likes me for who I am. And he wants to talk about us. Not only him and me, but you guys. What if...what if I tell him and he hates me after? I mean, he's so good and kind, I can't imagine him hating anyone, but it's just...it's the way he looks at me. Like I'm special, you know? And I've never been special to anyone, not like that. What if I tell him and he never looks at me like that again?"

Christ, this was painful. Like opening up a vein leading directly to your heart and bleeding out all your fears, insecurities, and dreams. Worse than any physical injury he'd endured.

"No pain, no gain, though, right, Kevin? No risk, no reward. That's what you told me whenever you'd hurt yourself running track. I guess I need to act like an adult." He flattened his palm on the ground. "I wish you guys could've met him. He's a pilot—cool, right? The opposite of me. Calm, levelheaded, and so goddamn sweet." Thinking about Schaeffer, Ren couldn't prevent the smile from breaking through. Being with him did that.

"He's got a great family who likes me. And I don't want to lose this…or him. For the first time, I feel like this whole fucking life is real and there's a reason I'm here. I think…I think I love him. Fuck. I don't even know what that means, but these past ten days with him gone, it was like I couldn't find myself because he was missing."

In the distance, he heard voices and the *buzz* of hedge trimmers. Self-conscious, Ren stood up and brushed the twigs and grassy bits off his jeans. "I'll be visiting more often now that I'm staying put for a while." Ren kissed his fingers, held them in the air, then to his heart.

"Love you always."

It took him twenty minutes to get home, and another fifteen to find a parking space. He unlocked the door and spied Schaeffer on the couch.

"What—what're you doing here? You weren't due back until tomorrow."

Schaeffer's lips curved. "Flight got canceled—mechanical issue—so I elected to come home rather than hang out and see if they needed me for another flight. I have enough hours. And you're here."

"Passengers' loss is my gain. You." Ren kicked off his sneakers and joined him on the couch. "I'm so glad you're home." He kissed Schaeffer's neck. "I missed you. So fucking much."

Schaeffer wrapped his arms around him and hauled him closer. "Me too. Hotels suck." Ren raised his brows, and Schaeffer chuckled. "Okay, when you're not with me, hotels suck."

"Are you hungry? I've been watching the Food Network and thought I'd surprise you by making meatloaf and potatoes."

Schaeffer's jaw dropped. "You? Cook?"

Ren waggled his brows. "I'm trying to learn and keep my man happy."

Schaeffer dipped his head and brushed their lips together. "You make me happy," he murmured in between kisses. "Very, very happy. I almost forgot how good you taste."

"Let me jog your memory," Ren said, his empty stomach forgotten, a different hunger overtaking him. His blood stirred, and he pulled off his sweat shirt and jeans, while Schaeffer undressed. Once they lay on the bed, lips locked, their cocks side by side, full and heavy, he ran his hands over Schaeffer's body. Shadows played light and dark over his torso, and Ren mapped the curves and dips of his muscled body with his lips. "God, I missed this. Missed you."

Schaeffer cupped his ass and played his fingers up and down the cleft. "I did too. You're like a drug. I'm hooked on you, and if you're not here, I go through withdrawal."

"I'm here now." Ren handed him the lube. When they'd moved in together, they'd decided to forgo condoms, and Ren wanted that heavy, slick length to fill him up. "And I need you just as much as you want me."

"Shh," Schaeffer crooned to him as he teased the quivering rim of his hole. Two cool fingers entered him for a bit, but Ren ravished Schaeffer's mouth with greedy kisses.

"More. It's not enough." He climbed on top of Schaeffer and sank onto his shaft, groaning as Schaeffer moved in deeper. Fully seated, Ren gripped Schaeffer's shoulders, and Schaeffer dug his fingers into his hips and flexed his hips, driving in farther.

"I can't get enough of you, Ren. I want more."

"Harder," he gasped. "Everything. All of you." He rose and fell, his dick aching and wet. Schaeffer slid a hand over the taut muscles of Ren's abdomen and up his throbbing length.

"You have me. You own me."

At those possessive words, Ren came, his orgasm wild and uninhibited, leaving him writhing with frenzied pleasure. Schaeffer climaxed a moment after, pulsing inside his passage. A heavy arm clamped around his waist, and he leaned in close to nuzzle Schaeffer's neck.

"Welcome home."

They must've drifted off to sleep, because when he opened his eyes, the room was pitch-black and he was alone in bed. A smile tugged at his lips listening to Schaeffer whistle in the bathroom. He rolled off the bed, and with his legs still a little shaky, he opened the door to see a glistening, wet Schaeffer, towel tied at his waist.

"You should've woken me up," he protested. "You know how much I love showering together."

"I know, but this time I needed to actually shower." Schaeffer winked. "It was a while. Besides, you were sleeping so deeply, you didn't even notice me getting out of bed."

"Okay. I'll shower myself, and we can eat. I haven't had a chance all day either, I was running behind. I was planning to when I came home, but you ravaged me."

"Do I hear complaints?"

"Not on your life."

He jumped in the shower, washed, then dried off and dressed in his boxers. He found Schaeffer lounging on the couch, checking the delivery apps. He glanced up when Ren entered and smirked. "I guess you can try cooking tomorrow night, huh?"

"Wise-ass. What do you want?"

"Chinese?"

"Sure. Get me something spicy."

"You sure? You're already hot as hell." Schaeffer

snickered, and Ren rolled his eyes.

"God, you're corny."

"All right, I ordered us a bunch of stuff. Were you running behind today? Is that why you didn't answer my texts earlier? I did try and let you know I was coming home, but you never answered."

Time to put it out there.

"I spent the whole morning with the magazine, going over the setups and photocopy. Toni and Samuel think I'll be fine. And even when Samuel needs to go in for treatment, Toni and Leroy, who's in Helsinki, will be a great help."

"I'm proud of you. Stepping in to help a friend in need is a wonderful thing." Schaeffer smiled. "What'd you do after that?"

"I checked on my storage, where I have some great photos for the new place." He took a deep breath and paced. "Then I went to the cemetery."

Schaeffer's smile vanished, his startled gaze holding his. "Oh?" His neutral tone didn't fool Ren. His face was filled with curiosity.

The buzzer sounded, and he jumped. "I'll get it."

The food came, and he set it on the counter, but neither of them made a move to eat. Ren resumed his pacing until Schaeffer grabbed him when he passed by.

"Hey. Sit, come on. Whatever it is, I'm sure it's not as bad as you think."

His knees hit the couch, and while he'd normally shift to close the gap between them, he kept it deliberately wide.

"It might be worse," he said, his heart heavy with impending doom.

"Ren," Schaeffer urged. "It's going to be okay."

"Yeah." He laughed bitterly. "I've heard confession is good for the soul." He rubbed his face. "Chris and Kevin…I told you they were brothers in foster care who came to live with my foster family when they were seven and nine. I was fourteen, and right away, we bonded. We became our own little family. We did it all together—played ball, went to the zoo and the movies…and they looked up to me. We had plans."

"I'd love to know more about them."

Despite his pain, a smile came to his face. "Chris, he was real tall and skinny. Always shooting hoops. He dreamed of being discovered at the courts and playing for the Knicks. Kevin was the runner—I used to call him Cheetah 'cause he ran so fast. He was a track star. Had his eyes on trying out for the Olympics one day. Both did really well in school too. They knew what to do. Had it all figured out." He struggled for control. "All pipe dreams." God, he was going to be sick. Maybe Schaeffer knew, because he felt his hand gripped tight.

"It's gonna be okay."

"It'll never be okay. They died because of me."

Schaeffer stared at him. "What?"

"I'd worked two jobs to save up for a camera and was taking tons of photos all over the city. You'd be amazed at some of the animals you can find—raccoons, opossums, coyotes. Even snakes, just hanging out, doing their thing. I made friends with this photographer I used to see at the zoo a lot, and he offered to print some and show them to his friends. I ended up selling a bunch, and I kept doing it and saved enough to buy a secondhand car."

"Sounds like you had the start of your own business. Something real."

"Maybe it could've been…I don't know."

"What happened?"

"When I turned eighteen, I aged out and left the house. I didn't go far 'cause they were my brothers and we were all going to stay together. I wanted to be close in case they needed me. I had a job in a camera store and was doing okay. Between the camera store and selling my pictures,

I made enough money to rent a crappy apartment, but it was mine. After school or on weekends, Chris and Kevin would come to visit, when they didn't have school stuff. Kevin had started to date, and he really liked this girl in his class, but he knew not to be stupid and take his eyes off the prize. Education. He was on his way to getting college scholarships for track. He wanted to be a teacher. Those two were so good. So good." He shivered, took a deep breath, and released it. "They were the first people I came out to, and neither cared that I was gay. They still loved me."

"I'm glad they were supportive."

"When I turned twenty-one, I got the idea to do a trip. Spend my birthday with my brothers. I'd rent a place upstate near a lake, and we'd go fishing and swimming and I could take pictures. It was going to be perfect."

"Sounds like it." Schaeffer's hand in his was warm and comforting, and he held on to it like the lifeline it was. Schaeffer was the strength Ren needed to hold together his broken pieces.

"We'd had a great day at the lake, and I met this guy— his name was Jayden, I think. He invited me to the pub in town for a birthday drink. I didn't want to go and leave Chris and Kevin, but they said I was crazy. Kevin said, 'We're not babies. I'm sixteen. Just do it, then tell us all about it when you get home. He probably wants to give you a birthday kiss.'

"So I went out, and it was when the guy walked me to my car that I heard the first sirens. I didn't pay much attention, and I got my kiss. He wanted me to come home with him, but I said I had to get back because I didn't want to leave my brothers alone too long. The drive was only about ten minutes, and I began to smell smoke in the air. I got this weird chill, and I sped like a motherfucker down that dark road. When I pulled up to the cabin…"

He couldn't finish. All he could see were the flames

tearing through the wood cabin, engulfing the entire structure. Schaeffer pulled him to his chest where he lay, listening to his heartbeat.

"I'm sorry. I'm so sorry."

"I left them when they needed me. I should've been there with them."

Schaeffer stroked his hair. "You couldn't have known. Did they find out what happened?"

He sniffled. "Yeah. Chris was always cold, because he was so skinny, and it was only November but already chilly up there at night. He'd found this space heater in a closet, but I had told him not to use it because they weren't safe. They found it next to his bed, plugged into an extension cord. It overheated and sparked a fire in their bedroom. Everything was wood, and it just lit up like a tinderbox. They found them together. They were trapped....I can't imagine..."

"Don't," he soothed. "Don't try. Hopefully they didn't suffer."

For fifteen years, every step he'd taken had been dogged by the memories, no matter how far he'd traveled. Guilt and recriminations consumed him. "I lost it—went wild and they had to restrain me from going inside. The paramedics gave me something, and I woke up in the hospital because they were afraid I'd hurt myself. I paid for their funeral and got them headstones. Every time I come to New York, I visit and tell them where I've been and all the things I've seen."

"I'm sure they know, and they're so proud of what you've done." Schaeffer kissed his hair and held him tighter. Ren needed that closed-in space with only Schaeffer and him. The two of them against the world.

"Today I told them about you. And me."

Schaeffer smiled, lips pressed to Ren's temple, and laced their fingers together. "Yeah? What'd you say?"

"That I hoped after you heard everything, you wouldn't leave me."

Schaeffer tensed and moved away so they faced each other. His expression was fierce and grim. "Is that what you think I'd do? After being with me all this time, you think I'd walk away?"

"I'd hope not, but I don't want to be a disappointment."

"My greatest disappointment would be if I lost you."

CHAPTER SIXTEEN

His poor guy. The crushing weight of Ren's guilt explained so much of his personality and life choices. And Schaeffer, more than he'd admit, understood. It was his private burden he'd never shared with anyone, a level of blame he assigned to himself and had borne since his mother's death, and Steve's as well.

But this wasn't about him.

"You were not responsible for the fire. It was a terrible, terrible accident that should've never happened. But you've honored their memories by creating beauty with your pictures and bringing attention to the decline of our wildlife. I'm sure Kevin and Chris would be so damn proud of you."

"You think?" Ren shrugged. "I hope so."

Schaeffer kissed his cheek. "I know."

Green eyes washed bright, Ren gazed at him with a look of hope that broke his heart. "I thought I was okay. I had a job I loved, helping get the word out about how we need to take care of our planet."

"You have. You're making an impact every time someone reads an article and sees your photos. They realize what's at stake of being lost if we don't protect what we have."

"I'm not a saint, you know." His lips twitched, and Schaeffer couldn't resist kissing him.

"I don't know about that. You've made me see God a few times."

Ren loved to tease Schaeffer about his face getting red, but it was finally his time to turn crimson as a cherry tomato. "Idiot. I just…they're with me every step of the way in whatever I do."

"But you used them as an excuse as well, didn't you? It's why you picked the assignments that took you far away for so long, sometimes to the point of danger."

He lifted a shoulder. "Yeah. I figured if it was my time, I was ready."

"But now?" Schaeffer dared the question.

"Now? Once you lose everyone in your life who matters, it's hard to take a breath. Now that I have you, I can breathe again."

Ren's confession left him trembling with wonder. Schaeffer had never had a lover be so honest. So raw. He skimmed the planes of Ren's face and locked their eyes.

"I love you." It was freeing to speak those words he'd never imagined he'd be lucky enough to say. "I love you. It doesn't matter if you go out and venture into the wilderness for however long you want. I'll always be waiting for you whenever you come home. To me."

"You love me?" Ren's eyes filled with wonder.

"Yeah. And I know it might be hard for you to say it—"

"No. Don't say that. Don't even think it." His voice shook. "For days I've felt this hole. An emptiness which grew in its depth and breadth the longer you were gone. I didn't understand it at first. I'd never been in love before.

But it was me, without you. When you're not here, I lose the time I get to love you."

Schaeffer's hand trembled as he cupped Ren's face. "Your words are as beautiful as your photographs. I've flown into combat zones, and that didn't scare me nearly as much as saying those three little words to you, hoping you'd feel the same."

Ren nuzzled into his palm and kissed it. "I feel it, think it, and I'm finally ready to say it. I thought I'd seen it all, and done everything, except I was missing the most important thing of all. Being in love. Until now. With you."

Schaeffer kissed him hard, holding him close, still in disbelief that this vibrant, lively man loved him back. Would he still, if he discovered all the fears that plagued him? Now, with Ren baring his soul, it would've been the perfect time for Schaeffer to share his secrets, but staying the course, he let fear dictate and kept quiet, justifying it by one revelation being enough for the evening.

I'll be Scarlett O'Hara for now. Tomorrow is another day.

Ren's stomach growled, and Schaeffer snickered. "So romantic. Here I thought you were going to ravish me."

"First the spareribs, then you." Ren jumped up, and Schaeffer caught his hand.

"Hey. Just so you know, I'm really, really happy right now."

Ren brightened and pulled him up for a hug. "Me too."

"Leaving me so soon?" Ren rolled over and played with Schaeffer's chest hair. "You've only been home a few days." The past month and a half they'd spent almost every moment together, but Schaeffer was greedy. He loved waking up and seeing Ren next to him, and going to bed wrapped in each other's arms.

"Yeah, but you know by now that's how the shifts go. I'll be home in a week or so."

"If you were a captain, would you get to stay home more? I would think with your experience in the Air Force, it would be a no brainer for you to be at that level."

"They're two very different types of aircraft. Plus, I'm not that anxious to be in charge. I've already piloted into danger on my own."

And failed spectacularly.

He tried to divert Ren's attention to avoid further questions. "Besides, I would've thought you'd had enough of me."

Ren slid a leg between his. "I'll never get enough of you. I think I've proved that." He climbed on top of Schaeffer. "But in case you forget what's waiting for you, I'll leave you with this."

Ren latched on to his neck and nipped his skin, then kissed and licked away the sting. Schaeffer held him close. "I won't forget. Be safe, and I'll see you next week."

Ren watched him dress. "Where to this time?"

"Dallas, Chicago, Atlanta…I think Las Vegas, but I'll have to check."

"Jesus, I'm tired just listening to that."

Schaeffer merely smiled, buttoned his shirt, and slipped on his jacket. "It's not so bad."

Better than flying into a war zone and seeing your best friend explode in flames.

"I'll call you when we land."

The ride to the airport was quick, and he knew to relish it. Once they moved, his commute would double in time. It was worth it, though, not only to be able to live in a beautiful place, but because Ren thrived being close to nature. He might not say it, or even realize the consequences of living in an apartment, but there was bound to be an adjustment period for him. He'd spent years wandering the globe, responsible only for himself. Schaeffer's frequent trips were actually the perfect mechanism to slip Ren into a routine. They were together night and day when he was off shift, but leaving for those extended periods gave Ren that independence he likely needed to fill his creative well.

He checked in with security and navigated his way through the airport to his gate, where he was greeted by one of the ticket agents.

"Hey, Schaeffer. How was your time off?"

"Great, thanks. Always good to get a break." He sipped his coffee. "Full flight?"

She scanned the screen in front of her. "Eh. Not too bad."

"Okay, thanks. See you."

He strolled down the jet bridge and into the plane, where he could see the captain was already present in the flight deck.

"Good morning," he greeted the captain with a nod. "Schaeffer Morgan."

Around sixty, with a receding hairline and a bit of a paunch, the captain nodded to him. "Wallace O'Brian. Let's get this bird ready to fly."

It appeared O'Brian was no-nonsense, and Schaeffer was as happy to fly with a silent captain as a chatty one. "Weather's clear except for some thunderstorms over Arkansas."

"Hopefully they're gone by the time we get there." O'Brian spoke to air traffic control, relaying the preflight information, while Schaeffer completed the preflight safety and maintenance checks and verified flight data. They went through the reports, and Schaeffer checked that the communication and software for the flight were working. O'Brian signed the flight release. Several minutes passed while they waited for air traffic control to give them the predeparture clearance form, when to his surprise, O'Brian became talkative.

"Never did like these damn early morning flights. Gotta get up in the middle of the night."

"I hear you." Schaeffer chuckled, thinking how on his days off he and Ren would reconnect by staying in bed, so middle of the night or day didn't matter.

"My wife hates it. Says it interrupts her sleep. You get a lot of complaints from your wife?"

"I'm not married."

"Well, your girlfriend."

The questions were getting a little too personal for him, and he struggled for an answer.

O'Brian smirked. "She must be a handful. I see those marks on your neck."

Heat burned through him. "Hey, the clearance came through. We can take off."

Shooting him a look, O'Brian turned into a captain again, shelving the gossip. He got on the intercom and made the standard announcements to the crew and passengers. They worked through the take-off together, and it went seamlessly. At least the man was a good pilot. Twenty minutes in, after they'd reached their cruising altitude, O'Brian activated the autopilot and settled in with a sigh.

"Can't wait to get home."

"Oh, you're not from New York?"

O'Brian broke out in laughter. "Hell, no. I'm from Texas—'bout two hundred miles south of Dallas. Wouldn't catch me dead living in that hellhole they like to call the greatest city on earth." He stretched. "Can't even take a piss in the bathroom without worrying if you got a man or a woman next to you."

Schaeffer frowned. "I don't understand."

"Come on. Those men who think they're girls and vice

versa. What do you think they got goin' on there? You know what I mean." He pointed at his crotch, and his lips thinned until they showed white. "All I know is, any of those bastards ever come near me, I'd kill 'em."

Those words were stated with such conviction, it left Schaeffer shaken. No doubt, O'Brian meant it. It frankly shocked him that O'Brian was spilling such crap, but instead of answering, Schaeffer pretended not to listen and concentrated on the dials on the dashboard in front of him.

"You won't find them in my hometown, that's for damn sure. They'd know." His lips curled in a sneer.

"Know what?" Schaeffer trembled with anger.

"We don't put up with freaks or queers. Man's gotta be a man."

That was his limit. There was only so much he could take, and he slipped off his headset.

"I'll be right back."

He opened the door and slammed it shut behind him. A few seconds passed while he stood breathing deeply. Sweat ran down his face. A flight attendant approached him with concern etched in his brow.

"Are you okay?"

Schaeffer ducked his head. "Yeah. I just needed to ah… use the restroom. He pulled open the tiny door and closed it. He splashed cold water on his face and wiped it off with a towel. He hadn't come across such ugly, outright hatred in years. Staring at himself in the mirror, Schaeffer wondered why he was such a coward. Ren would've told O'Brian where to shove his ugly opinions.

When he stepped out of the bathroom, the same flight attendant was loading the drinks cart. Their eyes met.

"Here, I figured you could use something stronger, but that can wait until we land."

He took the cold can of soda and opened it. "Thanks. I appreciate it."

"O'Brian can be a lot to handle. Especially when he goes off on one of his rants."

Startled, he drank some of the soda. "Oh, yeah…so you know. Have you had to deal with him before?"

"Unfortunately, yes."

"Dale, we have to get going." The flight attendant on the opposite side of the cart gave him an eye.

"Just a sec, Jessica." Dale put up a hand and shifted closer to him. "O'Brian is a raging bigot. He hates everyone he thinks doesn't belong here. He's gotten away with it for years because he's one of the airline's most senior pilots. It makes me sick that I let him talk to me like I'm a second-class citizen because I was so afraid of him when I first started. Now he just ignores me. People brush it off because he's part of the 'old boys' group." Contempt filled Dale's dark-brown eyes. "But what they don't realize is that their 'group' is getting smaller and smaller every year. And one day they're going to fuck with the wrong person."

Dale left, and he and Jessica rolled the rattly cart down the aisle. Schaeffer returned to the flight deck. O'Brian was checking the weather when he buckled into his seat.

"You were gone a long time." O'Brian winked. "Got your eye on one of the girls out there and hoping to score? That blond with the big tits looks like a screamer. Really fills out the uniform nice." He threw his head back, cackling with laughter.

Bile rose in his throat. Kendra used to tell them stories of when she was a server at the hotel and how patrons would slip her their room number with the tip or try and corner her to grab a kiss. All of it made him sick.

"I'm not interested." He began to sweat again.

"Oh, right. You've got a biter." He snickered and unbuckled his seat belt. "I need one of those." He tipped his head toward the soda can. "Can't wait to have a few cold ones tonight." He buzzed the flight attendants. "Hey, sweetheart. Can I get a soda and maybe an extra bag of peanuts? Thank you, darlin'."

A minute or so later, the door to their cabin opened, and the young, blond flight attendant—Marissa, according to her name tag—entered with the soda and an assortment of snacks. "Here you go, Captain." She handed him the soda and put the snacks between them. "I brought some for you both. Lunch is coming in a little while."

"Beautiful, thank you, sweetheart," O'Brian drawled, his lusty gaze traveling up and down her curvaceous body. "How long have you been flying with RWB?"

"This is my third flight." She threw Schaeffer a nervous smile, which he returned with what he hoped was reassurance.

"Very nice." O'Brian chuckled, still focused on her breasts. "Very nice."

"Thank you, Marissa," Schaeffer said. "We appreciate it."

"You're welcome." Another smile was sent his way, and from the corner of his eye, he saw O'Brian watching them. "I have to hurry, sir. We need to give the first-class customers their lunch."

"You go right ahead, honey. You'll get far being so conscientious." O'Brian grinned.

"Thank you, sir."

The door closed, and they helped themselves to the snacks.

"I saw the two of you staring at each other." O'Brian chomped on the pretzels. "You could get in that real easy. They don't call them layovers for nothing."

"I told you," he snapped, tight-lipped with anger and disgust, "I'm with someone."

There was a knock on the door, and then it opened with Dale carrying a tray. "Lunchtime. Captain, here you are." He set the tray in front of O'Brian.

A nod from O'Brian was all Dale received, lending

credence to what he'd confided in Schaeffer earlier.

"I'll be right back with yours, sir."

Dale kept his face neutral, and he left the cabin, returning a moment later with his food.

"Thanks, Dale."

"Not a problem."

They ate in silence, and Schaeffer concentrated on the puffy white clouds spread out beneath them. He finished and set the tray aside to check on the weather for the remainder of the flight.

"Looks clear ahead till landing."

"*Mmhmm*." O'Brian chewed a piece of chicken. "So how long you been with your girlfriend?"

It was the situation he'd always feared. But he shouldn't have to hide his love for Ren because he was afraid. Love should never be eclipsed by fear.

He licked his lips. "I've been with my partner for about eight months now."

O'Brian's brows rose high. "Partner? Are you saying—"

"Exactly what I said. Ren is my partner."

"Ren?" O'Brian scrunched up his face as if he were in serious thought, but Schaeffer could guess the ugly thoughts running through his mind. "What kind of name is that?"

As expected. Before he lost his temper, Schaeffer decided to be the professional he was and finish the flight with no further distractions.

"Captain, we're approaching our descent. Should I contact air traffic control?" He held O'Brian's stone-faced gaze.

"I'll do it. You talk to the passengers." The curt reply was nothing less than he'd expected, and O'Brian spoke into his headpiece.

Schaeffer took to the microphone and announced the beginning of their descent into Dallas-Fort Worth airport, gave the weather report and the usual thank-you-for-flying-RWB-Airlines. As talkative as O'Brian had been earlier in the flight, he'd shut down completely and barely looked Schaeffer's way for the twenty-five minutes to touchdown. The moment the jet bridge connected, O'Brian was up and out of his seat, as if he couldn't stand being in such a confined space with Schaeffer. He remained behind O'Brian, like a good first officer, and waited for all the passengers to leave the plane.

"Where are you off to after this, Schaeffer?" Dale asked.

"Layover tonight, then Chicago, Atlanta, Phoenix, then home. How about you?"

"Layover, then Miami, Charlotte, and home to New York."

"Always busy," he joked, aware of O'Brian's eyes on him. "What's his deal?" he murmured.

"I told you. He's a jerk," Dale responded. "I don't say anything more than necessary to him. Watch yourself—not that you have anything to worry about. He only hates people different from who he is."

Alarmed by those ominous words, Schaeffer vowed to keep his distance at the hotel that night. A night in his room didn't sound all that bad. He could FaceTime with Ren.

"Thanks, Dale."

They finished their post-flight paperwork and checks while the flight attendants prepared the plane for the next crew. On the shuttle to the hotel, Schaeffer remained silent, only speaking when spoken to. Once he'd checked in to the hotel and dropped his bags, he texted Ren to let him know he'd arrived, and received an immediate answer:

It sucks here without you.

He smiled to himself.

Same. Going to take a shower and get something to eat at the hotel restaurant.

Make sure you don't let some cowboy get you in his saddle.

Schaeffer snorted with laughter.

I'm still sore from the ride you gave me.

Ren sent him a winky-face emoji and a heart.

He checked his email, and with nothing needing his immediate attention, he undressed and took that shower. Dressed in jeans and a sweat shirt, he made his way to the bar and ordered a beer and a burger. Spotting Dale walking out of the elevator, he waved him over.

"Come on and sit. What'll you have? First one is on me."

"Just a Bud."

The bartender set out a coaster and poured him a tall one with a nice foamy head.

"To safe travels." He raised his glass to Dale's.

"You know it."

"You from New York?" he asked.

"Yep. The Bronx. I live there with my boyfriend. And you?"

Sweating, Schaeffer decided the time was never better to start being who he was. "I was born there, moved to California, but came back when I got discharged from the Air Force. My…boyfriend and I live there now, in Queens, but we just signed the lease on an apartment on Long Island."

There. He'd said it out loud for the first time to someone not in his family, and the world continued on as if nothing had changed. He gulped the beer.

"He in the airline business too?"

"No." Schaeffer smiled, thinking of Ren, who loved his space, cooped up in the flight deck for hours at a time. "He's a wildlife photographer. His specialty is endangered species."

Dale's eyes widened. "Cool. That must be an awesome job."

"Yeah. He's been everywhere in the world. But now he's going to be helping out a friend at the magazine he works for, so he'll be home."

"Wow."

"Yeah. That was my first thought when I met him. He's definitely a wow to me. What does your boyfriend do?"

"He's a bartender. Knows how to make all the drinks. Makes great tips when he does his flair."

"Have you been together long?"

Dale crunched a few more pretzels. "About two years."

"Ren and I have known each other about eight months, and most of that time he was on a shoot. He's only been in New York for close to two months, but it seems like we've known each other forever."

"Hey." Dale shrugged. "When you know, you know."

"Know what?"

Two of the flight attendants, Marissa and Jessica, stopped by their seats. Schaeffer's stomach dropped. He hadn't said anything to Dale about not being out yet.

"I was just telling Schaeffer how I knew my boyfriend was the one. It doesn't matter how long you know someone. You get that feeling in your gut."

All at once, the fear dissipated. Why should he be afraid to say what was in his heart? What was the worst that could happen? People like O'Brian would talk about him behind his back? The day he cared about what someone like that thought about his relationship with Ren would be the day hell froze over.

"Yeah. I met my boyfriend, Ren, only eight months ago, but we knew from the start that what we had was special." Nonchalantly, but with his heart pounding a hundred beats a second, Schaeffer finished his beer.

"That's the way it should be." Marissa nodded. "My brother and his husband met in law school and got married after graduation. They're the happiest couple I know."

They got another round of drinks, and everyone ordered food at the bar. Schaeffer wondered why he'd worried at all. Everyone around him was accepting—and he could ignore ugly looks and snide comments. In the grand scheme of things, people like O'Brian meant nothing to him. Time to start living his life.

CHAPTER SEVENTEEN

Funny how he'd spent so much time alone but now chafed at his solitude. Schaeffer was due home that night, and Ren couldn't wait to see him. He missed having his solid, warm body to hold and snuggle up to under the covers. He longed for the comfort of strong arms holding him. He had trouble falling asleep without listening to the *thump* of his heartbeat.

"God, you're a sap," he said out loud in the empty apartment, but with a smile on his face, as he stirred the pot of homemade tomato sauce. His phone rang, and seeing it was Kendra, his smile grew broader as he accepted the FaceTime.

"Hey, gorgeous! How are you?" He waved his wooden spoon at her.

"Look at you. Now you can add chef to your list of accomplishments."

He chuckled. "I'm not so sure about that. And spaghetti

and meatballs can hardly be considered gourmet."

"Listen, honey. Gourmet is highly overrated. Hasn't anyone told you comfort food is where it's at these days? And I happen to know meatballs and spaghetti is one of Schaeffer's favorite foods. Besides, he's going to love it because it shows how much you care, and that means more than any fancy meal."

"If the smell is any indication, it will be a success. Thanks for walking me through it."

"I'm happy to do it. He's coming home tonight?"

"Yep." He checked the clock on the stove. "He's due to land soon, at seven forty-three, so I'm hoping he'll be home by nine at the latest."

"Okay, so we can chat a little still." She sipped her wine. "How's your new job going? How's your editor feeling?"

Thinking of Samuel always made him sad. "He's trying to keep a brave face and a positive outlook, but it's hard seeing him deteriorate."

"You've known him a very long time. He's like a father figure, I'm sure."

It hadn't occurred to him to think of Samuel that way, but Kendra was right. "He is, but even more than that, he's one of the best friends I've ever had. I'm not sure what I'm going to do if he doesn't make it."

"You just keep doing what you're doing. He called you in because he knows you're the one who can carry on the legacy of the magazine and what it stands for. How do you like working from home and not running around the world? Are you missing the excitement of it?"

"Are you afraid I'm going to get bored?"

She set her wineglass on the kitchen island and leaned closer. "Are you? I can't imagine the change has been easy on you."

"An apartment in Queens is a hell of a shift from an encampment in Tanzania, that's for sure."

When Kendra didn't join in his smile, Ren understood she was protecting Schaeffer. This was his family, and they loved him.

"It's funny because I was sure I'd start getting restless and want to go somewhere new. But that hasn't happened. I'm enjoying waking up in a real bed, with the comforts of a shower and running water. I like the mundane life of going to the supermarket or a department store. I love being able to simply take a drive and walk through all the neighborhoods I haven't been to in years. If I want to go anywhere, I have my car. I've been to the beach almost every day."

"What about your photography? Don't you miss it?"

He turned down the sauce. "I spend hours studying wildlife shots for the magazine, and not once have I thought, *Damn, I wish I were there to get this shot.* If I want to shoot, I have the beach and lots of native wildlife here to capture. Beauty is wherever you find it."

"I'm glad to hear that. We've been waiting for Schaeffer to meet someone who cares for him like he deserves."

"He deserves the best. I don't need to fly all over the world anymore. I've found what I need right here."

Finally, he got the smile he was looking for from her. Kendra blew him a kiss. "We care about you too. I wouldn't ask all these questions if I didn't believe you two are good for each other. Schaeffer steadies you, while your energy gives him the push he needs to take a chance. You each bring out the parts of each other that needed finding and nurturing."

"I'm not planning on going anywhere. You can count on me. And if I do, Schaeffer is going to be at my side."

She gave a self-satisfied nod. "Good. Just so you know, we always have Thanksgiving here, so be prepared."

He laughed. "I haven't celebrated a holiday since I was a kid."

Her smile faded. "That's sad. I'm so glad you're part of us now."

His throat closed up.

Part of us.

He'd never had an us—a true family. What he'd tried to cobble together with guts and love for himself, Chris, and Kevin had been a desperate attempt to have something they could call their own. No one had ever said that to him, and he'd never felt part of the warm, loving family scenarios he used to watch on television. Like he'd told Schaeffer, he'd always imagined they were bullshit, and now to feel welcomed into one? It was overwhelming.

"I've never had a family." Aside from his brothers, but he couldn't talk about them to anyone but Schaeffer. Not yet.

"Now you do."

Without knowing it, Kendra had whisked away the last of his trepidations, whether he belonged with people and deserved his place.

"Thank you. I feel lucky."

"We all are. I gotta go and help the kids with homework before dinner. You give Schaeffer a big kiss from me, after you finish with him." A saucy wink, and she blew him another kiss. "Bye, honey."

He waved at the screen. "Bye."

Talking to Kendra always put him in a good mood. With a smile still on his face, he checked that the meatballs weren't overdone. He poured the sauce on top, sprinkled freshly grated parmesan over it, and slid the tray into the oven. The lock clicked, and in walked a visibly tired Schaeffer.

"You're early. I didn't think you'd be here for another half an hour."

"I speed-walked through the airport." He left his rolling case behind, and Ren met him halfway to the door. "God, I missed you." At the first touch of his lips, Ren wrapped his arms around Schaeffer's shoulders.

"Missed you too."

"*Mmm,* you taste like tomato sauce and garlic. Two of

my favorites." Schaeffer pulled off his tie and unbuttoned his shirt collar, then settled his mouth over Ren's again, their tongues teasing playfully.

"I made you dinner," he murmured.

Face flushed and breathing heavily, Schaeffer sniffed. "Oh God, it smells amazing. I thought it was delivery from Nonna's and got psyched."

Ren helped him take off his pilot's jacket and hung it over the sofa. "Nope, all me. With help from Kendra. I made spaghetti and meatballs. Homemade sauce too. I think it's pretty good, if I do say so myself."

Schaeffer pulled him close. "I don't care what it tastes like. You being here is a prize I never imagined winning, but knowing you care to do this?" He rubbed their cheeks together. "I don't know what to say."

"Nothing. Just having you here is enough."

Holding him tight, Ren let him work through his emotions, soaking up his heat and the delicious scent of his skin. Schaeffer kissed his cheek. "I'm going to shower and change, and then I need to taste the masterpiece."

"It's almost ready. I put it in the oven right before you walked in."

Schaeffer's eyes twinkled. "Who said I was talking about dinner? I've been away from you for over five days. I'm hungry for some Renaldo." He rolled the *R*.

"*Mmm*. You know, people only call me that when I'm in trouble."

Schaeffer's eyes glittered like moonlight on water. "You are. Just wait until I get my hands on you."

Ren's lips curved in a grin. "I'll turn off the stove and meet you in the shower."

By the time he entered the bathroom, Schaeffer was under the spray. Ren shed his clothes and stepped in next to him. Soaking wet and with shampoo lathered in his hair did nothing to diminish his appeal. He was still the sexiest man

Ren had ever been with, and pleasure cracked like a whip through him. Schaeffer splayed a hand over his breastbone, those long fingers resting against the pumping vein at his throat.

"Sometimes I wonder about fate. How if I'd taken an earlier flight that day, I would've missed meeting you and we wouldn't be here."

"Fate is like the snowflakes that fell on that airport, trapping us together. Fate is us. Meant to be." Ren kissed his wet jaw, caring little about the water streaming over his face. All he saw was Schaeffer.

"I love you so damn much," Schaeffer breathed, and grasped Ren's full, aching cock in his hand. "I want you in me."

They hadn't switched up much, and Ren never pushed because having Schaeffer inside him was perfection, but he couldn't help the jolt of excitement at hearing Schaeffer asking for him.

"Ready when you are." Ren gave Schaeffer's ass a squeeze and played along the cleft. "It's been a while. I'll need to make you ready for me."

"I'm ready the moment I see you."

They hurried out, their bodies barely dry, and tumbled to the bed together. Their kisses were eager, almost frantic, as they sought to reconnect.

"Did I tell you I missed you?" Schaeffer whispered, lips trailing against his bare skin.

"Yeah, but I wouldn't mind hearing it again. And again."

Schaeffer rose over him, his knees on either side of his hips. "As much as I missed you, I know I have you with me everywhere I go. Loving you is like my heartbeat—it's second nature and always there."

Overwhelmed, Ren reached up to touch Schaeffer's face. "Sometimes I wonder if this is all a dream. I can't believe I'm so damn lucky to have you for my own."

"If it is, then let's keep dreaming together."

Schaeffer's mouth settled over his, warm and familiar, yet because of the days apart, fresh and exciting. Their kisses grew demanding, and they rolled together, arms and legs tangled, until Schaeffer lay beneath him. Glittering gray eyes found his, and Ren was caught in their beauty.

"Nowhere I've ever traveled has been more beautiful than you, lying naked in our bed." He reached for the lube, coated his fingers, and slid them inside Schaeffer, whose eyes fluttered shut. "Feel me?"

"I feel you everywhere…my blood, my heart, my soul."

His body buzzing with desire and anticipation, Ren could only tease Schaeffer for so long. He slicked his shaft and Schaeffer rolled over onto his stomach. He pressed into Schaeffer, entering him slowly, allowing him time to adjust.

"Oh God, you feel incredible." He was gripped in a tight vise of warmth.

"So do you. Please, more. Everything."

Schaeffer's moans and gasps spurred him on, and soon he was fully seated in the hot clasp of his passage. Schaeffer raised on all fours, and Ren grasped his hips to thrust hard and deep. The friction was almost too intense, and it burned through him like a live wire, leaving him destroyed. "Fucking hell. Oh, fuck."

Schaeffer groaned loudly, his hand working his dick, and Ren lost himself in Schaeffer's fiery grip on his cock.

"Ren," he cried out. "Ren." Schaeffer climaxed, collapsing facedown on the bed, but Ren was too caught up in his own orgasm crashing through him. He lay over Schaeffer's sweat-soaked body, both of them trembling in the aftermath.

"Welcome home," he whispered, and pressed a kiss to Schaeffer's neck.

"I love you." Schaeffer reached out a hand, and Ren grabbed it. "Now get off me because I'm hungry."

"Guess the honeymoon is over, huh?" Chuckling, Ren slipped out, and Schaeffer peered up at him with a grin.

"It's just starting."

The next two days were a whirlwind of getting the apartment in Long Beach ready. Ren took his photographs out of storage, dumped a bunch of stuff he no longer needed, and he and Schaeffer went furniture shopping. Schaeffer's current bedroom was too small for a king-sized mattress, but not the new one, and they might've been having a little too much fun testing them out for firmness.

"This could be dangerous," Ren murmured as they lay on one of the mattresses in the store. "I can't get near you on a bed without wanting to jump you."

Schaeffer's eyes twinkled. "That would be a story for the salesperson to take home. After we get arrested, of course. Stop that." He inched away when Ren rolled next to him, and Ren cackled.

"You're no fun."

"Is that a challenge?"

Ren shrugged. "Take it any way you want. As long as I get you naked, I'm good."

"Ahem." The salesperson, a staid man in his midsixties, pushed his glasses up the bridge of his nose. "Have you decided yet?"

Ren smiled up at him. "We'll take this one."

The look of relief on the man's face was almost comical, and driving home, Ren couldn't help but laugh.

"I think he was afraid I'd ravish you right there in front of him and the rest of the store."

Schaeffer chuckled. "He's just happy we left and he's

made a sale."

They were driving along the Southern State Parkway when Schaeffer asked, "Would you like to come with me to visit my mother? I haven't been in a while."

Ren took his hand. "I'd love to."

They drove until they reached Calvary Cemetery. Ren's throat tightened. "My brothers are here."

Schaeffer squeezed his fingers. "I'd like to meet them too."

They had to pass by his brothers first, and he fixed the two bouquets of flowers he'd left the other day, picking off the dead petals.

"This is Kevin and Chris. They would've thought you're so cool, being a pilot. Neither of them had ever been in an airplane." He watched as Schaeffer brushed the top of each stone with his fingers. "Matter of fact, the first time they ever left the city was…" He dropped his gaze and unable to speak, Schaeffer pulled him into his arms.

"It's okay. I know, I know."

With Schaeffer's arms around him, he could be strong.

"Let's go see your mom."

It was a longer walk to where Schaeffer's mother was buried. Schaeffer took his hand as they stood in front of her.

"This is Ren, Mom. He's my boyfriend…that sounds silly from a man my age. Partner is more mature, right? Anyway, you would've loved him. He's crazy about animals, like you were, and has traveled all over the world, like you used to say you wanted to do when Dad retired and you'd have the time."

Like Schaeffer had done with his brothers, Ren rested a hand on the headstone. "Hi, Mrs. Morgan."

Schaeffer draped an arm over his shoulders. "When the hiding got to be a little too much, I'd drive here and just sit for a while and clear my head."

"I'd do the same, whenever I was in New York."

They stayed a few more minutes, cleaning up the twigs and dead leaves from the gravesite. The ride home was quick and once inside, Schaeffer got them both a beer, and they stretched out on the sofa.

"I have to tell you something."

Wary, Ren put his bottle aside. "Yeah?"

"On the flight to Dallas I was saddled with a captain who was so vile, I wanted to walk out. He was sexist, homophobic, transphobic, racist. Everything in one."

"Not surprising. When you're one, you're usually a package deal of reprehensible behavior and thinking."

"I decided, why the hell should I care what the opinion of someone like that means to me? Why give him any importance? He can't hurt me or change how I feel about you."

"Yeah. I learned a long time ago that when you stop giving assholes real estate in your head, life becomes much easier."

He chuckled. "The world according to Ren. I'll have to listen to that."

Ren shrugged. "It's worked for me. What do you want to have for dinner?"

Schaeffer's eyes lit up. "Any meatballs left?"

He snorted. "You're kidding, right? You scarfed them all up like a wild hyena. Nope. Not a one."

His happy face fell. "*Hmm*. We could order a pizza."

"Sounds good. Can you do it? I have to check my emails and see if I've gotten anything from the magazine."

"Sure. Just let me check my schedule for the upcoming week." Schaeffer picked up his phone. "What the actual fuck?"

Ren glanced over at him. "What's wrong?"

"I have a video call with HR tomorrow."

"Why?"

Schaeffer's jaw flexed. "I have an idea, but I'm going

to wait and see."

"I'd really like to know."

Schaeffer pinched his eyes before answering. "Like I said, I'm not sure, but it might have something to do with that jerk of a captain I flew with. He's the type who would try to get me into trouble for something completely minor just to make a point."

Ren frowned. "I hope you're wrong, but you kept your cool and said nothing. Unlike me, who'd probably have socked him in the jaw."

Schaeffer laughed. "Well, my way is certainly the easier way to handle it."

"Easy isn't always the best. But I understand why you did it."

CHAPTER EIGHTEEN

The more Schaeffer thought about Ren's words, the more he realized Ren was correct. Sometimes you had to make a difficult choice and stand up for what you believed in and what was right, even if the consequences threatened your safe haven.

Schaeffer decided he'd no longer bow to hate when confronted with it. He would stand up tall.

That night, he woke to Ren shaking his shoulder gently.

"Schaeffer, *Schaeffer*."

Sweat dripped from his skin, and his heart drummed so hard, he gasped. "I can't breathe. I can't…"

"Shh. I have you. I've got you. It's okay. You're safe."

Shivering and with his teeth chattering, Schaeffer burrowed into Ren's arms. Several minutes passed before his breath steadied and he could force the words past his lips.

"I'm okay. I-I'm all right."

But Ren continued to hold him, crooning soft words and

rubbing small circles on his back. "What happened? You seemed to be having a horrible nightmare." Ren let him go but kept a hand on him.

"It wasn't that bad." The first attempt at a smile failed, and it took a second attempt to get it right, but he could see the disbelief in Ren's eyes.

"Not that bad? Are you kidding me? You were flailing around in the bed and screaming. I was afraid you were going to hurt yourself."

"Did I hurt you?"

"Not physically. But I hated seeing you like that. It upset me to know you're in pain. What happened to set it off?"

He rolled away from Ren, hating the pity in his eyes. Exactly what he didn't want. "I don't know. I'm not hurting. I'm happier than ever."

"Maybe it was the visit with your mother? Or is it the move? Does it stress you out?" At the touch of Ren's hand, he faced him. Anxious eyes searched his. "It was upsetting to see you like that, and I want to do whatever I can to help you."

"It's nothing like that." It was time, especially now that Ren had opened up about the devastating tragedy of his brothers' deaths. If Ren trusted him enough to share the most important part of himself, he could and should do the same.

"I didn't join the military to fight. Maybe it was cowardly of me, but I couldn't see myself taking the life of another person, even in a wartime situation."

"Not cowardly," Ren murmured. "I doubt anyone would understand what it's like unless and until they're faced with the situation."

"You're right. I was in intelligence gathering, which meant I'd fly reconnaissance missions to give our fighter pilots the information they needed. It was exciting. Nothing compared to that thrill." He rubbed his face. "Until it all went to shit."

Ren wrapped his arms around him and kissed his neck. "Talk to me."

"I've mentioned my friend Steve. The best man I've ever known. Kind, smart as hell. He was the only one in the Force I'd ever told I was gay."

"And?" Ren asked.

Schaeffer's voice trembled. "Didn't care a damn bit. It never changed our friendship. He lived in Tucson and said when we'd finally make it home, he was planning on proposing to his girlfriend and he wanted me to be in his wedding party. He had his whole life planned out: put in his years, then open up a flight school and teach people how to fly."

"But he never got that chance."

"No, he didn't," he said, the bitterness choking him. "We'd gathered our intel for the mission and were on our way back to base when we took fire. I'd never been so scared in my fucking life." Ren held him closer, and Schaeffer sank into him. The tighter Ren held him, the easier it was for him to breathe. "I didn't think we'd make it out, and I was screaming for my mother, my father, Anson, praying to anyone who would listen to let me live. And then I heard it. The sound no pilot ever wants to hear. And I knew, even without the flash of hellfire exploding before my eyes. It was my worst nightmare. I watched my friend's plane get blown to pieces in front of my eyes and go down in a fireball. And all I did was zoom out of there like a bat out of hell."

"What else could you have done?"

"I don't know." He raised his eyes to meet Ren's and saw nothing but sympathy and concern. "I felt like the biggest coward."

"You weren't fighter pilots, were you? You had no weapons?"

"Not then. Now some do, but they mostly use drones— something that didn't exist." That sense of helplessness and lost hope reared its ugly head from where he'd kept it hidden all these years. "But you also don't leave anyone behind. We don't abandon our brothers. And I fucking left him to burn to ashes."

"Schaeffer, my God, are you serious? What choice did you have? Stay there and get shot yourself?"

Agonized, he hung his head. "I know it would've meant me getting killed. But it doesn't make what happened any easier to bear."

"Would it be better if two families were in mourning? For your father to have not only lost his wife, but a son? For Anson to lose his brother?" Ren kissed his cheek. "Babe, killing yourself with guilt isn't going to bring Steve back, and it sure as hell isn't going to help you."

Maybe nothing could. "Sometimes I think maybe I shouldn't fly anymore. I've lost the joy I once had being in the sky."

"You didn't have a break between the Air Force and becoming an airline pilot?"

His father had urged him to take some time off, but he'd ignored his advice and immediately enrolled in flight courses to begin training to fly with the airlines. "I thought it would be a good idea to jump right in and not dwell on my issues. Maybe it was a mistake."

Ren took his hand and laced their fingers together. Schaeffer loved how his need to connect was through touch. "I'd never presume to tell anyone who's been through a traumatic experience how best to deal with it. It's not as if I've handled it well myself." His smile was heartbreaking, and Schaeffer knew his thoughts were with his foster brothers. "But taking a break and talking to someone might help."

"You have. More than you know."

Unflinching, Ren met his gaze, determination in the set of his chin. "My love and support aren't a substitute for professional help. Therapy isn't a weakness, no matter what you were led to believe. It takes incredible strength to recognize you need it."

"I have been, at different times. When the nightmares disappeared, I'd stop, hoping they were gone forever. Maybe because I just wanted them to be. I guess I was wrong."

From his many years in the military, he'd learned to internalize so much of his life—his sexuality and the intermittent nightmares entwining the death of his mother with the crushing loss of Steve. Both events had left him with suffocating guilt that had only grown over the years. It seemed the faster he tried to run from it, the more his steps faltered, and now he was slogging through quicksand, unable to move forward.

"So…maybe you need to rethink that?" Ren pressed. "I hate seeing you twisted up in pain and self-doubt. Bad things occur when you blame yourself, and I can't stand the thought of something happening to you. Please tell me you'll look for someone." As if sensing the unease swirling through his mind, Ren hugged him and whispered in his ear, "I know you're used to handling your problems on your own, but I'm here now."

But would he always be? What would happen if Schaeffer's messy, ugly insides broke free, and Ren decided he'd rather be with someone who didn't need so much work? But somehow Ren, who knew him better than he knew himself, read his doubts.

"I don't know much about relationships, but I know that love isn't about being perfect. When you love someone, it includes all their imperfections because that's what makes them beautiful to you. I love you, and that makes you perfect for me. I'm not going to leave because of your nightmares. I'm only going to hold you tighter and love you harder."

"I think you know more than you believe. That was beautiful. I thought escaping enemy fire was the luckiest day of my life, but I was wrong. Finding you during that snowstorm was."

"I feel the same. Having you to talk to about my brothers brought me closer to them. I can forgive myself now because reflected in your eyes I see someone worth forgiving."

They held each other close, two lost souls recognizing life's fragility and the indisputable truth that love wasn't easy, but that the most difficult path often led to the greatest reward. He rested his head against Ren's chest. "I'll find someone. I'm ready to try again. First, though, I have to deal with the airline nonsense."

Ren's concerned voice rumbled through him. "If it is that bastard captain reporting you, do you think they're going to take his side over yours? I'm sure if he's offended you, he's done the same for years to other people."

"I guess I'll see. But I'm done with the hiding bullshit. This is me, and they'll have to take me as I am."

Ren kissed his head. "Whatever you choose, I'm with you."

"You have a right to union counsel, Mr. Morgan. I'm sure you know that."

Danita Washington, the RWB Airlines Human Resources director, faced him through the computer screen. He crossed his arms, and though he tried to remain pleasant, he failed to hide his irritation.

"I've done nothing wrong. What is this about?"

"We've had a complaint."

"A complaint? About me? From a member of the public?"

She shook her head. "No. An employee."

Of course. He'd been correct in his assumption. A sardonic grin tipped up his lips. "Captain Wallace 'Good Old Boy' O'Brian."

"You don't sound surprised."

He huffed out a sigh. "Because I'm not. The man is a walking billboard for misogyny, homophobia, transphobia, and I'm sure everything else." When she didn't respond, he continued. "Let me guess what happened. He said I came on to him, or that I was inappropriate with him."

"Why don't you tell me what happened on your flight?"

"He took his seat, and right away started making inappropriate comments about my personal life. When he asked me if I was married or had a girlfriend, I didn't answer because I don't discuss my personal life on the job. All during the flight, he made rude, demeaning remarks about one of the female flight attendants. He gave me his unwanted and unwelcome opinion about trans people using bathrooms, and he said that if any trans person ever came near him, he'd kill them. That he has no use for queers. Honestly, I should be the one filing a complaint against him."

"Do you want to?"

"What I want is for this nonsense to end and for the victim to stop being blamed. Near the end of the flight, he again asked about my girlfriend. When I told him I have a partner, he looked at me as if I were something to be scraped off the bottom of his shoe. I'm sure he guessed what I meant." Schaeffer raised his eyes to meet her gaze. "I'm gay, Ms. Washington. For years I've kept my sexuality hidden—first in the military, for obvious reasons, and when I joined RWB Airlines I decided to keep silent because it also didn't seem to be the friendliest place for someone like me. But understand this—I'm not ashamed of who I am. I chose to keep quiet about my sexuality because it's no one's business whom I choose to love but mine."

She'd taken notes while he spoke, and her facial

expression remained neutral, so Schaeffer had no idea if his words made any impact. Perhaps that was all part of her training. After all, she wasn't supposed to take sides, only consider the facts. "Is there anyone who can corroborate your story as to his comments?"

"Whatever was said, O'Brian made sure it was in the privacy of the flight deck, only between the two of us. I'd hate to have to ask people to speak negatively toward their colleague. They shouldn't be drawn into this ugliness."

She set her pen on the desk. "O'Brian is one of our more senior pilots, with over twenty years of service and thousands of hours of flight time."

"And?" He raised a brow. "Is that supposed to mean he's untouchable?"

"To the contrary. There have been whispers about his offensive behavior for years, but no one has ever come forward to complain."

"And you want me to be the sacrificial lamb. Ms. Washington, I'm not here to do the airline's job for them. If you heard whispers, it was your duty to investigate."

"We're taking the complaint very seriously."

"His complaint?" His jaw dropped. "Against me? This is how the airline protects its workers, by blaming the victim? Now you see why people keep their sexuality hidden. He's the bigot, yet I'm the one you're looking into."

"That's not the way it works. I've taken your statement, and now we will proceed to investigate it from both sides. That means speaking to the entire crew from that flight, as well as your other flights and Captain O'Brian's."

A bit mollified but still angry, he gave a sharp nod. "I see, but frankly, I'm not at all comfortable with this investigation. I don't want to be a bug under the microscope. I did nothing wrong."

Her gaze remained unwavering. "I understand that, but there are procedures we have to follow. We will do everything to protect you and make sure your rights aren't violated."

Thoroughly disgusted, he had nothing left to say. "Are we done? Is there anything you need from me?"

"Someone will be in touch. Don't be angry, Mr. Morgan. Hopefully a positive change will come out of this."

"Sure. Thanks."

The screen turned off, and he pushed away from the table to pace the apartment. Ren was off to Westchester that morning, and without anyone to vent to, he needed to leave. He decided the best thing to do was cool off, so he grabbed his wallet and car keys and headed for the diner. Maybe a cup of coffee and a change of scenery would help. God only knew, pacing the apartment and growing angrier by the minute wasn't helping.

Upon arrival at the restaurant, it was empty enough that he scored a booth in the corner, where he ordered his coffee and decided to splurge on breakfast, since he'd been too nervous before the video conference to eat.

Head down, he scrolled through his phone, searching the Internet to see if there were any airline court cases like his. Many cases involved flight attendants, and with disgust he recalled how O'Brian talked about and treated the female crew members.

"Schaeffer?" He glanced up to see Andy standing at his table. "Hi."

"Hi, how're you doing?"

Andy tipped his head. "Can I sit for a sec?"

He shrugged. "Sure." He hadn't seen Andy since their dinner, and it looked like he had something on his mind.

Andy clasped his hands on the tabletop and met his eyes. "I heard about O'Brian's complaint."

His stomach bottomed out. "Oh?" His lips twisted with derision. "So much for the privacy they promised."

Andy shrugged. "You know how it is. One little whisper

is all it takes. Trust me, I know whatever he's claiming is a crock of shit. He's been a prick to deal with for years. You have my full support."

"Thanks. It's so frustrating having to defend myself against someone like him." He propped his chin in his hand. "He should be the one under a microscope, not me."

"I agree, and the only thing I can say is, I have a feeling you won't have to bear that burden alone."

Andy's frank gaze surprised him. "What're you talking about?"

Leaning in closer, Andy lowered his voice. "Look. We've all put up with O'Brian for years. Lately he's been getting worse, and now he doesn't even try to hide how hateful he is. I've flown with him and heard firsthand his snide comments about women's breast sizes and how he'd love to have sex with them. He's made no secret he's homophobic, and he always treats the male flight attendants with derision, whether they're gay or not."

"None of this is making me feel any better, Andy."

A slight grin curled Andy's lips. "It should, because we're all going to stand behind you."

Schaeffer's jaw dropped. "What're you saying?"

"Maybe you thought you were alone in this, but you're not."

Falling in love with Ren meant he'd never be alone again, and it was an existence he wanted to embrace with his whole heart. Not only for the sexual part of their relationship, but for the ugly, broken parts of him he'd learned were worth loving as well. It had taken him years to get over losing Steve, but maybe now he was willing to truly open himself up and find new friendships.

"Thank you, Andy. I'm going to need all the support I can get, and with your help, I think I'm ready to take it on."

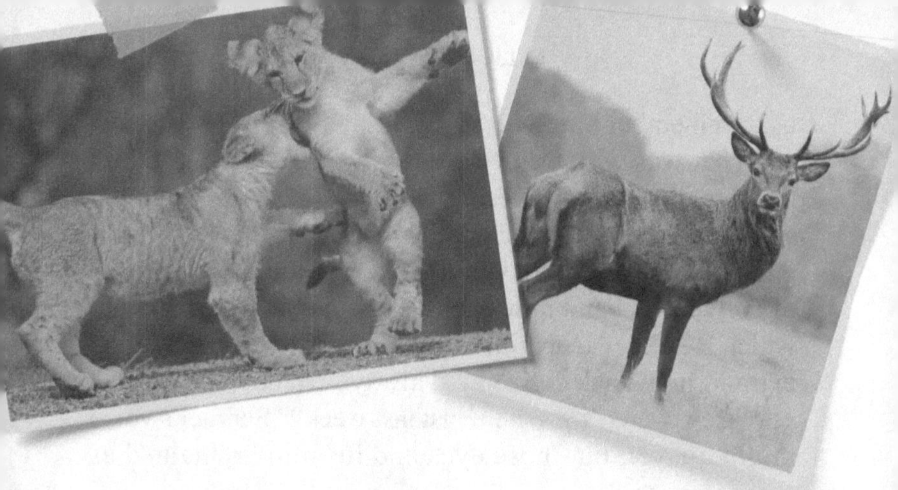

CHAPTER NINETEEN

There was nothing worse than watching someone you love wither away. In the months following his return, Ren's hope for Samuel to beat the cancer spreading through his body had waned. Fighter that he was, Samuel never complained or let on how much pain he was in, but Ren didn't need words to know the truth. He could see it in the shadows lurking in Samuel's once laughing eyes.

Each time he showed up at the office, Toni briefed him first before he'd see Samuel, giving him insight into his mood and ability to concentrate. And each time, Ren wanted to cry and scream at the unjustness of life, but he knew neither Toni nor Samuel would appreciate it. Both had taken a fatalistic approach to his illness, as Toni confided in him that morning.

"We're reconciled with whatever comes. I've loved him more than half my life and consider myself lucky for the time I was given. The last thing Samuel wants is for any of us to remember him with regret."

That was why Ren walked in with a smile pasted on his face, but felt it wavering when he saw Samuel. In the week since he'd last visited, Samuel had lost more weight and was too weak to even lift his ubiquitous giant mug of coffee. His hand now encircled a small Styrofoam cup, which Ren knew contained a watered-down version of the extra-strong black coffee he'd always drunk.

"Ren, weren't you here just last week?" Samuel's voice might quaver, but those eyes and his mind remained as sharp as ever.

"Yeah, but I miss your pretty face. I wanted to show you some of the shots I've chosen for the copy. There are some gorgeous ones of elephants I think we should feature on the cover."

Samuel nodded. "That's Doug Wilson's work. He's young and hungry. Kind of reminds me of you when we first met, although he needs to grow into his eye. Kid has to learn patience to get that one perfect shot, instead of a hundred almost-theres."

Funny, but when Ren had lived that nomadic life, moving from encampment to encampment, never thinking past the horizon of the next day, he couldn't have pictured himself in a steady relationship, not itching to fly off at a moment's notice to a destination across the world, hiding away for months on end to take that perfect, once-in-a-lifetime picture.

Now? He held his once-in-a-lifetime in the palm of his hand and planned on never letting go. Falling in love with Schaeffer had opened his eyes to see that the joy he poured into his work was a substitute for the painful past he'd been running from.

"He'll get there." He waited for Samuel to painfully manage the cup of coffee. "I'm thinking of taking a ride around upstate and doing some shooting. It's been a while, and I'm anxious to see what's out there."

"Looks like a beautiful day for it. The deer should be out and…I wish…well, never mind."

It didn't take much to guess what was on Samuel's mind, and Ren desperately wanted to give Samuel that wish and spend time with the man who'd given his passion the chance of a lifetime.

"Come with me. I'm sure Toni will let you play hooky."

A spark lit Samuel's weary eyes. "Are you sure?" But he was pushing back his chair from the desk, breaking Ren's already sore and aching heart.

"Let's go."

When he offered Samuel an arm to lean on, he took it, and Ren vowed to make this a day neither of them would ever forget. He texted Schaeffer to let him know he'd be home very late and why, and then, after Toni helped settle Samuel into the car and gave them a couple of folding chairs, a cooler filled with water, and Samuel's pain medication, they were off.

"Where're you taking me?" Samuel asked once they were on the thruway heading north. They'd stopped for some snacks and sandwiches, and recalling Samuel's love for Milky Ways, bought out the stock for him.

"I figured we could return to where it began and we first met. How does that sound?"

"Like you're as much of a sentimental fool as Toni," Samuel responded gruffly. A few minutes farther along the highway, he wiped his eyes. "It's perfect. I'd like to see it one last time."

Ran's hands tightened on the wheel. He wanted to yell and scream that it wasn't fair but if Ren knew anything, it was that just when you thought you had a handle on things, life had a way of kicking you in the ass. Tears blurred his vision, and he blinked them away. He wouldn't ruin his and Samuel's time together. If it was to be Samuel's farewell to their special spot, he'd make it the best damn day possible.

It was a long drive to the spot in the Adirondacks, and Ren knew Samuel could no longer manage the incline, so they stayed on a level footpath. Like the dedicated naturalist he was, Samuel's keen eye spotted several birds and flowers of note, and Ren took the pictures for him, showing him the shots. After an hour or so, Ren broke out the sandwiches and water, and though Samuel claimed he was famished, he managed only a few small bites before setting it aside.

"I want to tell you something."

A lump rose in Ren's throat. "Samuel—"

"Don't stop me." With a raised hand, Samuel glared as best he could. "It's something I've been meaning to say since you came home. Because I hope you realize it now, but you are home. You belong here, and after I'm gone, I want you to carry on the legacy of what I started."

"Don't think like that. You can still beat this." Tears slid from his eyes, but he didn't care.

A wistful, almost sweet smile, tipped Samuel's lips. "I'm at peace with it. I've done what I've set out to do with my life—make sure people understand we only have one planet and that we need to take care of the creatures living on it. And I can't think of anyone else I'd want to turn over the magazine to more than you."

Astonished, Ren wiped his face. "Me?"

"Who better? The son I always wished for. The first time I saw you up in these mountains, angling for the perfect shot of that spruce grouse, I knew you were as special as that rare bird. You had a broken heart but the soul of a warrior who would keep fighting. And you have—not only for the animals, but for yourself."

Unabashedly crying, Ren sniffled. "I-I don't know what to say. Toni—"

"Knows all about it and agrees with me one hundred percent. Because of the mumps I caught in my travels, we weren't able to have kids. No matter how many people we've hired over the years, you've always held a special place in her heart. She's so thrilled you've found someone and always hoped you'd eventually settle down, close enough to see you regularly."

"But take over?"

Samuel cracked a grin. "Being the boss can be fun. And you and Toni can run it together, with Hawk over in Helsinki."

"It will always be your magazine, Samuel."

They sat for a while, listening to the birds, and Samuel dozed in the warmth of the late-afternoon sun. Ren cleaned up their detritus and stowed it all away in the car. Earlier in the day, he'd taken some pictures of Samuel, and he added some of him sleeping with a peaceful expression. He knew Toni would appreciate them. After Samuel woke up, Ren helped him to the car, and they made the journey home.

He pulled up in the driveway of Samuel and Toni's home in Katonah. Toni opened the door, and the two of them assisted Samuel into the house. Once inside, they led him to his favorite chair, facing the floor-to-ceiling windows overlooking the forest. They weren't far from the New Croton Reservoir, and Ren had spent many happy hours exploring the wildlife surrounding Samuel and Toni's beautiful home.

"Come back soon, Ren. And bring Schaeffer with you. We'd love to meet him." Samuel had begun to fade, and Ren hugged him close.

"I will. I love you, Samuel."

Samuel's big hand rested on his cheek. "Goodbye, Ren."

Ren frowned. "I'll never say goodbye to you. I'll say what I always told you before I left for a shoot. I'll see you when I see you."

Samuel nodded, and Toni walked him out, her eyes shiny with tears.

"Thank you for giving him a special day. I know he'll

never forget it. And I assume he told you?"

"About taking over the magazine? Hopefully that won't be for a while. Take care of yourself, and I'll call you tomorrow."

She hugged him tight. "I love you. I'm so happy you've found someone who realizes how special you are."

"Schaeffer is the best man, and I'm lucky to have him. I hope you can meet him soon. Samuel too."

Toni's gaze was tearful. "I'd love that, but I'm not so sure."

He leaned down to press a kiss to her cheek. "I'm keeping the faith."

He watched her reenter the house, then texted Schaeffer.

On my way. See you soon.

The response was immediate.

Everything okay?

Yes, but no. I'll explain when I see you.

It took him over an hour to get home, and when he opened the door to the apartment, Schaeffer welcomed him with a hug. He sank into the familiar broad chest, needing the solace of that comforting hug. How damn lucky was he to have someone to come home to, and not an empty apartment, or worse, a hotel room? He held on to Schaeffer, soaking in his heat and love.

"I haven't felt this helpless since Chris and Kevin died."

With an arm around his shoulder, Schaeffer steered him toward the couch, where he saw a beer waiting. "I'm listening."

"I went up there to discuss the next issue, but instead ended up spending the day with Samuel. I took him to the place where we first met, and we just sat and reminisced about the past. I took some pictures too." His camera hung from his shoulder, and he pulled up the shots he took to show Schaeffer. "I have to remember to send these to Toni. Anyway," he sighed, the fatigue and frustration overwhelming. "Physically he's so weak, yet mentally he's as sharp as ever. He understands what's happening, and even though he said he's at peace with whatever comes, I know he's still fighting."

"I'm sure he is. He doesn't sound like a man who'd give up easily."

"No. Never." Ren paused. "He's asked me to take over the magazine. With Toni, of course."

"Permanently? Become its editor? Not only the photo editor?"

In Schaeffer's words, Ren heard optimism but with a tinge of fear. "Were you worried it was all just temporary and I wasn't going to stay?" Disappointed, Ren's shoulders sagged. "I thought you knew me better after all this time together."

"Hey, look at me. It hasn't been that long." Schaeffer met his gaze with complete honesty. "I know I love you and that you love me, but this is a huge lifestyle change for you. And I remember how you spoke of traveling the world and discovering the beauty of the endangered species and what a thrill it was."

"It still is. There's nothing like it. But none of it compares to what we're trying to build here. It's something almost equally as rare and precious. And just as I will never get over seeing the mother snow leopard with her cubs that day, I cherish you. I'm the happiest I've ever been right here with you, and I have no intention of walking away or leaving. Ever."

A beautiful smile broke out over Schaeffer's face. "I feel the same. And I don't want you to feel stymied, so if you ever decide you want to go out in the field again, I'm not going to hold you back. I can't imagine you want to give it up entirely."

Lucky was the day he found a man to understand him. "I might after I learn the ropes of running a magazine. Being out there today made me realize I do miss it. But, like I told Samuel when he first asked me to take the photo editor job, I can find plenty of wildlife here. And maybe when you're off, you can come with me."

Excitement brewed in Schaeffer's eyes. "I'd love to see you in action. I only caught a glimpse of it in California, since you haven't had too much time here."

Ren leaned on his shoulder. "Let's do it. I don't want time to slip away and us not share our passions. One day I want you to take me on a flight."

Schaeffer grew stiff. "I haven't flown solo since I left the military."

Ren took hold of his hand. "That's something you can discuss with the therapist when you find one."

After a moment's hesitation, Schaeffer nodded. "You're right. I used to enjoy going out with nothing but the sky in front of me. I'd love to do that with you."

He nuzzled into the warmth of Schaeffer's neck. "Speaking of shared passions…" Desire blazed through him. "I want you. Now."

Schaeffer pressed a hot kiss to his lips. "You read my mind. Come on."

They hurried to the bedroom and shed their clothes. Once on the bed, Ren wrapped himself around Schaeffer, eager for the touch of his naked body.

"The whole drive home I was thinking about you. How special what we have is and how I want to be here with you in fifty years."

"I want you forever. And beyond." Schaeffer rained kisses over his face and neck, licking and nipping at his feverish skin and latching on to his nipples. Ren writhed and moaned, his dick full and leaking between them.

"Please," he gasped. "Fuck me. I need you."

"Can't wait to be inside you."

A few seconds later, Schaeffer entered him, slick and

huge and perfect. Ren's groan of satisfaction echoed in the bedroom, and Schaeffer drove in deeper, stretching him to fullness, but even that wasn't enough. He craved possession, for Schaeffer to own him fully and completely.

"I want to feel you even when you're not with me. Come home in me."

Schaeffer bent his legs to his chest and thrust harder, lighting him up until there was nothing but the twisting, hungry need to come. He ached as Schaeffer hammered him into the mattress, burying himself fully, shaping his body to fit his cock. Schaeffer grabbed his dick, and that unexpected touch rocketed him to the stars. His toes curled, his blood sizzled, and golden sparks rained down on him as he came, spurting hot and sticky over Schaeffer's fingers.

"Oh God," he cried out, trembling as Schaeffer's grunts of pleasure increased. "More, more."

Panting, Schaeffer pinned his hands over his head, and with his tongue plundering his mouth, slammed into him and came, his dick pulsing and throbbing. He collapsed on top of him, and Ren held his sweating body tight.

"I love you," Schaeffer gasped. "So damn much."

Ren smiled against his mouth. "I love you too."

The call came at nine thirty the next morning, and Ren knew, without Toni saying a word.

"He's gone, isn't he?"

"In his sleep. The way he wanted it." Her tearful voice shook. "You gave him the best last day. That's what he said to me before we went to bed."

Grief overwhelmed him, and wordlessly, Schaeffer held him tight. "I loved him so damn much. What can I do to help you?"

"They've already taken him…the house is so empty. I keep expecting to see him in his chair."

"Would it help if we came over? You shouldn't be alone."

She managed a laugh. "Funny, isn't it? He's so much a part of everything in this house, I don't think of myself as being alone, but I guess I am now. For the first time in fifty years."

"We'll be there as soon as we can."

"Thank you."

He ended the call and sat motionless in bed, with Schaeffer pressed close to him. "I can't believe it. How is it possible for someone to be here one day and gone the next? Like he never existed. We spoke about so many things yesterday, and I thought we'd have a little more time."

"That's one thing I've learned we'll never have enough of. He'll continue to live on in your memories and in the legacy of the magazine you'll run. I'm sorry I never got to meet him."

"He knew you." Ren twisted around to face Schaeffer. "The first time I told him about you, he recognized you were going to be someone special in my life."

"He did? How?" Schaeffer's brows drew together.

"The way I spoke about you. How I wasn't itching to run and live in a tent for another six months to a year. He sensed something was different when I spoke to him in California, but I wasn't sure where we stood."

"Together. I hope you know that."

He laid his head against Schaeffer's chest. "Good. Because I need you by my side, more than ever."

"By your side is my favorite place to be."

CHAPTER TWENTY

"I know you've told me, but I forgot. How many days do you have at home until you leave again?"

"Two, not counting today."

Schaeffer sat next to Ren, who was driving them to Katonah. He checked his phone and saw several messages from Andy, who was keeping him up-to-date on not only the rumor mill, but any actual information he gleaned from his sources.

"Is everything okay? You keep checking your phone."

His problems with the airline would have to wait for the moment, as Schaeffer wanted to be able to give Ren his complete support.

"Yeah, sure. No problems."

Ren exited the Saw Mill River Parkway and drove on for about a mile or so past the leafy green trees lining the road, before halting at a red light.

"Why're you lying to me? Is it about that complaint?"

He blinked at Ren's harsh voice. "What? Shit, I'm not lying. Don't say that. I don't lie. I just didn't think the time was right to talk about me when you're grieving Samuel and you have to console his widow. It isn't as important."

A car behind them beeped, and Ren cursed and accelerated. He pulled into a gas station and shut off the engine. "I'm sorry. I didn't mean to call you a liar, but I don't want you keeping something important from me because you're afraid it might upset me now. Losing Samuel is horrible, but you don't have to put your problems aside."

He reached over and squeezed Ren's hand on the steering wheel. "I know. And I will tell you. Tonight. And it's really not bad. Right now, your concentration needs to be with Toni."

"Okay." Ren's mouth drooped. "I'm not looking forward to this." He started the engine, and they exited the gas station, driving down a road that looked to be leading deeper into the woods.

"I know. I can't imagine how Toni must feel."

"You'll find out in a minute. We're here."

The Tudor-style house was set back from the road, with beautifully landscaped bushes and flower beds surrounding it. Large trees threw welcome shade, and Schaeffer spotted a sprawling yard with bird feeders and a pool with a waterfall. Several cars were parked in the large driveway, and Ren pulled up behind one and cut off the engine.

"Gorgeous home."

Ren cracked a smile. "They lived here before anyone else practically, and Toni loves her garden. She has a whole section for vegetables."

"One of the things I remember most about my mom is how she was always trying to grow something in the little patch of land we had." He grew pensive at the memory. "She was so happy when she picked her first tomato from a spindly little plant."

Ren took his hand. "Come on. Let's go inside."

They didn't have to wait, as the front door opened and Toni waved to them. "Ren."

Together they joined her at the threshold. "Toni, I'm so sorry." He hugged her, and she held on to him.

"I know, but he's not in pain anymore. And he specifically told me that after it happened, there should be no crying and wishing what could have been. He wanted a celebration of life, and I'm going to have it for him." She brushed away the tears. "And you must be Schaeffer. I'm so happy to finally meet you."

He kissed her cheek. "I am as well. I only wish my schedule had allowed for it to happen earlier. I'm so sorry for your loss. Ren has told me what an incredible man Samuel was and how much he means to him."

Toni linked her arm through Ren's. "Ren is the son we never had. He means the world to us, and I can't tell you how thrilled I am that he's allowed himself to be happy. My sister and brother-in-law are here, Doug is flying in from Florida, and Hawk is on his way. He should be here tonight."

"Even with all the stories Ren has told me, I feel like I missed out by not meeting him."

"It's funny because after Samuel spoke to Ren when he was in California, he told me, 'Toni. Ren met someone. He's never been happy to stay in one place, and he told me not to rush his time off. I'd bet my last dollar.' " She sighed with the memory. "He had an instinct, not only for photography, but for people as well. He would've loved meeting you."

He followed Ren and Toni through the center hall toward the wide-open space surrounded by windows. All the ground floor rooms flowed so easily into each other, but Schaeffer was entranced by the gorgeous photography on the walls.

"These are so beautiful." He stopped between one of a mother and baby elephant's silhouettes against the setting sun, and another of a tiger, amber eyes gleaming, lying in wait in the grass. "Did Samuel take them?"

"Two of Samuel's favorites from when we first started working with World Wildlife. He spent weeks waiting for that tiger." Misty-eyed, she wiped her tears. Ren kissed her cheek.

"I remember him telling me the stories of those days before you decided to start a magazine dedicated to endangered species. In those days there weren't many publications like that."

"No, we were a group of renegades." Her laughter was merry. "No one thought it would last, but here we are, thirty years later and still hanging on. Now Ren and his vision can carry us forward."

"I think Ren is the perfect person," Schaeffer said. "I'm very proud of him."

"I am as well. And you're a pilot. How exciting. That must take you all over."

"Mainly the United States and Canada. I was in the military, so I did get to see other parts of the world."

"I'm sure you're happy for Ren to stay in one place now, instead of traipsing around the world like a nomad."

"Hey, that was my job," Ren protested good-naturedly.

"I know, but that time is over. Now you're here, staying in one place for good. Oh, here's my sister, Greta, and her husband, Paul."

Ren greeted them, and Schaeffer couldn't help wondering if Ren was unhappy with giving up the wandering life. It couldn't be as easy to walk away from as he claimed. Sitting behind a desk, choosing pictures and copy for a magazine, paled in comparison to the adventures he'd had. He'd said yes, but seeing Ren in his element, happily discussing his old shoots and ones he'd never managed to get, all of Schaeffer's old insecurities wiggled their way to the surface once again, and he began to doubt not only himself, but Ren.

The day passed quickly, with the small group reciting

their favorite stories and memories of Samuel. There was no funeral—he'd wanted cremation, and Toni was taking his ashes somewhere they'd decided together for his final resting place.

As night fell, Ren, who'd been occupied with speaking to Doug and several other magazine staff members, came to sit by his side.

"I'm sorry I haven't spent much time with you. I didn't mean to leave you alone."

"You didn't," Schaeffer reassured him. "I talked to Paul, who travels for his business in banking—he enjoyed telling all these stories of his flight mishaps. Everyone's been very kind, and they respect your work immensely. I love hearing people give you the accolades you deserve."

Ren chewed his lip, seeming uncharacteristically nervous. "I hope I don't let them down. I've never done anything like this before. I've always been on the other side and just sent my photos in and waited for the next assignment."

"And you're sure it's what you want?"

Ren cocked his head. "What're you talking about? Didn't we just have this discussion where I told you I was here to stay?"

"Yes, but…I want to make sure you're not settling and giving up what you love. Taking pictures. This is a huge lifestyle change for you. I see how excited you are discussing photography and taking those once-in-a-lifetime shots with everyone here, and I feel guilty." Frustrated and fearful, he had to lay it out there so he'd have no doubts, and he pushed a hand through his hair. God. At this rate he'd be bald soon. "All I'm saying is I want you to make sure you're ready for a desk job."

Ren shifted closer to him on the couch. "What I'm ready for is to be with you. Full-time. Sure, I love the travel and the high of getting that perfect shot, but there's only so much to see in the world. And nothing is more beautiful than the sight of you lying next to me in the morning. What can I do to convince you that I'm ready for a new chapter?"

"I've been alone for so long, I guess I need to convince myself I've got something to offer."

"All you have to do is be who you are. That man will always be more than enough for me."

Joy unfolded in his chest. He'd been trepidatious about their relationship all along because of his fear that Ren would grow restless and want to start globe-trotting again, but now he felt more secure.

"I'm glad. I can't wait to move into our new place."

Ren's smile broadened. "Me too. Next week. I have the movers set, and my photos are out of storage, framed and ready to be hung." He glanced around. "I think it's been a long day, and Toni looks beat. How about we call it a night, and we go home, order a pizza, put our feet up, and you can tell me what's going on?"

Suppressing a grin, Schaeffer took his hand. "You don't forget a thing, do you?"

"If it concerns you, no. You're the most important person in my life. No job or anything else could ever mean more."

When Ren had told him the story of his two brothers, Schaeffer knew then he was a man who loved with his whole heart, sometimes to his own detriment. But to be on the receiving end of something so beautiful was a gift he'd never grow tired of opening.

"Okay. And did I tell you today how lucky I feel to have you?"

"You showed me last night. I'm still sore. But loving every second of the ache." Ren took his hand. "Let's say our goodbyes."

Toni gave him a hug and a kiss on his cheek. "Thank you for loving Ren."

"He makes it easy. I'm lucky he loves me back."

"Luck has nothing to do with love. It's hard work and lots of laughter and tears. But if you respect each other and give as well as take, you'll be fine." She pulled Ren in for a hug. "I'll talk to you after I come home from my trip. Love you."

"I love you. Be safe." Ren's eyes shone with tears.

On their way out, he took the keys from Ren. "Let me drive. I think you've had enough for the day."

A teary-eyed Ren managed a smile and climbed into the passenger seat. "Thanks. It's really beginning to hit me that he's gone."

He turned on the GPS, concentrating on the directions onto the dark roads, and upon reaching the relative safety of the highway home, felt safe enough to speak. "It's a hard realization…knowing that someone who was such a big part of your life is gone."

"I'll never forget him. He made everything in my life possible. Even finding you, in a roundabout way. I plan to do my best every day to live up to the legacy he gave me."

"We both owe Samuel everything."

Ren rested a hand on his leg and closed his eyes. Several minutes passed in silence, and Schaeffer noticed him sleeping. Traffic proved to be light, and within forty-five minutes they were home. He shut off the engine. Ren opened his eyes and stretched.

"I conked out on you, didn't I? But now I'm wide-awake. And hungry."

"So the usual, you're telling me?"

Ren grinned, and Schaeffer followed him across the street and into their apartment.

They'd begun packing up, but he didn't have much—over the years he'd never acquired anything of value. He didn't like accumulating stuff for the sake of keeping it. The furniture would be picked up by Goodwill tomorrow, and their new bedroom set, couch, and television had already been delivered to the new place.

He placed an order for pizza, and they both changed into more casual clothes. He hadn't checked his emails or messages for hours, and now, scrolling through, he saw several he'd like to read, but instead he set the phone aside to talk to Ren, who sat waiting.

"So? Tell me. It's about that stupid complaint, right?"

He loved how devoted Ren was, and again, it was a startling realization, knowing he'd always have someone in his corner, besides his family. "Yeah. It's nothing bad, just surprising. It seems I have more support than I thought."

"I knew you would, but tell me." Alert, Ren shifted closer to him. "From everything you told me about O'Brian, you couldn't be the only one who was subjected to his bigotry."

He picked up his phone and opened the first message, from Marissa, who'd suffered through O'Brian's crude jokes and began to read out loud.

"Hi, Schaeffer.

HR called to ask me if I could make a statement about Captain O'Brian on the flight we had together, and if I had any complaints about how I was treated. I specifically said that you treated me with the utmost respect and I had no problem with you. Captain O'Brian was the offensive one. I was well aware of the comments he made about my body, and I let the investigator know that he constantly leered at me and brushed up against me and made me very uncomfortable.

Just wanted to let you know.

All the best,

Marissa"

"No one should have to suffer such disrespect on the job." Ren threaded a hand through Schaeffer's hair and curved it around his neck in a light yet possessive grip.

"*Mmm*, don't stop that. And of course I agree. I was

horrified when he said those crude things to me, but I kept my mouth shut. Now I'm sorry I did because if he said those things to Marissa too, it's guaranteed he was saying them to all the other women. I'm angry with myself for allowing fear to override what was right."

Ren's teasing fingers stilled on his nape. "Don't beat yourself up over it. You hadn't yet come out, and no one could blame you for keeping silent, especially if this is the type of environment the airline fosters. At least now it's come to light and something will be done."

"Maybe."

Ren's brows knitted. "Why so negative?"

He shrugged. "I guess because I'm not used to things going our way. After all those years in the military and hearing the snide, hurtful comments and worse, I'm not all that sure what the airline will do. What I do know is, I will never work with him again." Curious about another message, he picked up his phone again. "I have a message I'd really like to read, from the captain we met at the beach that time?"

"Yeah, sure. And of course I remember him." Ren peered over his shoulder. "What does he say? I bet he's on your side."

Without responding, Schaeffer opened the message and began to read.

"Hi, Schaeffer,

First, let me say at the outset, you have my full support. I can only imagine how upsetting it must have been for you to have to sit through a flight with someone like O'Brian spewing his bigotry and idiocy. While I wasn't personally contacted by HR, I unilaterally reached out to them to make sure I gave a statement as to my own experience with O'Brian, which was less than stellar. He's made a point of sending an email to each senior captain to try and persuade us to give statements on his behalf, but from what I've heard through the grapevine, he doesn't have many people on his side. He's made many enemies over the years with his bad behavior.

I let him know I don't stand for his ugly behavior. There are other pilots who belong to NGPA who'll stand up for you as well. O'Brian has been allowed to act unchecked for years with no repercussions.

I hope the actions of one bad apple won't stop you from achieving what you want. You're an excellent pilot, and it would be a loss to the airline if you leave.

Ron Vance"

"Wow," Ren exclaimed behind him. "Did you know he felt like this about you?"

"No." A swell of gratitude warmed his chest. "But it's nice to hear."

"Yeah? Well, listen to this." Ren hauled him close and kissed him so thoroughly, he almost forgot to breathe. "I'll tell you how much I love you every day." The buzzer sounded, and Ren patted his cheek. "Now go get my pizza."

"Bossy." Laughing, he pushed Ren off him and went to answer the door.

CHAPTER TWENTY-ONE

Running a magazine, sitting behind a desk, was a hell of a lot different than looking through a lens. A week had passed since Samuel's death, and Toni had messaged Ren from wherever she'd gone to say she'd decided to take another week, but not to worry, she had complete confidence in him that he could handle everything.

But could he?

Ren had rarely doubted his abilities so many times on so many different things. Photography was one thing. He knew he was good at what he did, but this was uncharted territory, and he couldn't admit it to anyone but himself: he was scared to death of fucking up.

Several times during the week he'd wanted to talk to Schaeffer about it, but he'd left for ten days of flying, and the one thing Ren wasn't going to do was waste their time together talking about his nerves. Like the night before, when Schaeffer had called from Chicago to say he'd landed, the last thing Ren had felt like saying was, *I'm not sure I know what I'm doing.*

Between his therapy for the nightmares and the complaint, Schaeffer was dealing with way more important problems, and Ren didn't want to dump any more weight on his shoulders. He kept quiet and said things were going fine and showed him the photographs he'd hung.

But now he had a meeting with Hawk, who'd agreed to stay in the country to help him and the rest of the editorial staff, and Ren wasn't even sure what the hell he was supposed to be doing.

He picked up the phone on Samuel's—his desk. That would take the most getting used to…

"Hawk? Could you come in, please?"

"Be right there."

Leroy Hawk was in his late forties. Slow to laugh, he had penetrating, honey-colored eyes that reminded Ren of a big cat staring down its prey. He rarely raised his voice, and he chose his words wisely, so when he did speak, people listened and reacted. Hawk had run the international division of *Nature's Beauty* for the past six years, and Ren knew he could be trusted.

His door stood ajar, and Hawk strode inside and closed it behind him. Ren sighed. "I guess you know why I want to see you?"

"Yes, but that's not why I closed the door."

"Oh?" Ren clasped his hands as Hawk took the chair in front of him.

"I know you're feeling overwhelmed and in over your head. For the moment. It isn't easy to come in and be expected to understand every nuance of what needs to be done."

Gratified and relieved, Ren blew out a breath of frustration. "But I feel like I should."

"That's where people make mistakes." Hawk leaned

forward, golden eyes earnest. "I'm here to help you, Ren. From the time Samuel knew he was terminal, he told me he wanted you to learn the ropes of publishing and for me to be the one to teach you. I'm here for as long as you need me."

"But you're leaving next week."

A smile, as rare as a snow leopard and almost as fleeting a sight, crossed Hawk's lips. "I informed my staff that my stay will be an extended one. They're thrilled to have me off their backs, and my wife is equally happy to visit New York City. Her old college roommate lives here, so they've been spending their days going to plays and museums and restaurant-hopping."

"I'm sorry you can't spend more time with her, seeing the sights."

"Don't worry about that. Marianne and I have a perfect marriage. We each give each other exactly what we need."

"Maybe that's why Schaeffer and I fit so well together," Ren mused. "When he leaves, I miss him like crazy, but then he comes home and it's like a celebration."

"You are very lucky."

"I know it. I still can't believe a man like Schaeffer loves me."

"You end up with the life you deserve. I truly believe that."

There was some message in Hawk's words Ren knew he was missing, but he didn't feel like he had the right to pry. He decided to keep things light.

"What you're telling me is you're here to be a life preserver, or in my case, a lifeboat, because I'm going to need all the help I can get."

"Use me however you want. I'm not concerned. Everyone has to start somewhere. The most important thing is not to try and do it all yourself. You have directors. Use them and their knowledge."

"I've met with them all, and everyone has pledged to lend

their support, except I feel like I'm getting pushback from the Features editor, Peter Jenkins. If I suggest something, he always has to make a change."

Hawk's eyes narrowed. "*Hmm*. Well, it is his job to make the articles as tight as possible. When do you meet with him next?"

"In about ten minutes."

"I'll sit in, how about that? Give you my opinion after the meeting."

"Thanks, I appreciate it." Relief flooded through him. "You have no idea how grateful I am for your help with everything."

"Good. Then I can ask a favor."

"Name it."

"I'd love a copy of one of your shots of the condors from your trip to Big Sur. They were spectacular."

"You got it. I'll send over the proofs, and you can have your pick."

"Thank you. I want it for home, right behind my desk."

"Whatever you want."

"How about a cup of coffee? Samuel had the strongest and best coffee."

"Coming right up."

Ren poured them each a mug, and Angie, the receptionist sitting in for Toni, buzzed him.

"Peter's here."

"Thanks, send him in."

Peter knocked and opened the door without giving Ren a chance to tell him to come in. Hawk's brows rose, and Ren didn't miss his surprised expression at this slight breach of civility. Ren knew Hawk demanded and received respect from his staff.

"Morning, Peter, come sit down."

He stopped when he saw Hawk, and frowned. "You didn't need to call in reinforcements."

Ren crossed his arms. "Meaning what? Hawk being here for our meeting? He's my international counterpart, and he has every right to sit in."

"I never said he didn't," Peter muttered, and sat in the chair next to Hawk.

"I'd like to know what we have set up for the final quarter's issue in terms of articles. They're due in three weeks."

Peter's jaw flexed. "I know. I have it all under control. I told Toni before she left."

"And now you can tell me." Ren's lips thinned in a smile.

The magazine was published quarterly, and their yearly issue wouldn't come out until the beginning of December, but they needed to get all the copy and photos in place. They'd sent Doug to shoot the perennial favorite, polar bears, but Ren debated putting the picture of the spruce grouse on the cover he'd shot so long ago. He thought it would be good for those new to the magazine to see it, and also as his personal tribute to Samuel. He'd submitted a short article on what the photograph and meeting Samuel meant to him, thinking it would make a great story for the holidays.

"I'm not sure your article is a good fit for the issue." Peter thrust out his jaw.

"Because? To me, it's a great story of finding one's beliefs again."

"That's just it. The story's almost too *new age* for a wildlife magazine. It's more about you and less about the grouse."

Perhaps he was right, and Ren had made it too self-reflective. "I can change it."

"I just don't think it's right. I have another article in place."

Hawk shifted in his seat. "Without running it by Ren first?"

Peter's gaze was defiant. "It's not like he has experience

with this. Samuel trusted me to make the right decisions."

"Samuel isn't running the magazine any longer," Hawk snapped. "And I know you were still required to get Samuel's approval before any changes were made. You need to follow procedure."

An ugly flush rose over Peter's face. "What does he know about it?"

"He? I'm sitting right here," Ren said mildly, trying to keep his cool.

Peter continued to ignore him. "I've been here for five years, working my ass off, and he waltzes in, thinking he can take over without paying his dues?"

"Waltzes in?" Ren responded in a low voice, proud of himself for containing his anger. "What are you insinuating? Speak to me directly."

"Oh please, spare me." Peter snorted, arrogance and dismissiveness dripping from his words. "You know exactly what I mean. Samuel took our work for granted. As soon as you arrived, he forgot the real staff existed. It was all about you, his favored one. Now that he's gone, you think you can come in and pretend to know what you're doing and question my authority."

"What authority?" Hawk lashed out. "You report to us, not the other way around. Or have you forgotten?"

Peter frowned. "Hawk, I've never had a problem with you."

"But you do with me," Ren asked.

"Because you haven't paid your dues," Peter shouted at him.

"The hell I haven't." Ren rose from his seat to point a finger at Peter. "I spent years alone in the bush or in the rainforest. I've gotten heatstroke and frostbite. I've been bitten, stung, half-drowned, and almost mauled, all in the attempt to get the perfect shots for this magazine. All the while, you've sat your ass in a chair, deciding whether it's a comma or a period. Don't you fucking tell me I haven't given my soul for this magazine, and I did it gladly because it's what I believe in. Samuel put his trust in me, and I will *not* let him down."

Pale-faced, Peter swallowed. "I didn't mean—"

"Yes, you fucking did," Ren cut him off, not interested in bullshit excuses. "I never doubted your abilities as an editor, but I am doubting that I can continue to work with someone with so much animosity toward me. I want the article you've substituted for mine on my desk after you leave this meeting, and we're going to go over every single article this afternoon. Understood?"

Peter nodded. "Yeah."

Head bowed, Peter took a moment, and Ren gave it to him. It wasn't like him to lose his temper, but Peter's lack of respect and snide comments grated on him.

"I'm sorry, Ren. I was out of line. I apologize."

Let the twit sweat a bit. Ren ignored his apology.

"I'll see you at two p.m. Sharp." He took his seat and didn't miss Hawk's lips twitching. "Better get a move on if you're going to be ready. I don't have anywhere to be tonight. I can stay past midnight if necessary."

He had no intention of keeping Peter at the office so late, but he knew Peter's wife was a jealous woman who called to check up on him constantly during the day, so if he stayed after normal working hours, there would be hell to pay.

"O-okay. I-I'll see you later," Peter stuttered, then jumped to his feet and practically ran out the door.

Hawk waited a second before slow-clapping. "You don't need me. That was a master lesson in takedowns. Good show."

"Damn, that felt good." Ren chuckled. "I am interested to see what article he intended to replace mine with."

"Could he be right? Was the article self-indulgent?" Hawk steepled his fingers under his chin.

Ren considered this. "Possibly. Those pictures were taken at a time when I was in a very different mental state. I might've gotten a bit in my feelings writing about getting the perfect shot and how it led me to Samuel." He relayed the story of his mother's death and Kevin and Chris, and how in losing them, he'd lost himself until he met Samuel. "I owe everything to Samuel. Things might've turned out much differently if we hadn't met on the mountain."

Hawk's stare was unblinking. "I'm sorry. I wasn't aware. How are you now?"

Thinking of the miraculous turn his life had taken the past year, he couldn't help getting emotional. "I never believed life could give a person a do-over, but I feel like I have a second chance. Meeting Samuel and working with him and Toni was the first step, but finding Schaeffer was the completion of my one-eighty turnaround. I have a home now."

Hawk's sigh came from within his soul, and Ren's heart pounded, sensing he was about to share something deeply personal. "I never thought I'd live beyond forty. I grew up on the streets of LA after running away from abusive parents. At thirteen, I found myself a pimp—or should I say, he found me. When I was fourteen, an older man brought me to Europe, where he not only kept me as his plaything, but rented me out for sex parties to his rich friends. He didn't know they'd give me gifts, and I squirreled away a little fortune in cash and jewelry over the years."

"Why didn't you leave?"

"And go where? To the streets? It was the only place. He had my passport, and I barely spoke French at that time. At least with him, I was fed, clothed, and had medical care."

In its own terrible way, it made sense, but Ren's heart broke all the same.

"The only thing that kept me sane were the animals surrounding his villa. There was such unspoiled beauty in the deer, foxes, rabbits…all the creatures roaming about. During the days, before I'd be sent to the private yachts for the parties, I'd sit for hours, writing stories about them. When Giorgio died, he left me a huge sum of money. I was only twenty-two, so I went to school, got my degree, and used a connection I'd made while I was with him to get a job with a wildlife magazine, where I learned at the hands of an incredible editor. He and I were lovers until he met someone younger and prettier."

A wry smile ghosted his lips, and Ren sat frozen as he listened to Hawk's story. Ren would've never imagined he'd lived such a harrowing life.

"You seemed shocked," Hawk said, and Ren hesitated, gathering his thoughts.

"I had no idea. But then again, we've never really talked until now."

"No, we haven't. And even if we had, I most likely wouldn't have shared this with you. But hearing your story, I knew you'd understand mine."

"Thank you for trusting me."

That fleeting smile crossed Hawk's lips. "Without trust, we have nothing. My ex, whom I won't name as he's still in the business, secured me a job with a naturalist magazine, and at an event I met Samuel. That was when he told me he wanted to start an international division of *Nature's Beauty*, and I jumped at his offer. I didn't need the money, but I knew I'd found my calling. A year ago I met Marianne and we married. She's fourteen years younger than me."

He had no idea why he asked, but the words tumbled out. "Do you love her?"

Hawk rubbed his chin. "I respect her, and we enjoy each other's company. She needed to marry to save face with her very Catholic family, but the truth is, she and her college roommate are lovers. Every month or so Laura flies to us or Marianne flies to New York, and they spend time together."

"And what about you? Do you have someone?"

"Yes. Myself. I don't want that type of relationship anymore. All those years of belonging to someone else…I need to be alone."

"I'm sorry, Hawk. I know the words are inadequate, but I hate how society lets down the lost children."

"Don't feel sorry for me. Remember I said that we end up with the life we deserve? I'm living one I never dreamed possible, and I'm happier than I've ever been. Maybe it's unorthodox, but that should only matter to me." He rose to his feet. "And now I'll leave you to your work and go catch up on mine. We will talk later. Enjoy your next meeting with Peter."

Shaken by their discussion, Ren found it hard to concentrate the rest of the morning. If it were anyone but Hawk, he'd think the story was exaggerated, but Hawk wasn't an embellisher.

Peter knocked on his door precisely at two, and this time waited for Ren to grant him entry. An hour earlier he'd sent over the copy he'd chosen for the issue, and Ren had read through it several times.

He pointed to the chair. "Have a seat, Peter."

Avoiding his eyes, Peter did as asked, and for all they'd argued earlier, Ren's anger had diminished.

"I read the article, and I agree with you. This story is clearer and more about the animal than the author. Run with it."

Peter raised his gaze. "Seriously?"

"Yeah. I see what you were trying to tell me underneath all your jealousy."

Peter flushed. "I'm sorry for losing my temper. You're right. I was jealous."

"Why? You're a senior copy editor. Samuel trusted you. I want to as well."

He fidgeted. "It's not me…my wife…she's very pushy.

She thought I should've been named editor in chief along with Toni."

"What do you think?"

Peter lifted a shoulder. "I don't think I'm ready. But Hailey says I need to be a go-getter and show that I'm looking for bigger and better things."

"It's nice to have a partner who believes in you, but you should be able to make your own decisions." Recalling what Hawk said, Ren decided to delve deeper. "How did you two meet?"

Peter gnawed his lower lip. "Uh, I was in rehab, and she was one of the group counselors. Not mine, because that wouldn't be cool, but after I left, she contacted me and we started dating. She's done so much for me—kept me straight and helped me find a job when I came out. I owe her everything."

"How did you get this job?"

"I was at the Bronx Zoo one afternoon. I just had to get away. I sat by the lions' area, and they were so beautiful and majestic. I started writing. Samuel sat next to me, and we started talking. He had a way of drawing things out of you that you never meant to talk about, but there was never any judgment about my past. He offered me a job as a copy editor."

A lump rose in his throat. He knew. So well. "Yeah. Samuel was like that."

"Before I got hooked on oxy, I wanted to be a writer. I graduated with an English degree from CUNY and had a job as an editorial assistant. I had a fiancée and a great future. Then the accident happened. I was hit by an out-of-state driver with no insurance. I had a fractured spine and was in so much pain. Oxy helped, but I kept needing more and more. I lost the woman I loved, my job, my apartment… basically my life. For three months I lived on the streets, begging for money, until someone from a social services agency offered me a chance at rehab. I was so sick, I knew it was my last chance. That or death."

A chill ran through him at Peter's words. "I think you're stronger than you know. And I hope we can put this behind us now and learn to work together. I'm not here to take Samuel's place. I'm here to continue his legacy and move the magazine forward. I'm always interested in new ideas. But Peter, you need to stand on your own feet in your marriage as well as you did here this morning. One person should never control the other. It should be equal."

"I don't want to lose Hailey." He blinked rapidly. "She says if she's not around, I'll start using again."

"Is that what you think?" Ren didn't like what he was hearing.

"No. Never." The answer came swiftly, putting Ren at ease.

"Tell her that. Be strong."

"Samuel said the same thing," Peter whispered. "And Toni told me if Hailey leaves me, they'd help me. That the magazine was like a family."

Lead by example. And he'd had the best teacher in Samuel to emulate. Ren smiled. "Nothing's changed in that respect. Now let's get these articles sorted and put together the magazine."

Peter mustered a grin. "You got it, Boss."

On the drive home, it hit him that Samuel had created a magazine made up of the outcasts in society—Hawk, Peter, and himself had all lived through the darkness, and thanks to their inner strength and the love and support of Samuel and Toni, had come out better on the other side of midnight. They truly were the family he'd never had, and he vowed to continue not only showcasing the animals disappearing from the planet, but the people who were tossed aside and rejected, through no fault of their own.

When he opened the door and saw the lights on, he

called out, "Schaeffer?"

"Be right out."

Thrilled he was home early but concerned it wasn't by choice, Ren waited, on edge to hear what happened. Schaeffer finally appeared, still in his uniform.

"Happy you're home, but you weren't supposed to be getting in until tomorrow. Everything okay?"

"Yeah. Mechanical difficulties in Austin, so I got to come home a day early. With the move and everything else, I got another first officer to take my shift."

"So you can be home with me."

Schaeffer held him close and rested his forehead to Ren's. "So I can be home with you. The only place I want to be."

Thinking of the remarkable conversations he'd had today, Ren knew how lucky he was.

CHAPTER TWENTY-TWO

"Good morning."

He rolled over and found Ren already dressed, with a camera around his neck and a smile as bright as the sunlight peeking through the blinds.

"Up early again?" He shifted to sit up and stretched.

"I can't help it. I woke up at six and wanted to see the beach at sunrise. I walked about two miles, found a tumble of rocks where some crabs were scuttling in and out of the water, and I had a great time taking pictures of them and the birds."

"I'm glad. I knew living at the beach would be good for you." His heart warm, Schaeffer swung his legs over the side of the bed, and Ren followed him into the bathroom.

"I love it. No matter where I am, I'm drawn to the sight of the ocean and I love listening to the waves."

He brushed his teeth and met Ren's eyes in the mirror. "You may not be as happy come winter, but we'll manage."

"I've spent January in the Himalayas. I think I can deal with it." He leaned against the vanity.

Schaeffer sniffed. "Do I smell coffee?"

"Oh, you're getting more than that. I made a breakfast run after I finished shooting at the beach."

He entered the living room and saw a whole spread on the kitchen island. There were bagels, lox, cream cheese, tomatoes, and onions. "Damn, old-school Sunday morning." He picked up half an onion bagel and tore off a bite. "God, these are amazing."

"Max Bialystok & Company. Doesn't get much better than them." Ren swiped a bite of Schaeffer's bagel, and Schaeffer jumped out of his reach.

"Don't even think of it." He shoved more of the bagel into his mouth. "What's with the big brunch?"

"I met Ron Vance on the beach this morning. We got to talking about the complaint and investigation, and he said he wanted to have a meeting. So I offered the apartment. And we might as well eat."

"A meeting? About what?" He finished his bagel. "I'm guessing about the complaint."

"He didn't say, but that makes sense." Ren poured himself coffee and took a sip. "He'll be here at noon."

Schaeffer checked his watch. "It's ten forty-five. I'm going to take a shower."

Ren gulped his coffee down. "Funny, so am I. And as a conservationist, I believe in saving water."

They stripped off their clothes and entered the bathroom. Schaeffer turned on the water, and they stepped under the spray. He kissed Ren hard, pressing him against the cool tile wall. Ren tangled his fingers in the wet hair curling at Schaeffer's neck.

"I can never get enough of you," Ren said. "I used to hate snow, but I'll always be so damn grateful for that storm that brought me to you."

"Whatever this complaint brings in the end, as long as I have you, I'm happy. I can find a job anywhere, doing anything, but I'll never be able to find another you."

"I love you. So damn much." Ren sought his lips, and they kissed.

"I love you. Now. Tomorrow. Forever."

They washed off and dried themselves with their fluffy new towels. Once dressed, he made a fresh pot of coffee and then paced, his nervous energy needing space to work itself free.

The buzzer sounded and he ran to press it.

"It's Ron."

Less than two minutes later, the doorbell rang, and when he opened the door, Ron stood waiting, but that wasn't what made Schaeffer's jaw drop. Four other people stood with him, none of whom he recognized.

"Come on in."

"I hope you don't mind, Schaeffer, but I've brought reinforcements. Let me introduce you." The five of them walked inside.

"This is Burton Roberts, head of the NGPA." A man in his midfifties with salt-and-pepper hair and an easy smile shook his hand.

"Schaeffer, nice to meet you."

"Nice to meet you as well."

"Casey Hardin," a second person introduced himself. He was tall, thin, and blond. "First officer, as well."

"Joe Desmond." A Black man in his late thirties or early forties nodded to him. "Captain with RWB for six years."

"Al Goldberg." The oldest man of the group waved at him. "Retired captain with twenty-seven years at RWB." His jet-black hair was swept back from a pronounced widow's peak, and sharp brown eyes met his from behind black-framed glasses.

"Nice to meet you all, though I'm not really sure what

this is all about. But please, sit down. We have bagels and lox and coffee."

"It was worth the drive from Mamaroneck for a real New York bagel," Goldberg joked. "I never come into the city if I can help it."

They gathered around the island, and after the coffee was poured and the cream cheese spread, Ron fixed him with a frown.

"I'm sorry if you think I'm out of line, but after talk started circulating about O'Brian's complaint, I spoke with Burt here. We started together and we're pretty close. I know you were tight-lipped about your personal life, but I gather that's changed?"

"Yeah. I'm not willing to hide who I am anymore. I don't care what bigots like O'Brian think. I never should have."

"Sometimes we need to step out of our heads to see what's important," Hardin spoke up. "I also hid my sexuality until I decided my mental health was more important than someone who thinks I don't deserve the right to exist. Once I did, it all became easier. My second flight was with O'Brian, and he's a nasty SOB. Wouldn't stop talking about the queers ruining the country and how glad he was that he lived in a state with real men. I laughed and asked him if he didn't think gay men lived in Texas, and he smirked and said, 'Not for very long.' "

"And you didn't say anything? Not that I'm one to criticize, just curious." Schaeffer had no right to question anyone when he'd been in the closet for so long.

"I didn't, no. But I asked never to be assigned to work with him again, and I joined NGPA." Hardin braced his hands on the island. "We don't have to take his crap, Schaeffer."

"I personally have experienced his racism—he claimed Black pilots are only hired to make the airline look good and that we aren't as well trained as others." A slight smile lifted Desmond's lips. "He might be right about the airline hiring us to make them look good, but I'll be damned if I let him say I'm not as qualified as anyone else."

Goldberg finished chewing his bagel. "For twenty years I've heard the name-calling and slurs about all of us—Blacks, Jews, gays…I complained a few times, but back in the day it went in one ear and out the other. It's hard to stand up and do the right thing, Schaeffer, because it feels like you become a target. But ridding the airline of a cancer like O'Brian will show others that change can happen. I think we've learned throughout history that if we remain silent, we're the only ones who lose." He took a sip of his coffee. "All of us have come here to tell you that we've gone to Human Resources to file our own complaints about O'Brian. I'm retired, so my complaint most likely won't be allowed because it happened too many years ago, but I'm also here for moral support. O'Brian's days are numbered. Mark my words."

They all nodded in agreement, and for the first time, Schaeffer felt a comradery with the people he worked with. Ren sat next to him, a hand resting casually on his thigh, and a future he'd almost given up on now seemed closer than ever.

"Listen," Desmond said. "I can't hide the fact that I'm Black. And I'm damn well sure not going to make it easy for him to show his face."

Burton spoke up for the first time. "You're not as alone as you think, Schaeffer. The number of LGBTQ pilots has increased every year, and we're becoming an important group in the industry. We have legal teams at the ready, should the airline not handle this case to your satisfaction."

"What do you want? Do you know? Have they asked you?" Ren's questions raised an interesting point.

"No, actually, they haven't, which concerns me." He faced Burton. "Don't you think if they were going to rule in my favor, they'd want to talk to me?"

"I think when it comes to these kinds of accusations and the seriousness of the charges, the airline is going to do its due diligence and interview as many people as possible."

"Makes sense," he admitted, albeit begrudgingly. "But I do want to thank you all for coming here today and sharing your stories and willingness to go to bat for a total stranger."

"We're not strangers. We're all family." Goldberg took another half a bagel. "Airline family and the family of man." He spread a hefty chunk of cream cheese and plopped a hunk of lox on top. Schaeffer grinned, and Goldberg caught his eye. "Remember. Family doesn't rat out their elders. Especially to their wives. Shari would kill me four times over if she knew I was eating this."

Schaeffer put his hands up as the rest of them laughed. "Hey, I don't see anything."

Ron waited until they settled down, then hitched his chair toward Schaeffer. "I have a friend in Human Resources, and I've heard the complaint is being taken very seriously and they've already collected a lot of evidence. There's enough against O'Brian, not only from everyone here, but the crew from that Dallas flight where you were the first officer. We're going to get this bastard and make sure he never pulls this shit on anyone again. I wanted you to know you're not alone, and after this is over, we'll still be there for you, and each other."

"He's never said anything to you before, has he?" Schaeffer was curious.

Ron's eyes narrowed to hard slits. "We were in the break room a few weeks ago. I was early for a flight, so I was checking my trip reports. He sits at the opposite end of the table with someone else and starts commenting on gay marriage and how it should've stayed illegal, and that they shouldn't be allowed to have kids. I was already supporting your complaint, but I decided right then to actively make sure that bastard doesn't have a job by the time this investigation is over."

Hearing Ron's story, the last fragments of doubt and concern melted away. No more would he be ashamed of who he was or who he loved. Seeing Ren chat with the other men, Schaeffer realized he had one life to live, and he could choose to hide and hurt himself, or overcome his fear and show the world how proud he was. Because he could never be ashamed of loving Ren.

"I'm hopeful it will all turn out the way we want, and the airline can rid itself of someone like O'Brian."

"Don't expect him to go away without a fight," Goldberg said darkly, all earlier traces of his easy good nature gone. "People like him, the ones who've been allowed to go unchecked for years, tend to think they're invincible. They believe in their narrative. But don't worry. Every year, less and less people are afraid to speak the truth."

Goldberg's words replayed in Schaeffer's mind when he received an email two days later, inviting him to a video conference with Danita Washington. His bags sat packed and ready for a late flight out to Denver, and Ren was at the magazine. He texted Ren to tell him, and Ren called immediately.

"I'm coming home."

"Why?"

"Because you shouldn't be alone when you talk to her. What if something upsets you? I should be there with you."

"You should be at your job. You have a magazine to put out. I'm a big boy. I can handle it myself."

"I know you're a big boy—you prove that to me every night and most mornings. And I like handling you." Ren's low, sultry words sent a thrill of desire through him. "But I don't like the thought of you alone, listening to whatever she has to tell you."

"I promise to call you as soon as I finish speaking with her," Schaeffer reassured him. "I can't imagine it will be news I don't want to hear."

"I hope so, but I never assume anything. Dammit, I hate being here when you're there."

Love welled in his chest. "I love you, and that's all the support I need, whether you're with me in the room or not."

"You're in my heart. I carry you with me wherever I am."

After reassuring Ren again that he could handle the call on his own, Schaeffer puttered around the apartment and took a walk on the beach. Chilly as it was, the pounding waves and fresh salt air helped clear his head, and he returned to the apartment for the meeting, convinced he would prevail.

At two, he logged on to his computer and answered the video call. Danita Washington appeared on the screen, her face, as always, revealing nothing.

"Thank you for meeting with me on such short notice, Mr. Morgan."

"It's not a problem. I have a flight tonight but not until later."

"I'll get right into it. We've interviewed a number of people O'Brian gave us for his defense—captains and flight attendants you've worked with over the years. Only one person has backed up his claim, and before you ask, no, I can't tell you who."

"May I ask what they claimed I said?"

"It was more your demeanor—overly friendly with the male flight attendants was how they put it."

Face burning, Schaeffer took a deep breath and fought for control. "Okay, go ahead. I hope you know that's patently false."

"In your defense," Washington continued, ignoring his comment, "we had over twelve employees come forward to be interviewed, and twenty more provided written statements claiming they too were harassed or intimidated by Captain O'Brian."

Justified but angry, Schaeffer crossed his arms. "And

so? What happens now?"

"We're having a meeting with O'Brian and his union rep right after this phone call. He'll be informed of all the evidence and asked to retire, and if not, he'll be charged."

Schaeffer sighed with frustration. "So in reality, nothing will happen to him, because of course he'll retire. He gets off scot-free, and nothing will change."

"Not exactly. He'll be told that in order to retire, he must admit his wrongdoing, and there will be a disciplinary record on his file. All RWB members will have to undergo sensitivity training, and we're making our reporting methods much easier with online forms and offices in every hub city, staffed with people to take complaints."

An unsatisfying ending, but Schaeffer hadn't expected much more. "Thanks, Ms. Washington. I appreciate your quick response to this."

"I know you're unhappy with the results. But it is better to have someone like O'Brian out of the picture. He'll know that the reason he was forced to retire was his own bad behavior, and so will others."

"I guess I'll have to learn to live with it."

"I'll inform you by email of the outcome of the meeting. Thank you."

"Thanks. Bye."

He closed the screen and sat for a moment. Did he care that O'Brian would be able to retire? Not as much as he was glad to know he'd never fly with RWB or any other airline, most likely. He was grateful for the people who'd taken a risk to go up against an older, well-established pilot who thought he was invincible and speak their truth. He was thankful for a family that had always stood by him and for a partner he loved and trusted.

Speaking of…he picked up his phone, and he didn't even hear it ring before he had Ren's anxious voice in his ear.

"Well? What happened?"

After he relayed the conversation with Danita Washington, Ren huffed out his displeasure.

"They're getting away easy. You could've sued them and won big, and they know it."

"I have no desire to sue anyone. All I want is to be able to do what I love."

"You mean me?" Ren teased. "You do me every day."

"You're a who, not a what, silly." He laughed, and as always, talking with Ren made everything better. "By the way, you do remember we fly out next week to California for Thanksgiving?"

"Do I ever. Kendra put me on potato duty—mashed and sweet."

"Just so you know, those happen to be my father's favorite part of the meal, along with the stuffing."

"Uhhh, are you trying to freak me out?"

"You'll do great. He loves you. Everyone does."

"All that matters is that you love me."

"Every single hour of every single day. Now I have to get ready to fly out tonight. I'll call you when we land."

"I'll be waiting. Maybe we can have video sex."

"I'm beginning to think you have a one-track mind."

"Nope. I think about things other than having sex with you. Like the wild animals I used to see. Did I ever show you my photos of mating lions? And did you know that a male lion will have sex with a lioness in heat up to fifty times in twenty-four hours?"

"That poor female." Schaeffer chuckled.

"I'm only asking for about fifteen minutes. Imagine having to get hard fifty times in one day."

"It's easy to be hard around you."

Ren snorted. "God, that was bad. Go fly your plane. I'll talk to you later."

"Love you."

"Love you too."

Ren had made him superstitious about their farewells, but all he had to do was look into his eyes and see forever. And forever meant no goodbyes.

CHAPTER TWENTY-THREE

They touched down in Santa Ana a little after noon, and Ren yawned. "God, I hate sleeping on planes."

Schaeffer gawked at him in amazement. "You were out as soon as we hit thirty-four thousand feet. My shoulder is numb."

He poked Schaeffer. "Stop whining. Let's go get the car."

They took their carry-ons from the overhead bin, and within ten minutes were on the freeway. Schaeffer drove while Ren stared out of the open window.

"Have you really not celebrated the holidays since Chris and Kevin?"

It was a chilly day in Southern California, and Ren drew close his leather jacket with the shearling collar. It had traveled with him all around the world, and as battered as it was, he found comfort in it. "Yeah. I made sure to cover for people who had families and actual places to go to celebrate. Samuel and Toni would always invite me, but I didn't want to intrude on their family time."

Schaeffer took his hand and squeezed it. "We'll make this one special."

"It already is."

It wasn't simply talk. In Kendra and Anson, he'd discovered the true meaning of family, and he loved their weekly FaceTimes, where they'd catch up on their lives. The kids had readily accepted him, and he planned on taking tons of pictures during the week they were there. Mini had a dance competition, Scotty had a swim meet, and Ren would be there cheering them on.

"How are you feeling about what happened with O'Brian? I can't believe he's choosing to go ahead with a trial and everything, rather than retire."

"I can," Schaeffer said grimly as he switched lanes. "Which made my decision to take some time off even easier. I gave my testimony, and frankly, I have no desire to sit in the flight deck, wondering what the captain is thinking. The time away will do me good."

Ren leaned over to kiss his cheek. "It'll do me good too. I get my man all to myself. No flying off for half the month."

"Does it bother you more, now that you're home all the time? You can tell me the truth."

"No. Of course I miss you like hell, but I'm so busy, my time isn't even my own. Plus, I'm tired at night, so I just grab something to eat, take a shower, and go to bed. The weekends give me a chance to recharge, and I've been taking my camera out and getting some good shots."

"Now we get to share that for a while."

"Can't wait. Maybe I can scare up a few days away."

Schaeffer's bright smile was all he needed to make a note to himself to do exactly that.

When they pulled up to Anson and Kendra's house, the door opened and the kids ran out yelling, "They're here." Mini ran to him, and Scotty to Schaeffer. He picked her up and hugged her tight.

"You got so tall, I don't think we can call you Mini anymore. Maybe Biggie is a better name."

She giggled. "You're so funny, Uncle Ren."

He froze and let her down gently so she could greet Schaeffer. Scotty ran up to him next.

"Uncle Ren, I took so many cool pictures of the lions at the zoo. Wait till I show you."

"Can't wait to see them, buddy," he replied faintly.

Kendra nodded, her eyes tender.

"Mini's been telling everyone at school all week that her uncle who takes the animal pictures is coming. And Scotty asked for a camera for Christmas so he can learn to take cool animal pictures like his uncle Ren. They love you and missed you. Like we did."

She wrapped her arms around him, and he held her close. "Thank you. That means more than you'll ever know."

"Oh, honey, I do."

Schaeffer hugged Kendra, and Anson slung an arm over Ren's shoulder.

"So how's the big-shot magazine editor doing, huh?"

"Not sure about being a big-shot, but I'm enjoying learning a different side of the business."

"Do you miss going out and taking the pictures?"

Before he could answer, a voice called out from behind them, "Stop hogging the merchandise. Let a father say hello to his boys."

All smiles, Walter walked out, a bit grayer than the last time. Schaeffer caught Ren's eye and winked, but Ren couldn't even respond. The impact of Walter's words—*his boys*—left him speechless and blinking back tears. Once again, he saw that little boy sitting in one of his foster homes on the couch, wishing he could have a family like the kind he watched on television. Walter hugged Schaeffer first, then approached him.

"How's the famous editor?"

"I don't know," Ren joked, looking over his shoulder. "When you see one, let me know."

Walter brushed him off. "Jokester. Schaeffer's been telling me about all the work you're putting in. I'm very impressed. I'm sure you're doing a great job. I can't wait to get the next issue to see your name on the masthead."

It touched him that Walter had taken an interest in his work. Knowing Walter's reservations about his globe-hopping—understandable, as his disappearances for months at a time would make a relationship hard to navigate—Ren had been a little intimidated, despite Schaeffer's assurances that his father truly liked him. All Walter's concerns seemed to have been washed away by Ren stepping into the role of editor in chief and choosing stability over the impromptu lifestyle he'd lived for so long.

"Thanks, Walter. That means everything to me."

They traipsed into the house, Anson helping him with his bag, as Ren had brought along his photo equipment. Schaeffer wheeled in his own suitcase. They were staying with Walter, but Kendra had prepared a welcome dinner, so the plan was for a lazy day spent in the backyard, hanging out with the kids. If anyone had told him a year ago that he would be in love, living with the man of his dreams, and spending the holidays with a family who considered him their own, Ren would've told them they were high. Now it was coming up on the anniversary of the snowstorm, and with Samuel gone, he was almost afraid to think where he would have ended up without that serendipitous meeting.

Kendra had a beautiful breakfast spread ready, and he accepted the cup of coffee from her. "Thanks, gorgeous."

"Are you ready for tomorrow? First holiday with the family can be a little overwhelming. Even this family."

Ren watched as Schaeffer and his brother and father were pulled into the backyard by Scotty, who wanted to show them his prowess at the backstroke.

"Is that how it was for you?" he asked Kendra. They'd touched only briefly on her chaotic home life as a child. "Did you ever feel…"

"Not good enough? Like I didn't belong?" Her brow wrinkled. "As much as Anson loves me—and Walter never made me feel uncomfortable—I was wary. When we married, we'd go to Aunt Eileen's house—Walter's sister. Her husband died years before Anson and I married. Eileen was sort of a *grande dame* and would always have a big group for the holiday. Let me tell you, it isn't easy being the only Black one at the table."

"Did people say hurtful things?"

"Nothing was ever said in earshot of Eileen or Anson. They made sure of it. But there were comments in passing. 'You're so lucky you don't have to worry about sun damage to your skin,' or, 'What do you do to get your hair so straight?' Subtle, but othering, if you know what I mean."

Ren did. His experience was as a gay man, but the "separate but equal" remarks he'd heard through the years always made him feel different.

"And you never told Anson?"

"And start a war? Honey, that man would've marched into that group of women and said some things he couldn't take back. They were old and foolish and set in their ways and weren't going to change for the likes of me. Maybe I was wrong, but I didn't want that. Besides, once Eileen passed, I never had to see those ladies again. Now I have a wonderful group of friends, and I never have to think twice."

"You're a good person."

"Not that good," Kendra said with a mischievous twinkle. "One lady once asked me for a recipe for fried chicken. I have never made it in my life, but I said I'd email it to her and looked up a recipe online that called for Scotch bonnet peppers to be chopped up in the crumbs."

Her eyes danced. "I doubled the amount. She never spoke to me again."

He busted out laughing. "I love you."

She set her coffee mug on the counter. "I love you too. We all do. I've never seen Schaeffer so happy and content. We know something bad happened to him in the Air Force, but he refused to talk about it. Now? He's like a new man, freed from whatever pain was dogging him."

A chorus of clapping and cheers sounded from outside, and a dripping-wet Scotty rushed in.

"Mommy, Uncle Ren, come on. I want you to see me swim too."

"We're coming, sweetie." Kendra took Ren's arm as they joined the others. "You belong here. With us. Don't ever forget it."

Thanksgiving Day, Ren awoke and left Schaeffer sleeping. He showered and took his cameras and found Walter in the backyard, watering his roses.

"Mind if I take a few pictures?"

"Of me?" Walter turned off the hose.

"Yeah. This time I'm not after the animals. I'm commemorating the holidays."

Walter's thoughtful gaze rested on him for a moment. "Sure," he said gently. "Take any pictures you want."

He snapped freely, and though he'd thought he wouldn't capture any wildlife, the gentle flutter of a monarch butterfly's wings caught his eye. Walter's flowers and bird feeder attracted a host of colorful species, and before long, he'd become caught up in their activities and taken a slew of photos of hummingbirds, goldfinches, and blue jays. When he finished, he found Walter watching him. Through the glass sliders he saw Schaeffer drinking his coffee, making no attempt to come outside and join them. Ren guessed he was giving Walter and him time together.

"I've never seen you in action like that, only around the family."

Heat rose to his face. "Sorry, I kind of forgot I wasn't on the job."

"Don't apologize. I was fascinated. You were so into it, I don't think you even remembered I was here."

His lips twitched. "Yeah, you're right. I get in the zone and lose all track of time."

"I'd love to see them." Walter had put away the hose and stood waiting. "But now we'd better get ready to go. Kendra has our chores lined up, and I don't want to be late." He eyed Ren. "I hear you're in charge of the potatoes this year."

Ren gulped. "Yeah. I'm going to try my best."

"See that you do," Walter growled playfully. "I'll be tasting for sure."

Once inside, Schaeffer handed him a bagel, but he only took a few bites. He wasn't that hungry. "I'm saving my appetite. I'm going to get ready."

Schaeffer trailed behind him and sat on the bed as Ren placed his cameras inside their cases. "You and my dad had a nice talk?"

"Kind of. I was surprised to hear he subscribed to *Nature's Beauty*."

"He's into everything us kids were, and now with Mini and Scotty, he makes sure he goes to all their meets and competitions. He'll drive them if Kendra or Anson can't, and makes sure to take them out for ice cream after each time. As a father, he was overwhelmed being the solo caretaker and wasn't always sure how to handle us, but as a grandfather, he's the best."

Ren kissed him. "I think you both turned out pretty

great. You especially."

Schaeffer held him close and nuzzled his neck. "Yeah? I think you're pretty great as well."

Heat blazed through him. Maybe they had time for a quickie, and he pushed Schaeffer onto the mattress.

"You boys ready?" Walter called from the hall. "Don't want to be late."

Guess not.

Schaeffer's eyes twinkled. "Keep it for later."

Laughing, Ren pressed another kiss to his lips. "I love that you can read my mind."

Schaeffer patted his ass. "It's not your mind, trust me."

Dinner preparation was in full swing when they arrived at Anson and Kendra's, and Ren was put to work right away with the potatoes. He pulled up the recipes he'd found online. Schaeffer and Anson were in charge of the prime rib and stuffing, and Kendra had the turkey and apple pies going.

"This place smells amazing." Ren mashed the potatoes and poured in the fried onions, butter, and sour cream. "I can't wait to eat."

"Don't think we haven't noticed you taste-testing all along the way," Schaeffer teased.

"Hey," he protested. "Just making sure it's good enough for Walter."

"Now that's what I like to hear," Walter called out.

Finally everything was ready, and they sat at the table. All but Walter, who remained standing with his glass of wine in hand.

"You have no idea how grateful I am to have everyone I love at this table. There were some terrible times, hard times, but through it all, we knew we always had each other to come home to. And the best thing for me is to see how we've grown over the years. First Anson brought home Kendra, my darling daughter. Next, Scotty and Mini, the two lights of my life. They give me a reason to get up every day, knowing I get to see them. And now we have Ren, who's dazzled us with his photographs and hopefully his potatoes."

They all laughed but him. He knew if he opened his mouth, he'd start crying.

Walter wasn't finished. "Most importantly, Ren is the partner I always wanted for Schaeffer. Someone who loves him unconditionally and never wants to change him."

A warm hand curved around his nape, and his shattered pieces settled like stars in Orion's Belt. All he was then, and all he was now, could only be the foundation for who he and Schaeffer were meant to be.

"We're very happy we're all able to be together." Schaeffer lifted his wineglass. "And thank you, Dad, for doing everything you have over the years for all of us. Now you get to sit back and reap the rewards."

Walter settled into his seat and rubbed his hands. "Which I plan to do right now. Hand me those sweet potatoes." Ren watched as Walter took a bite and his brows flew up. A smile broke over his face. "They're delicious. Are you sure you made these?"

"I did. Try the mashed. They've got fried onions, and I was told those are your favorite."

"Buttering me up with mashed potatoes. Smart."

Platters of food were passed, but Ren didn't need the turkey with all the trimmings. His heart had never been so full.

CHAPTER TWENTY-FOUR

"Oh God, I think I gained ten pounds this week," Ren groaned, and Schaeffer grabbed his hip and gave a squeeze.

"*Mmm*. More of you to love."

"We need to start exercising." Ren pushed him and jumped out of bed. "Let's go biking."

Schaeffer held out his hand. "I know something better that'll use up calories and is way more fun."

Ren snickered. "Your father's up, and you know you get noisy." Blood rushed to Schaeffer's face, and Ren winked. "Wait until tonight when he's asleep." His phone rang, and with a frown, he answered it. "Toni? What's up? Everything okay?" He listened for a few moments. "Hold on, hold on. Let me put you on speaker. I'm here with Schaeffer."

Toni's voice filled the room. "I hate to bother you while you're away with your family, but we have a little emergency."

Schaeffer didn't know why Ren wanted him to listen in

on his conversation with Toni, but he decided he might as well be productive, so he left their bed and picked out his clothes for the day's outing.

"What do you need from me?" Ren sat on the recently vacated bed.

"Doug was with his family for Thanksgiving in Vermont, and they took a trip to Canada for some skiing. He fell and broke his arm and ankle."

"Ouch, shit. That sucks." Wincing, Ren's eyes widened. "Oh, crap. He was supposed to go to Florida to see if he could find the panther for the summer issue."

"That's right. And everyone else is already on assignment. I have a favor to ask."

Schaeffer had an idea what Toni wanted.

"You want me to go to Florida in Doug's stead."

"Is that a possibility?"

Ren cut a glance to him, and Schaeffer could see a hint of longing in his eyes. He nodded and mouthed, *Do it.*

Ren wriggled his fingers between the two of them. "I'd love to. But I'd like to take Schaeffer with me. He's got the next few weeks off, and I'd planned some alone time for us. And nothing says alone time more than the possibility of weeks cooped up in a blind, waiting for an endangered wild animal to appear."

It was nice to hear Toni laugh. "I think it's a great idea. I used to love going with Samuel when we first started out."

Schaeffer's jaw dropped as a thrill raced through him. Go on a shoot with Ren? How amazing would that be? He'd get to see Ren in action and spend day and night with him, like their first time in the hotel. Before they knew each other and fell in love. He nodded with vigor, and Ren gave him a thumbs-up.

"He said yes. We have another two days here, and then we can fly directly to Florida. I'll pick up some equipment for us. Good thing I brought my cameras."

Ren was like a kid on Christmas Day, his excitement palpable, and after he ended the call with Toni, Schaeffer caught him by the arm.

"So you do miss it. I knew that would happen."

"Are you kidding me?" Ren gaped at him. "I'm excited at the prospect of spending time alone, just the two of us. How awesome is that going to be? I get to show you my world and have you at my side."

"I can't wait to see it all. Everything. I want to learn as much about your world as I can, since we've been so wrapped up in mine with complaints and ugliness." He kissed Ren's cheek. "Besides, Florida's pretty nice this time of year."

"How many days of rain has it been?" Schaeffer asked, huddled in their blind somewhere in Collier County, Florida. The incessant *drip, drip, drip* against their tiny space hadn't abated in what seemed like forever.

Ren shrugged. "Three? Four? I don't know. Don't worry. They say it'll stop soon, and then we'll have a good chance to see the cats. They like to come out after a good storm— it tends to flush out the smaller animals who've been in hiding." He squeezed Schaeffer's arm. "This is the not-so-glamorous part of the job that no one likes to hear about."

"It's not all bad. I get to be here with you." He cast a rueful glance around their tight quarters. "It must be love if we can share this and still not kill each other."

Ren cocked his head. "Wait. Listen. Do you hear that?"

Schaeffer waited, but all he heard was birdsong. "No. I don't hear anything."

Ren grinned and grabbed his camera. "Exactly. The

rain stopped. See, I told you good things come to those who wait."

Disbelieving, Schaeffer stuck his head out of the blind and blinked. White clouds scuttled along the blue, blue sky, and they were surrounded by a sea of lush, green foliage, sparkling in the now-bright sunlight. He breathed deep of the fresh, clean air.

"God, it's gorgeous. Nothing but us and the land."

Ren snorted. "Don't you believe it. Try a billion mosquitos, other weird and ugly bugs, alligators, snakes, birds, lizards, and hopefully a panther or two."

"Sounds…great," he said, his gaze darting about wildly in case one of those reptiles Ren mentioned decided to make an appearance.

"Aw, don't worry. I'll protect you," Ren cackled and kissed the back of his neck. "I'm going to take a walk, then get set up. Want to come with me?"

"Sure."

Hand in hand, they exited the blind, and for the first time since they landed, Schaeffer surveyed their area. Although less than 250 panthers were known to be in the wild, they'd been spotted most frequently in this part of Florida. Ren had explained that the rapid population growth had encroached on the big cat's habitat, and cars were their number one cause of death.

They tramped through the grassy area, and Schaeffer lifted his face to the sun, soaking in its warmth. After a two-mile hike, they returned to the blind, ate lunch, and Schaeffer watched Ren set up his equipment. There was little to no cell service, so he'd made sure to download enough books.

"How long do you think we'll be out here?"

Ren, who was focusing his camera through the slit in the blind, peered over his shoulder. "Getting tired of me already?"

"Never. Just wondering if we're going to be here past

Christmas."

"Definitely not. If I don't get the shot, we can either use something else, or I can come down here in the winter and try again. I'm not going to cancel Christmas with your family. I've been looking forward to having them come visit. Think positive. We'll get what we came for and be home by next week at the latest."

His brother and father hadn't been home to New York since his mother died, and Kendra and the kids had never been, so Schaeffer had a full itinerary planned. Wintertime in the city could be magical, and he wanted to share it all with his family.

"I hope so, but I don't want you to think I'm not enjoying myself." He slipped his arms around Ren's waist and kissed his nape. "I love spending time with you and seeing you in your element."

"Hey." Ren turned to face him. "You're my element. My gold standard. The oxygen I need to breathe. The sweet water when my throat turns too dry to tell you I love you enough times so I can never stop saying it. The spark that lights me on fire. The ground beneath my feet to steady my crazy ass when the world spins out of control."

Schaeffer touched his forehead to Ren's. "I love you so much. No matter where you go, I'll follow you."

They kissed, and Schaeffer sucked hungrily at Ren's tongue. The bad weather and confines of their blind hadn't allowed for much in the way of intimacy, but now the familiar longing burst open, and he wanted Ren. His fingers fumbled with Ren's pants, when a growl split the air. Like he'd been burned, Ren jumped from him and ran to the camera perched on its tripod.

"Is it—"

"Shh," Ren cut him off, waving a hand behind him, while the other remained on the camera. "It's a mother with her kitten. God, so beautiful."

Schaeffer remained rooted to the spot, afraid any sound or motion might scare away the big cat. He could hear the rapid clicking of the camera and Ren murmuring to himself. After about three minutes, Ren whispered, "Come here." He crept over to Ren's shoulder. "Look." Ren moved aside, and through the immense telescopic lens, he spied the large, sinuous, tawny cat with a miniature of her running at her heels.

"Oh, wow," he breathed.

Ren took his place behind the camera, but continued to speak. "This is incredible. Almost makes up for that damn fox."

At that moment, the mother panther turned her head and gave them the full force of her amber stare. The kitten also stopped its gamboling behind her, and Schaeffer caught the gleam of blue eyes.

Click, click, click.

"Amazing, right?" Ren's lips brushed his ear. "The kittens are always born blue-eyed."

Before their eyes, the two cats disappeared in the grass, and he and Ren stared at each other. Schaeffer knew he'd seen something rare and beautiful that not many people were privy to.

"Thank you for bringing me with you. Not only for the time spent together, but for opening my eyes to the world around me I might've ignored."

Ren cupped his cheek. "We ignore what's precious, and then in the blink of an eye, it's gone forever. The final goodbye." He touched his lips to Schaeffer's. "Now we can say goodbye to this little spot and go home where we can enjoy ourselves, because I don't know about you, but I'm dying here. Three days lying by your side without touching you is three days too long."

Schaeffer grinned. "Pack up."

"It'll be a year soon," Ren sighed. They'd awakened early, and even though it was cold, they stood on the balcony, watching the sunrise. Ren held him tight, and Schaeffer nuzzled the warm space between his neck and shoulder. They'd been home for ten days and were expecting his family in a week. They had a thousand things to do, but at the moment, all he could think about was kissing Ren.

"Seems like I've loved you forever."

Whole. I'm finally whole.

"Forever isn't nearly enough time," Ren said as they cuddled closer.

"You never told me. Was Toni happy with the panther pictures?"

Like a big cat himself, Ren rubbed against him with a satisfied rumble. "She said if I want to do this, I should take you with me, that you must be my good-luck charm. The pictures, especially the one of the kitten jumping on the mother, are exceptional. It's going on the summer cover."

"I'm glad. I had a great time with you. I'd love to go with you."

"One day."

Something in Ren's tone was off, and from beneath lowered lashes, Schaeffer studied his serious face.

"What's wrong? Do you want to go out on another shoot?"

"Not really. I like learning about the business end of the magazine, and being out in the miserable weather made me realize I don't want to spend weeks cooped up by myself anymore. But it makes me wonder…shouldn't I miss it? I've spent my whole life caring about the animals, and now all I do is sit behind a desk."

"And you think not taking the pictures shows less of a commitment on your part to the cause? Ren, you're getting the stories out there for the people to see. The photos are beautiful, but without the words behind them, people can't know the dire situation. Magazines like yours enable knowledge."

"I suppose."

He rubbed Ren's back, sensing he hadn't yet convinced him. "How about every month or so, when I'm home, we go off somewhere together and you can take pictures, just for you. And for me, because I'm selfish and I love seeing you in action. We can go anywhere you want—Europe, South America…anyplace."

"Just like that? On the fly?" Doubt coupled with interest perked up the sadness in his eyes. "You wouldn't mind that?"

"Are you kidding? A surprise vacation with you to a foreign country? Us together exploring? I'd love it."

Ren's eyes brightened. "We could do that."

Schaeffer kissed him. "We can do anything."

Ren shook with laughter. "Except, apparently, go food-shopping. Because we've both been putting it off for days, and now we have nothing in the house to eat."

He made a face. "Wild elephants and lions are nothing compared to people after a sale on canned tuna at Stop and Shop. Let's go shower and prepare for battle."

He'd begun seeing a therapist and the first two sessions had been a painful journey. Like onion layers, his grief and sense of responsibility waited to be peeled apart and reveal the truths buried in his core.

"How have the nightmares been, Schaeffer?" Dr. Pintano

asked. "Have they diminished at all since we've started our sessions?"

"Yeah. I almost didn't realize it had been a few weeks since I had one, and even when I did, it wasn't all-encompassing and terror filled. It was more a sense of grief and loss."

"And what do you attribute this to?"

"It's not one thing but a combination. I've come out at my job, which was always a terrifying thought."

"And it's going well? No backlash?"

He hadn't gone into great detail about his dealing with O'Brian, so he filled the doctor in on the entirety of the situation.

Dr. Pintano frowned. "I hope you feel safe. With such a high-stress job, it's imperative to have trust in the people you work with."

"I do. People have been very supportive. And frankly, the subject of my sexuality rarely comes up."

"It shouldn't, unless you want it to. It's your prerogative to be able to say—or not say—anything you choose without repercussions."

"I agree, and so does Ren. He's never made a secret of who he is, and I'm trying to adopt that attitude."

The doctor's serious expression softened. "I don't have to ask how your relationship is going. I can see it in your face."

He knew his smile was wide and silly but didn't care. "I've never been happier. I thought I'd be alone forever because I wasn't ready to be free, but once I met Ren, none of it made sense—not the hiding, nor the pretending I'm something I'm not."

"That's good. But Ren didn't solve your problems, you did, by letting go of your fear. You must learn to lean on yourself and your inner strength. It's there, waiting for you."

"I'm trying."

"I know you are. Which is why the nightmares are dissipating. Now, there's no guarantee they'll be gone forever, because everyone experiences suppressed emotions of fear or failure, but our goal is to make them manageable so they don't make it impossible for you to work or sleep."

It made sense. "So I can control them, instead of the other way around. It's normal to have them but then to move on." Intellectually, he knew this, but it was hard to let go of the pain and sense of guilt that dogged his every step.

"Absolutely," Dr. Pintano said firmly. "Each step of our lives will put us in a situation where we question ourselves. But if you inspect what you think is your responsibility, you'll be able to see that neither of the two instances that shaped your life—your mother's death and Steve's—were in your control, and nothing you would've done differently would have changed the outcome."

He hung his head. "I know you're right. But I feel guilty that I was mad at my mother and I never had the chance to say I'm sorry."

"If you could, what would you tell her?"

"That I love her." Tears welled up in his eyes. "And I didn't mean what I said. I miss her, and everything she should've had." He wiped his eyes.

"Let me ask you something. You had arguments with your parents before, right?"

He shrugged. "I mean, yeah, of course. Every kid does."

"And then all was back to normal."

"Yes."

"So this would've been the same. Maybe you would've been punished for disobeying her, and you'd think her mean and unfair, but after a while, it would all have been right between you."

"If she hadn't died, we would've brushed it off. But because I never got that final resolution, I've built it into a huge wall between us." A bit of the great weight pressing on his chest for all these years eased as he spoke.

"Yes, exactly." Eyes bright, Dr. Pintano leaned forward. "And now? What do you think?"

He rubbed his eyes, and in his mind, he could see his mother's smile and feel her hug of approval. "Now I think it's time for me to break the wall down."

Later that evening, as he always did after a session, he talked it out with Ren, who sat listening with shining eyes.

"I think this was my biggest breakthrough session yet. I know I still have things to work out regarding Steve's death, but I don't feel the weight of suffocating guilt when I think about him."

"I am so fucking proud of you." Ren grasped his hands tight. "You're so strong to take this head-on."

"I don't know about that, but it's feeling like the right time now. Instead of the sky weighing so heavily on me, I feel open. Like I can finally rise above it all." He squeezed Ren's hands. "I know the doctor said it wasn't because of you, but I need you to know how much you've helped me. Maybe that snowstorm was fate, putting you in my way so that I could find not only love, but myself. Now we have the rest of our lives together."

"I can't wait to share every moment with you."

And just like that, it was the holidays and their apartment

was filled with family. They'd done the obligatory tour of all the New York City landmarks, and now were watching the kids ice skate at Rockefeller Center. Walter had decided to go inside the coffee shop to wait for them and have something hot to drink. Kendra and Anson were with Mini and Scotty, and Ren had taken a slew of pictures over the course of the day. The next day was Christmas Eve, and it would be a quiet one. They planned to go to the cemetery and visit his mother and Ren's brothers. The kids had been hoping for snow, but though it was cold enough, nothing was forecasted.

"This has been the best week," Ren sighed, dropping next to him. "I think they're having a great time."

"I know they are. I'm just loving doing it all with you."

Ren's eyes sparkled like the lights on the tree towering over them. "That makes it even more special."

Schaeffer held out his phone and took a selfie of them kissing.

"Nothing's more special than you."

A tiny wet flake drifted down and settled on Ren's lashes. Then another. Soon the snow was falling all around them. "Looks like the kids got their wish." Ren waved to them on the rink, and they were pointing up to the sky and laughing.

"They're not the only ones," Schaeffer said and kissed Ren's smiling lips.

EPILOGUE

Six months later

"Come out and see the birds." Camera in hand, Ren stood on the balcony. "The sky is filled with them." Unable to resist, he began to take pictures, capturing the morning flight of black skimmers.

Schaeffer's breath hit his neck. "I brought you coffee and some news."

"What?" He turned to face Schaeffer, whose eyes glowed with excitement as he handed him the mug. "Thanks." He took the mug and waited.

"I just heard from HR. O'Brian lost his final appeal."

Ren knew the case had been winding through the courts, but it was impossible to say when a decision would come down.

"What does that mean? Is he finally gone for good?"

"Yes. The airline plans to terminate him, but they're

guessing he'll put in his retirement papers before that happens."

Ren set his coffee on the table and flung his arms around Schaeffer. "I'm so happy. You must be thrilled."

Schaeffer's eyes brightened. "Yeah. I am. No one will ever have to put up with his behavior again."

"I'm so proud of you," Ren said, enjoying the blush rising up to stain Schaeffer's cheeks. "Tons of people only complain, but you made change happen. It takes courage."

"It was the right thing to do," Schaeffer mumbled.

Ren knew Schaeffer wasn't the type to like the spotlight, but with only the two of them, Schaeffer would hear how wonderful Ren thought he was.

"I'm glad you heard the good news now, instead of during your birthday trip."

"Me too." Schaeffer hummed with pleasure. "Look at the ocean. It's so endless—like possibilities. All we have to do is reach out for them."

"I'll never get tired of it. Makes me grateful to be here."

"I'm grateful too. For you."

Ren chuckled. "I know. I feel it." They sipped their coffee. "You have everything packed for later?"

"Yeah. Only five days away this time, but they're jam-packed. Then I get the days off with you."

"I know. I have your birthday weekend planned."

Schaeffer arched a brow. "So you've said, but you aren't telling me where we're going."

"I'm not. It's a surprise."

"Hmph." Schaeffer's lips trailed along his neck. "How will I know what to bring to wear?"

"Nice try," Ren teased. "Doesn't matter to me. I like you best naked. But you can wear anything you like outdoors."

He knew how much Schaeffer missed his family, and he did as well, so he'd arranged for them to go to California. The kids were out of school and hadn't started camp yet, and best of all, Kendra was off for the summer, so they could all spend lots of time together. He'd managed to rent the same house he'd had the year before when he'd run into Schaeffer. No one except Walter knew they were coming.

He and Walter had become very close. Over Christmas, Ren had confided to everyone about the fire that killed his brothers, and it was Walter's words that gave him the most comfort.

"For years I blamed myself for working and leaving my wife at home, even though that was foolish. I worked. There was no reason for me to stay home. Same with you. It was your birthday trip, and you went out to celebrate. You told your brother to stay away from the space heater, but he didn't listen. Life and death aren't within our control. That's why we have to make the most of the time in between. We never know what's waiting."

That was Walter—hard-line, gruff-talking—but ultimately, it was what Ren needed to fully heal. Every week or so after they'd left, he'd email Walter, sending him the photos he'd taken by the beach or on the trips he and Schaeffer had taken. So far, they'd been to Maine, Nova Scotia, and Iceland, and Ren loved sharing his love of his life's work. In return, Walter, who'd become somewhat of an amateur photographer with Scotty, would send him pictures they'd taken. Then they'd FaceTime, and Ren would give him tips about lighting and angles. It was a relationship he would never have thought possible but which he cherished, and it gave him a fatherly figure now that Samuel was gone.

"Who knew you could be so sneaky?" Schaeffer poked him.

"Come on. Let's go inside and have lunch."

Once they ate and cleaned up, it was time for Schaeffer to leave. Ren kissed him at the door. "I'll see you in a few days. I love you."

"Love you too."

With Schaeffer gone, he finished up the last few bits of their travel detail and got Walter, who always woke up early, on FaceTime. Ren waved at the man in his chair out by the pool. He could see the roses in the background, bobbing in the breeze.

"Everything set?" Walter brought his "Best Grandpa" cup to his lips, and Ren couldn't help smiling.

"All systems go. He's going to be totally surprised once we get to the airport."

"Thank you for this. We haven't been able to celebrate his birthday as a family in a long time."

"I know. He told me it's been years. I'm glad you'll all be together."

"We." Walter frowned. "It might only be a year or so that you two have been a couple, but you're as much a part of this family as Kendra. I've seen Schaeffer open up more now than he has in the past twenty years. I know his mother's death hit him very hard, and I tried my best, but I couldn't break through and get my boy back. You gave him what he needed, and I'll always love you for that."

"Thank you," he whispered.

"All I ever wanted was for my kids to be happy. I might not've gone about everything perfectly, but I tried as best I could, with the world knocked out from under me."

Ren thought about Walter's words. "It must've been awful for you. I know everyone was concentrating on the children, but you lost the person you loved as well."

"Never found anyone like her," he said gruffly. "But I'm good. Have my kids, my grandkids, and my health. That's all I need."

"You never wanted to remarry?"

A quick, firm shake of his head. "No time when they were young, and no desire to now that they're grown. Too old and set in my ways."

"You're never too old for love."

"Now you sound like Kendra, always trying to fix me up with one of her teacher friends at the school."

Ren grinned, imagining how those conversations went. Personally, he thought Walter would enjoy some female company, but he wasn't about to get in the middle of that. Better off leaving that mission to Kendra.

"I'd better get going. I'll see you this weekend."

"Okay. And Schaeffer still has no idea?"

"None." His grin broadened. "I can't wait to see his face when he realizes where we're going."

"Santa Ana? We're going to California?" Schaeffer's joy threatened to overtake his entire face.

"Yeah. I thought six months was long enough between visits. Too long."

"Thank you." Schaeffer hugged him. "I haven't been home for my birthday in over four years. This...you...I love you."

"I love you too."

They both slept on the plane, and Ren woke first, thrilled to see Schaeffer peaceful, without lines of pain etched across his face. The nightmares had faded in both frequency and intensity, and while Ren knew Schaeffer wanted them gone forever, he was aware it would take time. They deplaned, and having no checked bags, went directly to get their rental car. Schaeffer held out his hands for the car keys, but Ren kept them in his grasp.

"Nope. You don't know where we're going." He opened the door and slid into the driver's seat. A smile of pure delight curved Schaeffer's lips as he got in on the passenger side.

"We're not staying with my dad?"

Ren started the car and drove out of the lot. "Nah."

"Anson and Kendra?"

Ren signaled to switch lanes. "Nuh-uh."

Schaeffer huffed. "Okay, then where…*ohhhhh*." His eyes widened when Ren drove onto the 55 Freeway. "The same house?"

Ren nodded. "I figured for your birthday we can come here, and for our anniversary we can rent the room at the hotel airport." He snickered.

"Very funny. But no." Schaeffer rolled his eyes.

Twenty minutes later, they pulled into the driveway of the same house he'd rented the previous year. They entered and left their bags, Schaeffer reaching for his hand. Without a word, they walked the length of the space and opened the glass slider to the deck.

Ren leaned against the railing. "I'll never get tired of hearing the waves. It's my second favorite sound."

Schaeffer stood behind him and rested his cheek to Ren's. "What's your first?"

"You. When we're making love and you call out my name." He faced Schaeffer and kissed him. "That desperate, needy sound turns me on like nothing else."

Schaeffer cupped his jaw. "You'll be hearing that a lot this weekend."

"Why do you think we're staying here? I love your family, but I want to be able to make love to you and hear you scream."

Schaeffer tightened the grip on his chin, and Ren's breath caught at the glittering intensity in his beautiful storm-gray eyes.

"It doesn't matter whether it's a hotel room at the airport or a beach house by the water, you're the only thing I need, Ren. It all makes sense now with you by my side."

"Side by side. Hand in hand." Ren kissed his fingers. "I'll never get tired of walking into forever with you."

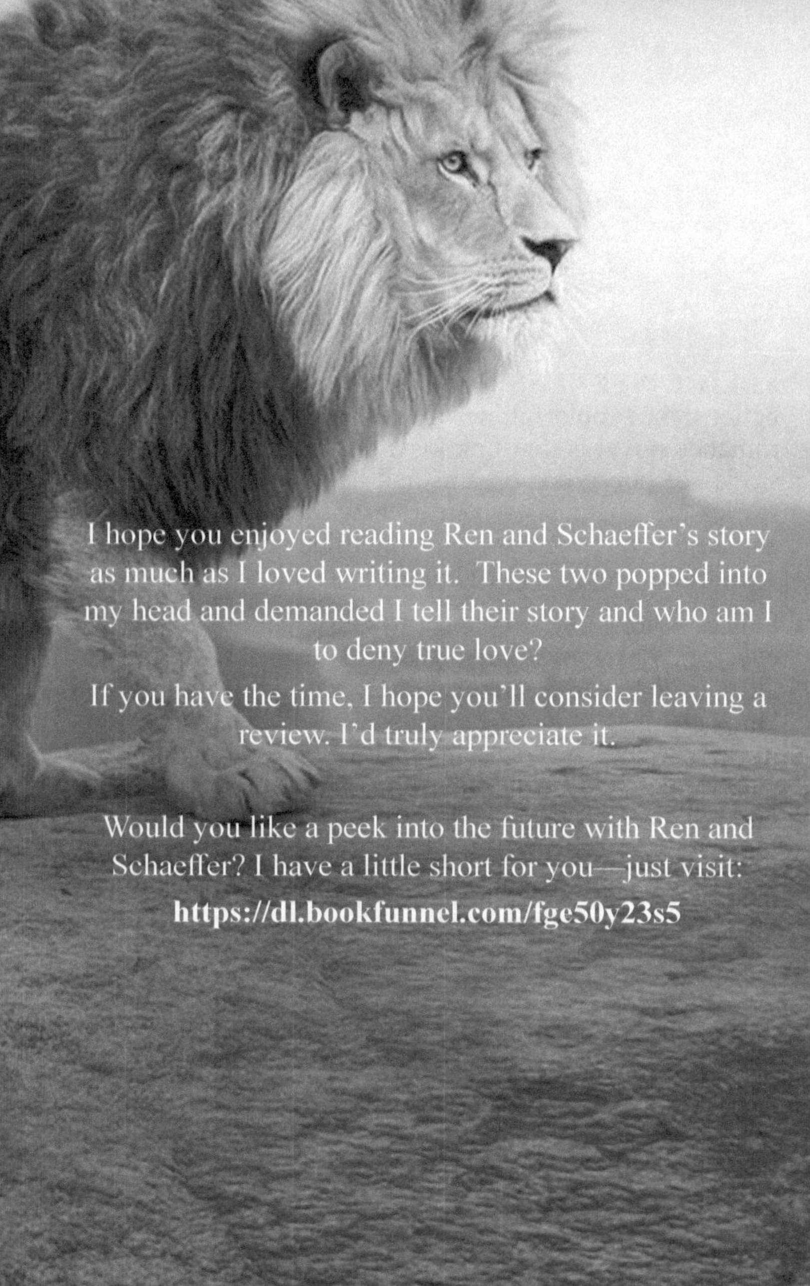

I hope you enjoyed reading Ren and Schaeffer's story as much as I loved writing it. These two popped into my head and demanded I tell their story and who am I to deny true love?

If you have the time, I hope you'll consider leaving a review. I'd truly appreciate it.

Would you like a peek into the future with Ren and Schaeffer? I have a little short for you—just visit:

https://dl.bookfunnel.com/fge50y23s5

FELICE STEVENS writes romance because what is better than people falling in love? Her favorite part of a romance novel is that first kiss…sigh. She loves creating stories of hopes and dreams and happily ever afters. Her stories are character-driven, rich with the sights, sounds and flavors of New York City and filled with men who are sometimes deeply flawed but always real.

Felice writes gay romance because she believes that everyone deserves a happily ever after. Having traveled all over the world, she can safely say that the universal language that unites people is love. Felice has written in a variety of sub-genres, including contemporary, paranormal, and she has a mystery series as well. You can find all her book listed on her website.

Felice is a two-time Lambda Literary Award nominee and the Lambda award-winner in Gay Romance for her book, *The Ghost and Charlie Muir*.

BOOKBUB
https://www.bookbub.com/profile/felice-stevens

NEWSLETTER
https://tinyurl.com/y85e69ab

READER GROUP
https://www.facebook.com/groups/FelicesBreakfastClub/

FACEBOOK AUTHOR PAGE
https://www.facebook.com/felicestevensauthor/

INSTAGRAM
https://www.instagram.com/felicestevens

GOODREADS
https://www.goodreads.com/author/show/8432880.Felice_
Stevens

WEBSITE
felicestevens.com

PAYHIP STORE
https://payhip.com/FeliceStevensAuthor